The moon shone as full and lucent as a spotlight

The dogs had trotted along and threaded underfoot and the boys were as bad as Granny's billy goats, leaping around on the jagged rocks in the dark. Seth had to grab at a couple of shirt collars and haul them back from the ledge. Finally they all settled down under the vast night sky for some stargazing.

"Boys, look," Rainey said. "That's Arcturus." She pointed. "And that's Andromeda. Orion. And those— Granny calls those the seven sisters."

While she was speaking a shooting star cut through the dark sky low on the horizon.

"Wow! Did you see that?" Dillon poked Seth's shoulder excitedly. Maddy signed his wonder near Rainey's face in the dark.

Even Aaron looked enthrall‍‍‍y was watching Aaron, Seth w‍‍‍oint they exchanged a g‍‍‍the boys' heads, a‍‍‍d be like, how it wo‍‍‍n the kind of man who wo‍‍‍a mountain to look at the stars.

Dear Reader,

Seth Whitman and Rainey Chapman form a family with three needy young boys under most unusual circumstances in a most unusual setting.

The Winding Stair Mountains in southeastern Oklahoma have an enduring mystery and beauty that civilization cannot touch. Just hearing the names of the landmarks in that area stirred my imagination: Black Fork Mountain, Talimena Drive, The Runestones.

I had to see this remote corner of my state up close. So with my best friend from high school riding shotgun, I took off on a road trip. As we checked out the towns, the historic sites, the flora and fauna, the dark rivers and hidden waterfalls, we discovered that the real treasures in southeastern Oklahoma are the people. The preachers and the cowboys and the artists who live there today are as fascinating as the outlaws and the Native American chiefs and the Vikings who passed through in the old days.

All this color and beauty and lore became like a kaleidoscope that I twisted and twisted until I came up with Granny's mountain home and the town of Tenikah…the perfect place for Seth and Rainey to fall in love and find a family.

I'd love to hear from you! Contact me at P.O. Box 720224, Norman, OK 73070 or visit my Web site, www.darlenegraham.com. While you're there, be sure to take a peek at my upcoming Texas trilogy.

My best,

Darlene Graham

An Accidental Family
Darlene Graham

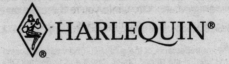

HARLEQUIN®

TORONTO • NEW YORK • LONDON
AMSTERDAM • PARIS • SYDNEY • HAMBURG
STOCKHOLM • ATHENS • TOKYO • MILAN • MADRID
PRAGUE • WARSAW • BUDAPEST • AUCKLAND

ISBN 0-373-71270-7

AN ACCIDENTAL FAMILY

For my lifelong friend, Susan Camp.
Thank you for exploring the Winding Stair Mountains
with me. Our adventures seem never to end!

Books by Darlene Graham

HARLEQUIN SUPERROMANCE

812—IT HAPPENED IN TEXAS
838—THE PULL OF THE MOON
904—UNDER MONTANA SKIES
958—THIS CHILD OF MINE
994—THE MAN FROM OKLAHOMA
1028—DAUGHTER OF OKLAHOMA
1091—DREAMLESS
1126—NO ORDINARY CHILD
1152—ENCHANTING BABY
1202—TO SAVE THIS CHILD

Don't miss any of our special offers. Write to us at the
following address for information on our newest releases.

Harlequin Reader Service
U.S.: 3010 Walden Ave., P.O. Box 1325, Buffalo, NY 14269
Canadian: P.O. Box 609, Fort Erie, Ont. L2A 5X3

CHAPTER ONE

THE FACE OF HIS BROTHER rose up to haunt Seth Whitman as he crouched alone in the dark. For some reason he always envisioned Lane the way he looked in the old black-and-white photo that hung on the wall of the field house, a cocky seventeen-year-old football hero, immortalized along with every other All-State player to graduate from Tenikah High. There was no black-and-white portrait of Seth's face up on that wall, and he was glad of it. Since the day Coach Hollings had ripped his picture down, Seth had been the outsider and always would be.

The snap of a twig somewhere in the dark rock formations that surrounded him snuffed the memories. Alert to any sound that might be the movement of humans, he listened but heard nothing except the throaty roar of the river below, and from behind, the tinkle of seeping water inside the caves.

He eased back down into the dark niche to resume his vigil.

His sweat-soaked uniform chafed like leather beneath his Kevlar bulletproof vest as the fingers clutching the stock of his shotgun tightened into a choke hold. An old hatred burned suddenly alive again in the pit of his gut.

He sensed the presence of his brother's murderers as palpably as he sensed the dying traces of summer in the air. Waiting for them was excruciating.

He swiped at a trickle of sweat slithering down his throat. The temperature had spiked above a hundred today, rare in the densely forested mountains of south-eastern Oklahoma, even in August. When it got this hot, the trees seemed to wilt and the sandstone cliffs and winding blacktop roads refused to release their heat even after the sun slid behind the ridgelines. He'd bet his pickup that the temperature hadn't dropped ten degrees since sundown.

Another twig snapped.

He pinpointed the sound to one of the smaller caves up the ledge, and made his way to the entrance with the deadly focus of a mountain cat. He shielded himself behind a rock, leveled his shotgun at his shoulder and yelled, "Freeze!" as he snapped on the halogen light mounted on the gun.

Snared in the cone of light were three boys. Middle school age, maybe ten or twelve. One looked slightly older. They were huddled just inside the mouth of the cave, the one in front wielding a knife in his bloodied hand. The way the big one pressed the other two back with one arm, glaring at Seth, reminded him of the time he and Lane had trapped three baby raccoons when they were kids growing up in these Kiamichi hills. The coons had toddled into the trap in one hungry clump, and when Seth bent down to peer into the cage, the male had herded the two little females behind his back and hissed. Seth and Lane had collapsed laughing.

But this wasn't funny. The Slaughter brothers were up in these caves somewhere, and now he'd stumbled on a bunch of freaked-out kids.

"Police," Seth said calmly. "Drop the knife."

"Police, my ass," the bigger boy snarled. "You want this knife, buddy? You come and get it." Seth realized the boy couldn't see beyond the glare of light.

He switched on his shoulder mike. "Jake, come in."

When the radio crackled back with Jake's voice— "Any sign of the Slaughters?"—the boy looked astonished.

"Drop it," Seth repeated. The kid tossed the knife at his feet.

Seth hit the mike switch again. "No, but I found three kids in a cave. One's hurt. Come on around."

The boys looked roughed up—dirty, sweaty, scratched. The big one had bled all over the knife. The smaller two were bound, hands behind their backs, with duct tape.

Seth sheathed the shotgun at his back as he approached them. "Are you kids from the camp?" Big Cedar Camp was for troubled youth, but these guys looked too shell-shocked to be a threat.

"You're a cop?" The tall one's voice was deep one second, high-pitched the next. He was a good-looking kid, with even, darkly Hispanic features and well-developed muscles. Right now he was as agitated as the devil. "Then listen! Some creeps tied us up! You got to catch them."

"First things first," Seth said as he used the knife to cut the tape off the other two. One was thin as a reed, with messy brown hair and frightened brown eyes. The other was a little chunk—curly red hair, deep-set blue eyes that had a spooked look about them. Neither one said a word, but as soon as their hands were loose they started flashing sign language.

"Yeah." The bigger kid nodded as he read his friends' signing. "They're twins or brothers or somethin'. Look-alikes. Big red beards." He made a pulling motion at his chin.

There were more hand signals from the other two. "Yeah. Real weirdos," the Hispanic kid agreed.

Seth knew, without even hearing the description, that the kids were talking about the Slaughters. "What are you guys doing up here?"

The Hispanic kid shot his comrades a guilty look. "We didn't mean no trouble. We just sneaked out to explore the caves, and next thing we knew, those guys caught us and tied us up. They're way back in one of those caves up there." He pointed up the cliff. "Aiming to dig up those *bones*," he blurted, before his eyes shifted, and he clammed up.

Seth narrowed his gaze at the kid. He suspected some kind of lie here. How would the boy know what the Slaughters were *aiming* to do? Seth would get to the truth sooner or later. He usually did. The last seven years had been one long pursuit of the truth. Many times he had searched this endless warren of caves, looking for bones himself. And many times he had come up empty-handed, ending up staring out over the valley, torturing his mind, seeing Lane's young face on that wall.

If Seth could find those bones, he'd have the evidence he needed to nail the Slaughters for Lane's death. The famous missing motive. The defense attorney in the Slaughters' manslaughter trial had argued that the twins had no motive to intentionally kill a cop. And Seth was never allowed to tell the story of his last conversation with his brother to the jury. "Inadmissible hearsay," the judge had ruled. That's when Seth had started to give up on the law. Or rather, that's when he'd begun to *use* the law like a weapon to punish the Slaughters.

Although the kid's statement did not surprise him, it sickened him. So Lane was right. And now Lonnie and Nelson Slaughter had returned to this high, rock-embedded cavity in Purney's Mountain to finish what they'd started. The place was shaped like a giant grotto, with jagged, towering walls of layered sandstone black with age, etched by seeping water and pocked by caves that had hidden the brothers' dirty secret well—until now.

"They hit Maddy on the head," the boy said urgently. "He's hurt bad."

Sure enough, the skinny kid had a pretty sizable goose egg developing under his tousled brown hair. Seth checked the big one's cut hands, too. Then he hit the button on his shoulder radio for dispatch.

"Amy, come in. I've intercepted some runaways from Big Cedar Camp. One's got a bad bump on the head and another needs stitches. Send paramedics with transport, bottom of Purney's Mountain."

Jake arrived, wheezing and out of breath from the climb. Unfortunately, Seth's partner didn't keep himself in shape the way Seth did. There were a lot of guys like Jake in Tenikah, former defensive players on the football team. Encouraged to bulk up as teens, they found their muscle turned to fat they couldn't shed as they aged.

"Now here's a fine situation," Jake drawled as he eyed the three frightened youngsters.

They got the kids' names. Dillon. Maddy. Aaron. Found out the reason the big kid was doing all the talking. Maddy was deaf and mute. Aaron was just plain mute. "He don't talk to nobody. Not never," was how Dillon explained it. So that's what all the hand signals were about.

They could describe the Slaughters, but they couldn't tell Seth which cave they were in. "It's dark back in those caves," Dillon said, "and they was dragging us around like feed sacks."

The kids had escaped because Dillon was sporting a contraband knife. "But I couldn't fight 'em both," he explained. "So we waited, and when those guys went back to finish digging up the...uh, we put our backs together and Maddy wiggled my knife out of my boot and cut my hands free." That explained the lacerations. "I cut our feet loose and we ran. We hid in here when we heard a noise. We thought you was some more bad guys."

"Good thinking," Seth said. But now they had to get the kids out of here. "Jake, you take them down. I called for an ambulance."

"You're not going after Lonnie and Nelson by your-self," Jake challenged. Seth knew this was coming.

"You have a better plan?" He pulled his shotgun out of the sling. "If somebody gets shot trying to escape, so be it."

"You know how that'll look? You bringing the dead bodies of the two guys who killed your brother down off this mountain? Seth, it could cost you your badge—"

"Then they can *have* my badge."

"What about Rainey?" the Dillon kid interrupted.

"Rainey?" The two cops turned on him.

"Our counselor from camp. Rainey Chapman. She might be out looking for us right now. She's done it be-fore. What if those guys find her, too?"

"That settles it. I'm going up." Seth turned the vol-ume down on the mike. "I'll stay in touch by radio."

Jake gave him a grudging nod. Then he and the boys went one way—down—and Seth went the other—up.

Rainey Chapman. As Seth crept along the ledge, he tried to imagine what kind of woman would go tearing through these woods alone in search of three runaway boys. Whoever she was, he would have to get to the Slaughter brothers before they got to her.

He turned to peer upward over one shoulder, toward

the edge of the high cliff that surrounded him in a dark horseshoe. A late August moon rose high above the ridge, and against its white spotlight, Seth couldn't make out any movement under the black cowl of trees. But if the Slaughters were in one of these caves, they could only get out by coming down this ledge, or by using ropes to scale back up the cliff. If the woman came looking for the boys in the caves, she'd have to skirt this ledge, as well. He positioned himself strategically for either occurrence and waited again.

It seemed as if he'd spent half his life waiting, trying to assemble the pieces of a puzzle that refused to fit. He'd waited for Lonnie and Nelson Slaughter to get out of prison. Waited for them to come back here and make a move. Waited for the day—or the night—when they'd lead him to the last piece. This day. This night.

He ran a sweaty palm over his thigh again. His quad muscles were knotting up like bundles of barbed wire. He'd pulled them good scrambling up over the boulders at the base of the cliff in the dark. But years of ignoring rodeo injuries had disciplined his body well. If only he could ignore the memories churning through his mind.

His decision to avenge his brother's death had seemed so cold, so clean at the time. But now that it had come down to this—hiding in these rocks, ready to kill or be killed—the weight of it all closed in. He glanced at the badge that gleamed dully in the moonlight like a shiny lie.

Despite certain well-honed skills, Seth didn't feel like a lawman. He knew that in truth he was nothing more than a predator, seeking one thing and one thing only—now going on seven years past. Sometimes he could actually feel his fingers closing around the Slaughter brothers' beefy necks.

A stealthy sound from above made his spine tense.

Slowly, he eased up, clutching the shotgun, and stepped out of his cave, listening.

The skin on the back of his neck prickled as he heard labored breathing, then a harsh curse, then excited shouting. "Lonnie! The kids got away!".

A second guttural voice hissed a foul curse. A ray of light flared over the edge of the cliff and Seth flattened himself against the rock. "We'll have to catch 'em later. We gotta get the stuff up first."

Rustling. Grunting. The strained voice calling, "More rope!"

Seth saw a rappelling rope bouncing out over the side of the cliff not twenty feet to his left. By damn, the fools were right above him.

As he listened to the crunch of boots on the wall of rock above, a new sound demanded his attention. Someone down the slope, gasping for breath. He spotted the flare of another flashlight ricocheting off the rocks below, as a female voice—high-pitched, hysterical—called out, "Dillon! Is that you up there? *Dillon!* I see your flashlight! Answer me!"

Great. Now the little counselor, or social worker, or whatever she was, shows up. Seth focused on the flare of the light as it grew brighter, closer. She was on the ledge now.

He eased himself around a boulder and in the next instant she "turned into his hand," as bull riders liked to say. Before she could lurch away, he'd clamped her firmly in the vise of his arms. With one hand clasped across her mouth, he dragged her backward into the small hole in the wall.

She flailed wildly, skinny arms and legs and the flashlight dangling from its wrist strap all whacking him in the arm, in the head and certain other places that made a man grit his teeth. When he removed the hand from her mouth long enough to wrest the flashlight out of her grip, she screamed, "Boys! *Help!*"

He flicked off the light, tossed it on the ground.

"Let me go!" she howled.

"Shh," he hissed as he clamped the hand back over her mouth. With the shotgun pressed across her middle like a crowbar, he forced her to be still against him. She was so small that he could have broken her in half if he had a mind to, which only galvanized his urge to protect her.

"It's okay," he whispered in her ear. "I'm a cop." He folded his arms tighter around her and was relieved when her struggling ceased. He held her backside pressed against his trunk in that fetal embrace for a few endless, tense seconds while he listened to Lonnie and Nelson above, yelling curses and scrambling away, back up the cliff. Then came the sound of a rattletrap engine firing to life, tires spinning away on a gravel road.

When at last there were no more sounds, Seth maneuvered his foot to scrape her flashlight within reach. He bent to snatch it up, switched it on and twisted the ray around so he could get a good look at her.

He raked the beam up and down her slender form. She was fully clothed—jean shorts, baggy white T-shirt, running shoes. No visible blood. But she was covered in dirt, and every inch of her was trembling. Her long blond hair was a tangled mess. She wasn't wearing any makeup or jewelry, as far as he could see. Except for some scrapes and the dirt, she looked like a woman who'd just climbed out of bed. Even with terror contorting her features, he could see she was a genuine beauty.

And she was strong, too. She managed to wrench one hand free, tearing at his fingers on the shotgun.

"Woman!" He thrust the gun up high, out of her reach. "This thing's loaded." He flicked the safety on. "Listen to me," he demanded, but held his voice to a harsh whisper. "I said I'm the law. And those weren't your boys up there. Those are dangerous men who'll likely kill us if they find us in here." He turned her jaw toward the glint of his badge in the oblique light. "I am not gonna hurt you."

"Mmmfp!" Her eyes bugged at the badge. She twisted her face against his hand and looked into his eyes, trying to speak.

"Okay. But keep your voice down. They could circle back."

She nodded and he slid his hand away.

"A c-cop?" she coughed out. Her face was flushed and her full lips looked parched from thirst.

"Yes."

"Well, you scared the hell out of me!" For a second Seth thought she might hit him, but instead she whirled to face him, and clutched the bulletproof vest in both fists. He reared back. He wasn't used to people messing with his person, at least while he was on duty. "Lady—"

But she only yanked him harder. "You have got to help me...the boys...I can't find them!"

She started babbling ninety miles a minute about the three boys, how she'd found their beds empty again, how they couldn't be far. About pennies on the railroad track. About getting lost in the caves. The woman was near hysteria. For one irrational second a shot of adrenaline hit Seth as he wondered if the Slaughter brothers had harmed her. Harmed her the way they'd harmed KayAnn Rawls.

"Did they hurt you?" He shone the light up and down her body again. No welts. No cuts and bruises from a beating.

"Who?" She winced as he shoved her hair back to get a better look at a scrape on her forehead.

"Those men."

"No!" She batted his hand away, seeming annoyed by his examination. "No one's hurt *me*. You're not *listening!*" Her voice rose. "Some *little boys* are *missing!*"

He lowered the flashlight. "Keep your voice down. The boys are fine."

Her jaw dropped. "The boys—"

Seth pressed the switch on his shoulder mike. "Jake. Come in."

Instantly, his partner's voice crackled in response. "Where are you, buddy?"

"In a cave. I've got the counselor. I'm bringing her down. But the Slaughters got away. Call for some backup to intercept them. Probably coming down Purney's Road."

"Got it. I haven't gotten much out of the kids. The talkative one clammed up. And I don't know sign language."

Rainey Chapman seemed to be still recovering from her shock. "The boys are…? You're…? You mean you found them already?"

"Yes. They're in an ambulance, at the base of this mountain."

"Oh, thank God!" She pressed a palm over her heart, wilting with relief. He steadied her with a light hand to her back. She was shaking worse than his aunt Junie's nervous poodle. The counselor looked up at him and her eyes grew wide as something hit her with such impact that he could see, even in the oblique light, their unique green shade. "Did you say they're in an ambulance?"

"One of the boys got a bump on the head. Nothing serious. One's got some cuts on his hands. They're more scared than hurt. They'll be okay."

Her lips trembled as if she were struggling not to cry. "No, they won't. You don't know these children. They shouldn't have been running around in these woods. I should have called—" Her eyes grew wide. "Who called the police?"

"Nobody. We were up here on a manhunt and came upon the boys by accident."

"A manhunt? After those men?"

"I was hoping to apprehend them. Unfortunately, I didn't get them before they tied up your boys."

She gasped. *"Tied them up?"*

"With duct tape. Luckily, the kids escaped. Like I told you, those men are dangerous."

"But why would they tie up the boys?" She stared at him with a look of wild-eyed horror.

"Because the kids saw some things they shouldn't have seen, some things those men have been hiding for a very long time, I'm afraid."

"Hiding something? What?"

"I'll explain once we're safely out of here." Once he decided how much she needed to know. He pulled on her arm.

But she resisted, pressing a shaky hand to her temple. "Oh, this is all my fault. Those kids have suffered enough trauma without this."

Seth frowned. A little on the dramatic side, wasn't she? She was the boys' counselor, not some savior, and certainly not the one who'd caused the trauma that had put the boys in her care in the first place. "Aren't you being a little hard on yourself?"

"No. I should never have tried to find them by myself." She started to tremble so hard he feared she'd collapse.

He slid an arm around her shoulders. Not the most professional thing to do, maybe, but he wasn't inclined to let the poor little thing shake her teeth out without offering some support. His days as a cop were about done, anyway.

"I'm sorry." She yielded in his arms as she reflexively turned to his chest.

He reached around and pressed the arm that held the shotgun to her back. He could feel her pliant softness even through his bulletproof vest. The rest of her felt as delicate as a bird. Suddenly the air inside the small cave felt too close. Suddenly Seth's skin grew prickly with sweat.

"Come on." He flicked the flashlight off and guided her to the fresher air outside the cave.

She had started to cry.

"It's okay." He held her firmly, feeling out of his depth. Crying females always made Seth want to hightail it to the barn, but he had to deal with this one. He had to find out exactly what this Rainey Chapman knew, what she'd seen. And he had to protect her. "Don't you think the kids had some responsibility in this deal?" His voice was gentle as he ducked his head to look her in the face. "Nobody forced them to run away from the camp. They're not exactly little."

"They're not adults, either," she sniffed. "He looks mature, but Dillon's only thirteen. And Maddy and Aaron are only eleven. They are *children.*"

"They look like pretty good-sized boys to me," he said.

She straightened away from his embrace and her voice took on a note of fierce protectiveness. "These are damaged children who need special care."

"Like some boundaries, maybe? They're plenty old enough to know not to sneak out of the camp." Seth was thinking about how he and Lane had both held down odd jobs by that age.

"Age has nothing to do with it. You can't expect children to accept boundaries until they feel loved."

Seth didn't agree. He believed in accountability, even for kids. But this was hardly the place for a philosophical debate.

She mistook his silence for disapproval. "You can think whatever you like, but I am the one who's responsible for these children. And it was *I* who handled this all wrong."

Seth could understand how she was blaming herself for running off in a panic and searching for the children in the dark woods on her own, without notifying anyone. That was definitely a stupid thing to do. What he couldn't understand was why she'd done it. But there would be time to sort out all the details when they got to the bottom of the hill.

"We've got to get you out of here." He stuffed the flashlight in his vest and took hold of her arm, leading her forward on the ledge, craning his neck to look down the slope. "The moonlight's too bright. They might see us on the footpath. We'll have to stay under cover of trees. Think you can climb back down between those rocks?"

"I came up that way, didn't I?"

He turned, and in the moonlight he could see her eyes. Again it struck him that they were very pretty.

"Just get me to that ambulance." She met his gaze dead-on, even though there was quite a difference in their heights. "I need to see the boys right away."

He was thinking how climbing up the open footpath with a flashlight and going down between the huge boulders in the dark were two different things, but all he said was, "Stay close then."

As they climbed over the first of the large boulders he heard her suppress a little yelp. Instinctively, he reached back to her. "You okay?"

"I just slipped."

"Here." He bracketed her waist with his hands and helped her down. She felt like a tiny doll in his grasp. Her hot breath brushed against his temple as he lowered her to the ground, and he was startled by a surge of attraction.

He set her a respectable distance from him and decided keeping her engaged in talk would calm her—and him—down. "Ms. Chapman—"

"How do you know my name?" she asked.

"The boys. They figured you'd come looking for them." He glanced back up the dark wall of rock that rose above them. "What made you come all the way up here, anyway?"

"I've found them here before. Twice, actually."

"Doing what?"

"Exploring the caves." She sighed and swiped at her sweaty brow.

"Did you see anyone else on either of those nights?" She shook her head. "No."

"And what about tonight?"

"Nothing except the lights. I should have realized the boys' flashlights wouldn't be that bright. But all I could think about was finding them so I could get them back to camp before Lyle realized they were missing."

"Lyle Hicks?" Seth had dealt with the officious jerk, who made a big deal out of the fact that *he* was in charge at Big Cedar Camp. The guy's body language always screamed "hostile." He crossed his arms like an umpire, issued demands, didn't like to be inconvenienced. Seth could imagine the effect a guy like Lyle had on wayward boys. He decided that for Lyle Hicks, the embarrassment of having three kids picked up by the cops would undoubtedly be more of an issue than the kids themselves.

"Lyle." Rainey lowered her head. "Lyle and I aren't exactly singing on the same page of the songbook. I guess you know that most of the boys who end up at Big Cedar are wards of the state. All have behavioral problems. Many have physical problems, as well. I try to help them, but Lyle, he only wants to warehouse them. He'll never let me live this down."

"The guy's a prick."

Rainey's head snapped up, the expression in her green eyes keen now. "Yeah. He is, actually. But how'd you know?"

"We've been called about incidents at the camp before. Lyle seems to be more worried about damage control than the kids. Once he asked me if the media monitored our police radios." Seth took her hand and led her on. "Is Lyle the reason you didn't report it when the boys ran off?"

"Partly. I thought it would be enough to chastise them."

Chastise them? If it were up to Seth, he'd *chastise* their backsides. Coach Hollings and his famous paddle flashed to mind.

"You have to understand how harsh the system can be," she added. "I didn't want them to end up…I thought I was keeping them safe with me."

"Right." Seth's tone was sarcastic. *"Safe."*

He had pulled her along until they reached a drop-off. He lowered himself over the edge and put the shotgun on the ground to help her down off the rock. When she had her footing, he picked up the gun and pulled her into a narrow cleft between two giant boulders. "Stay close," he said. "It gets a little rougher now."

The claustrophobic passage was pitch-black and so treacherously steep that they were forced to half scramble, half slide down.

Rainey used her free hand to steady herself against Seth's back, and her touch communicated tremors of fear.

"Can't we turn on the flashlight yet?"

"No. Even between the rocks a beam might be seen. I know where I'm going."

Seth could find his way through these passages with his eyes closed. From the time he was old enough to ride a bike, he and Lane had explored every nook and cranny of this part of the Kiamichi Range. And he had made many trips up and down this exact passage in the years since Lane's death, sensing that the answer he sought—KayAnn Rawls's bones—lay up at the top of these cliffs.

KayAnn Rawls. Her name filtered through the dark passageway like an echo that he couldn't silence. KayAnn Rawls. The trouble had started with KayAnn Rawls. For years, Seth had made it his mission to find out what had happened to Lane's girlfriend on the night she'd disappeared. He told himself he did it for Lane's sake. But lately he wondered if he'd carried this obsession around for so long he couldn't let go of it even if he wanted to.

And now these boys were involved in this mess. And this woman.

"We're okay," he reassured her. But in his mind he had to add, *for now.* Because navigating down this treacherous path was sure to be the least of their problems.

CHAPTER TWO

AS MUCH AS RAINEY LOATHED confined spaces, she had bigger worries. Inching her way between giant rocks that felt tighter than a tomb, she clung to the back of the cop's vest and hoped she wasn't making another stupid mistake.

This guy *was* a cop, wasn't he? With her imagination conjuring up thoughts about serial killers pretending to be cops so they could lure their victims into remote, dark places like this one, she forced herself to review the facts.

Badge. Bulletproof vest. Shotgun. But anyone could get their hands on such items, couldn't they? The voice on the radio. He couldn't fake that, could he? And he'd known her name…and Lyle's.

Breathe, she told herself, trying to calm down. But that was hard to do when she was practically plastered against his back. His hands had been all over her from the minute she'd slammed into him, but if he hadn't kept a firm grip on her, she would have fallen off these rocks ten times by now.

What alternative did she have but to trust this guy, at least for now? Running off into the woods like a crazy woman again?

Finally they emerged onto a level moonlit patch in the path, and she relaxed a fraction.

He resumed his questions. "What drew the boys up here?"

"Those caves. Dillon's idea, I'm sure."

Seth nodded. "He's obviously the leader."

"Some leader. He's always getting the other two to sneak out of their cabin, steal things, vandalize property, whatever he can dream up. These aren't normal boys, Sheriff. I suppose you figured out that Maddy is deaf."

"Yes, ma'am."

"And Aaron...well Aaron's hard to explain. His problems are complex. Basically he's a psychological mute. But don't let his silence fool you, Officer— I'm sorry, I didn't get your name."

"Whitman. Seth Whitman."

"Officer Whitman—"

"Just Seth." Seth had never been comfortable with that "Officer" bit. His motives for becoming a cop were far from pure.

"Okay. Seth. Aaron takes in everything around him like a sponge. Maddy's been hurt time and again because of his disability. And Dillon's one angry boy. He can explode for no reason."

"Yes, ma'am. I'm familiar with that kind." He'd been that kind himself once upon a time, before Coach had taken ahold of him.

"Honestly, that *child.*"

"He's no child." Seth reminded her, and felt a jerk on his hand for the mumbled remark.

He glanced back to see Rainey Chapman's pretty mouth tight with disapproval. "Yes, he *is.* And even if I'm the only one who understands that, I still intend to see that he gets the same loving care that any child deserves."

In Seth's opinion what boys Dillon's age needed was a little more discipline and a little less TLC. The "child" was nearly as tall as Seth, though lanky, and Seth had even noticed the beginnings of a mustache on Dillon's upper lip. "But I take it he's a real handful."

She finally favored Seth with a smile. That flash of pretty teeth in the moonlight sent another surprising ripple of sensation through him. He was definitely becoming captivated by this sprite of a woman.

"More like a budding sociopath. Dillon is creative and charming and athletic. He's everything a boy that age should be. Except he's also a manipulative little liar."

Not entirely, Seth suspected, although parts of his story hadn't added up.

The terrain was not as steep now, and they were hidden from view of the cliffs by the thick canopy of trees, so he flicked on the flashlight and aimed it at the trail. She came up beside him, and he released her hand, missing her delicate clasp immediately. "So, you last saw the boys in their cabin?"

She nodded. "Around midnight."

It was now well past two in the morning.

"When I got up to go to the bathroom. I've gotten in the habit of doing a bed check every few hours since the last...incident."

"When was that?"

"Two weeks ago."

Maybe night after night of bed checks for the last two weeks explained Rainey Chapman's impulsive behavior. Maybe the woman was too sleep-deprived to think straight.

"What happened that time?"

"They went skinny-dipping. I happened to look in on them once, but they had made up dummies in their beds. I would never have caught them if Maddy hadn't slipped up. He was signing to Dillon at breakfast the next morning. Aaron and Dillon learned ASL so they could talk to Maddy—"

"ASL?"

"American Sign Language. Maddy prefers it to Signing Exact English. The boys are quite clever with it. They do it so fast, it's almost like a secret language, you know? Anyway, Dillon slapped at Maddy's hands, but not before I saw that he was saying something about swimming at the old train bridge—that's where they'd gone that time."

"So you can read sign language—ASL—as well?" That would be useful.

"That's part of the reason I got this job. But boy, was I wrong about helping these kids. I was living in la-la land. Reliving my own childhood."

"You had a troubled childhood?" Seth frowned at her. He could identify with that.

Her expression clouded for only an instant before she covered up with a light laugh. "No! I'm talking about how I played in the out-of-doors. Out here, in these mountains."

"You grew up around here?" He'd guess they were about the same age. There was only one high school in the area—the massive one in Tenikah. He would have remembered any girl this beautiful. He was certain he'd never seen Rainey Chapman before tonight.

"Only in the summers. Long story. Anyway, I thought it would be so wonderful to be out here in the country, helping disadvantaged children get in touch with nature. Helping them heal and grow and reach their potential. Turning lives around. Saving the universe, et cetera, et cetera." She let out another little self-deprecating laugh.

Seth smiled. He liked the way this woman talked, the way she laughed.

"Ouch!" She stumbled on the dark path and clutched his arm.

"You okay?" He pressed a steadying palm to her back.

"Yeah." Her voice was tense. "Just stubbed my toe."

Seth took his hand off her back but didn't release her fingers, justifying the lingering touch to himself—then to her. "Maybe you'd better hold on to me a little bit longer."

"I guess so."

As they walked on she sighed heavily. "Anyway, so much for helping the kids. Now it looks like the boys are in worse trouble than they were before I took charge of them."

Seth ignored her self-recriminations and got back to his point. "So, Dillon reads sign language, as well?"

"Yes. Maddy taught him fairly quickly."

Seth frowned. So why hadn't Dillon interpreted for Jake? Trying to control the interview? He was obviously used to manipulating adults.

Seth glanced at Rainey, involuntarily tightening his grip around her slender fingers as he thought about how this impulsive bleeding heart of a woman had spooked the Slaughter boys right out of his grasp. He just hoped the twins hadn't spotted the commotion at the bottom of the hill. And he hoped they weren't circling back to get the bones this very minute.

He found himself dragging Rainey along faster as anger and worry drove him. As annoyed as he was at this woman for blowing his stakeout, his fear for her safety and the safety of three young boys was greater.

"Officer? Seth? You're hurting my hand."

"Sorry." He relaxed his grip.

"I'm the one who should be sorry," she said, as if she'd just read his mind. "I should never have covered for the boys the way I did. I'm afraid I was too soft-hearted. I always gave them one more chance. You see, the rule is if a boy causes trouble at Big Cedar, the next step in the system is the reform school at Werner. I didn't want boys this young to end up in that awful place, especially with their disabilities. The other in-mates there would rip Maddy and Aaron to pieces." She came up short. "I imagine they won't let me near children now. And the boys will end up trapped at Werner, anyway."

Seth frowned, thinking, *Not so fast*. He was already planning to place the boys under his protection. This woman might have connections that would help accomplish that. "What, exactly, was your job?"

"I work for the DHS—the Department of Human Services."

"I'm familiar with it."

"I did casework in the Tulsa office at first. I hated it. It was so bureaucratic. Worse than being an attorney."

"You're also an attorney?" Seth had a thing for smart women. He found himself getting more interested in this particular smart woman than he probably ought to be—in more ways than one. It had been a long time since he'd felt this charged up around a female. He glanced back and caught a glimpse of model-trim thighs below the snug jean shorts.

"I *was* an attorney. In my mother's law firm."

"Your mother's a lawyer?"

"One hell of a one. For a while I followed in her foot-steps like a good little girl. It wasn't exactly a healthy relationship."

She sounded so disappointed when she said it. He supposed nobody escaped disappointment in this life. He sure as hell hadn't.

"So somewhere along the way you decided to be a

counselor?" When he glanced back her jaw looked stubborn.

"I'm a pretty good one, despite what you may think about this particular mess. I wanted to be closer to the kids, to make a personal difference with them. And I wanted to relocate out here in the Winding Stair, where I was born. Like I said, it's a long story."

"Maybe I'll get a chance to hear it someday." When he looked back again, the moonlight caught in her eyes and their gazes locked. In that instant, it was as if he knew, and she knew that he knew, that someday he would, indeed, get to hear it all.

She stumbled on a rock and he caught her again. "Thanks," she said as she wiped the sweat at her temple. "Is it incredibly hot out here tonight or what?" She lifted her pale, tangled hair off her neck, twisted it up, tucked in some stray strands.

"Yeah, it's hot," he agreed, studying her. He wondered if she realized how attractive she looked. "The lower the elevation, the worse it gets, but we're almost there," he said. "Take a second to catch your breath." As she propped one hip against a boulder, he was glad it was too dark for her to see him sneaking a glance at her trim little backside. "Mind if I ask how old you are, Ms. Chapman?"

"Call me Rainey, okay? Ms. Chapman reminds me of my days at the firm. Twenty-nine."

He gave her another once-over, then trained his mind back on the case. "How'd you track the boys up here?"

"I had a pretty strong suspicion that they'd come

back. We had taken the children on a field trip to see the Rune Stones. Dillon kept wandering off in the direction of the caves that day. He tried to act jaded, as always, but I could tell he was fascinated by the idea of Viking carvings on the rocks.

"You can see these formations from miles around. It's like tacking in a sailboat," she explained, "traveling in one general direction, but in a zigzag pattern." She chopped her hand in a rising Z. "Eventually you hit your target."

He nodded. Hunters in these mountains used that strategy.

"And I know this area—somewhat. I spent a lot of summers up in these mountains with my gran." She stopped, surveying the moonlit valley that opened below. She turned her head to the east, toward Big Cedar Camp. The base of Purney's Mountain, where they now stood, was well over two miles from the facility. "Dillon claimed the caves were as far as they'd ever gone. But he's such a colossal liar. It's hard to say where they've been, what they've done, what they've seen."

Seth frowned. He hated to tell her what they'd seen. She'd find out soon enough when she helped him question the other two kids.

"Come on." He took her arm, leading her onto a fork in the path that led down to a clearing. "I need to know what this Maddy kid has to say."

CHAPTER THREE

WHEN THE AMBULANCE CAME into view, Rainey broke into a run. The sight of the blue-and-red strobe lights smacking against the dark trees brought a fresh lump of fear to her throat. In the passenger seat a paramedic sat, writing calmly on a clipboard.

"The boys?" Rainey breathed as she approached the lowering window.

"Cut those lights!" Seth ordered from behind her.

"Yes, sir." The paramedic leaned forward to flip a switch. Rainey could hear a man and woman's muted voices coming from the back.

"She's the counselor." Seth's voice was nearer to her now.

Rainey found his physical presence overwhelming again, as if she were almost preternaturally aware of his every movement. She was dismayed to realize she'd felt off-center ever since he'd first grabbed her in the woods.

She tried to tell herself that she was frightened, but there was more to it than that. She was starting to recognize all the signs in herself. That old jittery euphoria that bubbled up around an attractive man.

And this was one extremely attractive man. She tilted her head to give him a covert look in the light from the ambulance window. Tall, dark and handsome, as they say. He looked like he might have some Indian ancestors. His brows were dark, his skin was bronzed, and what she could see of his hair under the brim of his Stetson looked thick and jet-black. When he caught her looking at him, his dark eyes glinted from the depths created by his high cheekbones.

She quickly looked down.

He was handsome, all right. Possibly the best-looking man she had ever seen. But she couldn't actually be *attracted* to this…Dudley Do-Right. It was as if some kind of sick kismet had thrown her together with a good-looking cop. A combo of her best dream and worst nightmare. Because long ago, she'd sworn off cops, and with good cause. No cops. Never a cop.

They made her nervous, these guys who took control of every situation and never admitted even the slightest weakness. Her father's kind, that's what Seth Whitman was.

"Oh, the counselor. I *see*." The paramedic looked her up and down with a judgmental frown that clearly questioned Rainey's competence. But when his eyes flicked up to Seth, the guy's expression became abruptly respectful. "The boys are okay, ma'am." He jerked his head. "In the back."

Rainey trotted around and found the double doors at the rear of the ambulance locked. She knocked on the panel.

Seth came up behind her again, reaching above her head to bang on the metal impatiently. "Jake! Open up!" he boomed.

A heavyset, ruddy-faced man peeked around the curtain in the ambulance window, then cracked open the door as he holstered a sidearm. Rainey noted the badge and uniform identical to Seth's. "Sorry, bud." The cop looked pointedly at Rainey. "Glad he found you, ma'am. Kath and me were just discussing who to call about these kids." His gaze slid back to Seth. "Did you come up with anything out there?"

"Not much." Seth jerked the door open fully. "Let us in."

The cop flung the other door wide and Rainey felt a wave of blessedly cool air pour out. The ambulance engine was running, with the air conditioner pumping.

"Careful, hon." The chubby cop offered Rainey a hand up onto the metal step. She looked around, trying to find another place to take hold and then flushed when Seth grabbed her arm.

His grip was strong and warm, and just touching him sent a tight awareness through Rainey's middle that made her wish she had accepted the chunky cop's hand instead. Attracted. Definitely attracted.

"Thank you." She tried to say it with detached dignity, but it came out breathy. Not detached.

As she squeezed past the chubby cop's potbelly, he emitted an inappropriate hum of approval and she caught him giving Seth a randy little smirk.

"Rainey Chapman. Jake Gifford. My partner." Seth's tone was long-suffering.

"So I gathered." Rainey favored the man with a flat smile and a cool look that caused his leering expression to dry up. She'd been dealing with goatish men all her life.

"Shut the doors," Seth ordered as he propped a boot on the metal step and hoisted himself inside.

"Think I'll wait out in the cruiser," the heavyset cop said. "It's getting kinda crowded in here."

With the three boys and a female paramedic, it was actually more than crowded inside the ambulance.

Maddy lay with a cold pack pressed to the side of his head. He looked pathetically thin, with his oversize, white-stockinged feet sticking up at the end of the stretcher.

While Seth had a mumbled exchange with the paramedic, Rainey dropped to her knees beside the child, brushing back his wavy hair to cup one palm on his forehead, signing frantically with her other hand. Maddy signed back.

"What're they saying?" Seth asked Dillon, who was squeezed onto a narrow bench next to the stony, silent Aaron.

Dillon held up palms with pink-tinged dressings taped on them. "Beats me," he lied.

Rainey heard Seth unzipping his bulletproof vest. "Ms. Chapman told me you can read sign."

Dillon shrugged. "Okay. He's telling her about the two big dudes. How we ran from that cave and all."

Rainey could only peripherally note what was taking place around her. Her focus was on Maddy, the most vulnerable of her charges. Unlike the other two, Maddy didn't have his anger to shield him. When she heard how one of the men had struck him with a shovel, she pressed shaky fingers to her lips, feeling unbearable guilt.

Seth took off his hat and squatted beside her. Rainey noticed he winced as he arranged his legs, knees spread wide, around the foot of the stretcher. He was a massive man, but he moved with such grace that his bulk didn't seem overpowering unless he was actually in your space, as he was in Rainey's now. He tilted his huge shoulders and an involuntary image erupted in her mind: herself clinging to those shoulders. Feeling guilty for even thinking such thoughts at a time like this, she snapped her gaze back to Maddy.

"Maddy's okay," Seth reassured her quietly as he touched a warm palm to her shoulder. "The paramedic said the bump's not a concussion or anything serious. His pupils are reacting normally."

Rainey nodded and turned to concentrate on Dillon now. "Let me see." Gingerly, she lifted the dressings on Dillon's hands to have a look.

Seth eyed the back of Rainey Chapman's tangled blond hair, wondering what had come over the woman just now. Her lightly freckled cheeks had turned as red as a rodeo clown's, and as she replaced the dressing, he noticed her fingers were trembling. Maybe the gravity of the situation was sinking in afresh now that she'd seen the boys.

"Did they bleed much?" she asked Dillon.

"Yeah. All over the place." Dillon seemed proud of that fact.

"Did they give you something for the pain?"

"Nah. It don't hurt."

"I offered him some Tylenol." The paramedic spoke up from where she wrote on her chart.

Seth watched the boy. His body language said he was a little sidewinder. For instance, right now he was unnecessarily swiping at his nose. And why did the kid feel the need to gain more of Rainey's sympathy? Were the other boys getting too much of her attention or something? No. It was more likely that he was hiding something. Seth eyed the huge pockets of the boy's baggy shorts. Another knife, maybe?

Rainey turned her attention to Aaron. "And are you okay?" she asked.

Seth studied the third boy in this trio of misfits, trying to figure out what made this kid tick. The redheaded child looked as if he liked his groceries a little too much. His freckled face was about as expressive as a fence post, though he showed some responsiveness to Rainey. When she ruffled his hair, he gave her the barest, most pathetic smile, a mixture of adoration and trust.

"Can he write down his version of things?" Seth asked Rainey.

"He can hear you, *Sheriff,*" Dillon interjected sarcastically.

"I'm a cop," Seth clarified. "Not a sheriff."

"Whatever," Dillon said. "I already told you what happened. Those two guys was aiming to kill us."

Seth turned calmly to the boy. "And I won't let that happen. So now I want you to be quiet unless I ask you a question."

"You think I'm lying, don't you? Well, I'm not!" Dillon jumped up, suddenly agitated. "Let us out of here! We ain't done nothing wrong!"

"Nobody said you lied," Seth said, though now he was pretty sure the boy had, somewhere along the way. "Sit down." He kept his tone quiet, but firm. "Now."

Dillon sat and slouched back against the bench, crossing his arms over his chest in a gesture of defiance.

Rainey leaned around Seth's shoulder. "Dillon, it's not that we don't believe you. Officer Whitman just needs to know the other boys' version of things. They may have noticed something you didn't."

"They didn't see nothing," Dillon muttered.

Seth let out a pressured breath and scrubbed a hand over his face. This was going to be, as his uncle Tack would say, like herding squirrels. Seth was suddenly grateful for his experience with kids. Volunteer coaching. Junior Rodeo. Boy Scouts. Only these kids weren't exactly Boy Scouts. "Okay, Ms. Chapman. Ask Maddy where they were and exactly what happened when they first saw the two men."

As Rainey's delicate hands signed the question, Seth couldn't help but note the absence of rings on her fingers. He was already hoping she was unattached.

Before Maddy answered he shot Dillon a secretive look, then his hands started reluctantly moving. After Maddy had finished gesturing, Rainey said, "They were up on the old railroad bridge again. This time they were planning to tie a rope off of it so they could swing down into the river."

"And?"

"And…" Rainey watched Maddy's hands "…they saw lights up in that hollow area of the mountain where the cliffs and caves are. Dillon switched off their own flashlights and led them up."

"I already told all of this to your partner!" Dillon interjected.

"Quiet," Seth warned again. "Could they tell what the men were doing?" he asked Rainey.

"I said they were rappelling down the cliffs!" Dillon jumped up, practically shouting in Seth's ear. "And they took some tools into the cave."

Seth struggled to keep his patience. "Son, sit down before you make your hands start bleeding again."

Dillon did so, but with a defiant thrust of his shoulder in Seth's direction.

"What else does Maddy have to say?" Seth urged.

Rainey spoke as she watched the child's hands. "They made their way to the opening of the cave and Dillon sneaked inside, but Maddy and Aaron hung back at the entrance."

"They never went inside," Dillon claimed. "And I didn't go very far. I stopped when I saw the men digging back in there."

Maddy started to sign something else, but Dillon's hand flashed and the deaf child's abruptly halted.

"What did Dillon say to him?" Seth's gaze shot to Rainey.

"I have no idea. I wasn't watching his hands. Dillon, don't play games. This is serious."

"I didn't say nothing," Dillon lied.

"Ask Maddy to repeat it." Seth wanted to stay on point.

But Maddy wouldn't answer. After looking at Dillon with trepidation, he shook his head. But his darting brown eyes betrayed him.

"See?" Dillon shouted. "They didn't see nothing." He leaped up in the confined space of the ambulance again, this time bumping his head against a low cabinet. Rainey jumped up, trying to examine the injury, but the boy jerked away from her and turned his angry countenance on Seth.

"You should be out there going after the bad guys! They was gonna kill us. They was gonna take us back to the bridge and make it look like a accident." Dillon's arms flailed like an agitated monkey's as angry tears spurted to his eyes. "We didn't do nothin' wrong and those guys were gonna kill us. You gotta believe me!"

"Calm down." Seth clamped a hand on Dillon's shoulder and levered him back to the bench. "Right now I want you to sit down." He returned his attention to Maddy. "Ask him what happened next."

Rainey frowned at his sharp tone. Her green eyes glared at him as if *he* were the bad guy in this deal. "Officer, these children are really very frightened."

"I'm aware of that. But right now a couple of extremely dangerous men are running around on the loose. Anything the boy knows that might help me catch them has got to come out. *Now.*"

Rainey turned to face Maddy, and started signing again.

"He said he's sorry," she interpreted when the child answered. "He says that if it hadn't been for him the men wouldn't have seen them. He said he must have made a noise or something that made them look up."

She turned her gaze up to Seth. "Maddy can't hear himself when he makes noises."

"I understand," Seth replied. He didn't have her ask why Maddy might have made a sudden noise. Obviously the boy had seen something. Obviously the boys had all gone into the cave. But Seth was going to have a hard time getting a straight answer out of this bunch. "Then what?"

"The men chased them and grabbed Aaron first."

Seth glanced at the obese child, who probably couldn't move all that fast. The one most likely to get nabbed.

"Maddy told me he and Dillon could have gotten away," Rainey continued as she watched Maddy's agitated hands and facial expressions, "but Dillon turned around to help Aaron."

Seth frowned, wondering why the child wouldn't own up to his heroism.

Rainey was steadily watching Maddy's hands. "They bound them up with a big roll of duct tape and dragged them to the front of the cave—"

Which was where Dillon claimed the other two had been all along, Seth noted.

"—and he says the men were fighting about something."

"Ask him what they said."

Rainey turned to Seth with an impatient frown. He felt briefly captured by the beauty of her huge green eyes again before the meaning of her stare hit him. What an idiot—forgetting that Maddy wasn't capable of hearing anything. "Never mind," he muttered.

"They were fightin' about *us.*" Dillon jumped up again, spitting the words as he jabbed a finger at his own chest. "About how exactly to waste *us.* And you ain't doing anything about it." Beneath the youth's blazing anger, Seth read genuine fear, and he sympathized, but a cop couldn't permit any disrespect. This time it only took a sidelong look to make the boy sit down.

After Dillon quieted, Seth glanced at Aaron. The kid had sat slumped in a trance, except for an occasional flicker of interest over something Dillon said, when it seemed like a kind of silent signal passed among the three boys.

Rainey had said the redhead was a psychological mute. From some sort of trauma, Seth assumed. Uprooting these kids again—even if it was for their own protection—was not going to be easy.

He moved to the front of the ambulance and spoke quietly to the paramedic, who had been busily making notes on a clipboard. "Has that kid talked at all?"

The woman shook her head sadly. "Looks to me like

he has no intention of talking anytime soon. Better watch that one, Seth."

Seth had no experience with such things, and no time to gently pry information by other means from a child who would not, or could not, communicate. He'd have to rely on Dillon's version of the conversation for now.

"Okay, Dillon." He turned to the taller boy. "Tell me what they said."

"They were fighting about how now that we saw them, and how we seen what they was doin', we'd most likely tell. And one said they would have to give us the business—that means *kill* us—"

"Dillon," Rainey interrupted, shooting a look of concern in Aaron's direction. "Just tell what you heard."

"Look, *Mizz* Rainey." Dillon's emphasis of the title was not respectful. "They had us all trussed up with duct tape. They wasn't takin' us to no picnic." He threw up his bandaged hand and signed at Maddy. "They was gonna make us part of their bones collection."

Maddy made one of his involuntary noises. "Dillon, hush," Rainey hissed. "You are scaring Maddy and Aaron, and I won't—"

Seth put a palm up to silence Rainey. He didn't want Dillon to hush. "Bones?" This time he questioned it.

The lad blanched. "Did I say bones?"

Seth gave him a sharp look. Earlier the boy had said the Slaughters were *aiming* to dig up some bones, as if he knew in advance what they were going to do. Then he'd claimed he'd caught them in the act. If he let the boy keep talking, he'd eventually get to the truth. "What else?"

"They was arguing about whether we was town boys or not, meaning from Tenikah, I guess, and how long it would be before somebody noticed we was gone, and all that. And one of them said something about how Howard was really gonna be pissed."

"Howard?" Seth's pulse kicked at the name. "Are you sure he said *Howard?*"

"Yeah. There's nothin' wrong with *my* hearing. They was talking about how he'd know what to do or he'd be mad or something, like, you know, 'We're gonna have to tell Howard about this.' Talk like that."

"Go on."

"Then one of them—like I told you, they looked exactly alike, if you ask me—except one was big and one was kinda regular."

"They're twins," Seth stated.

"Twins?" Rainey glanced up at him.

"Afraid so." That fact had complicated matters in the wonderful world of the law. "The Slaughter brothers have used their identical looks to escape punishment more than once."

"Punishment? For what?"

He let his gaze slide to Aaron to indicate that this was not something to discuss in front of kids.

Rainey's freckled cheeks flushed. "And now these two men are just running loose in the countryside?" she accused.

Seth didn't want to tell her that apprehending Lonnie and Nelson Slaughter wasn't as easy as walking up, ringing their doorbell and slapping the cuffs on. He didn't want to tell her that he was looking for crucial evidence, and that the closest he'd come to obtaining that evidence had been when *she* had crashed through the woods and scared them off. He certainly didn't want to tell her that finding that evidence now involved these boys. "We'll discuss this later. What else did you hear, Dillon?"

"Well, then one of them said first they'd have to go back and get the…get the… I don't remember." Dillon looked down, picking at the dressing on his hand.

Maddy tried to sit up, his fingers flying like one possessed.

Rainey frowned as she saw what he signed.

"My hands really hurt!" Dillon bellowed.

"Excuse me, Seth." The paramedic, a robust-looking young woman with a bushy auburn ponytail and melon-size breasts that strained her uniform shirt, stepped forward with a suture kit. "I'd better tend to those cuts now."

As she squeezed past Seth, she eyed the way he was rubbing his jean-clad thigh. "Something the matter with your leg?"

"Pulled a muscle."

"How?"

"Jumping off a rock."

"I see." She drew the words out in a flat Oklahoma drawl as if stuff like this happened every day. "Want me to take a look at it?"

"No need."

"Suit yourself." She rolled her eyes at Rainey. "I guess it's pointless to waste any sympathy on a bull rider who's pulled every single muscle in his body at one time or the other."

Dillon sneered at Seth. "So you're some kind of *cowboy?*"

"More boy than cow," Seth deadpanned.

"More boy than—oh, I get it!" Dillon's laughter was forced, but Seth gave the boy a wry grin.

"I was a bull rider," he admitted.

"Cool!" For the first time all night Dillon sounded sincere.

"I'll tell you about it sometime, but right now, Kathy's ready to fix your hands."

"You won't feel a thing," the paramedic said to Dillon brightly.

"Let's step outside." Seth took Rainey's elbow. When she hesitated, he said, "Kathy will take good care of the boys, won't you, Kath?"

"You bet." The paramedic gave Rainey a reassuring smile. Then she lowered herself beside Dillon. "Let's get you fixed up." She removed the blood-soaked dressing.

"Ms. Chapman and I will be back in a minute," Seth said to Dillon and Aaron as he took Rainey's elbow. "Then we're going to see if we can take you guys someplace more comfortable for the night." He looked down at her. "Would you tell Maddy all of that?"

She nodded, but she seemed distracted again, and

Seth realized he was holding her arm maybe a little too tightly. He let it go.

When he took Rainey's hand again as she hopped down off the metal step, she thanked him politely and withdrew hers quickly. Seth slammed the door. So he wasn't the only one who was attracted. But why did that bother her so much?

He braced a palm high on the back of the ambulance, shielding her from Jake, who was sitting in the cruiser. "Okay. What did Maddy just sign?"

Rainey gave a visible shudder. Her pretty green eyes rose to meet his, and the fear radiating from them unsettled Seth. She swallowed. "Maddy never signs in exact English, but this time he did. It was like he was trying to finish what Dillon said without Dillon catching on."

"Maddy can read lips?"

"If he wants to, yes."

"What did he sign?"

Rainey frowned. "He signed that the men were going to kill them *after they dug up the bones.*"

CHAPTER FOUR

"WHAT ARE THEY TALKING about?" Rainey shuddered again. *"Bones?"*

"I think that's what the Slaughters came back to that cave to get."

"Human bones?" Rainey hugged her arms to her middle.

"Yes. I'll explain later." Seth looked down at Rainey Chapman's trembling shoulders, and wanted nothing so much as to wrap his arms around her again. But Jake was looking on, he was sure. Instead of touching her again he said, "Wait here."

After checking with Jake and finding that the road-block had not stopped the Slaughters, Seth knew what he had to do.

He walked back to Rainey, frowning as he considered how to say this without freaking her out.

She stepped toward him. "We are going to have to move the boys," he said. "Right away."

"Move them? Where?"

"I don't know. I was hoping you could help me with that. Someplace safer than that camp."

"You mean you don't intend to take them back to the camp?"

"That's right."

"Does Lyle know this?"

"Nobody knows it. Not yet. I'll decide who gets told what."

"Officer Whitman—Seth—listen. These boys are wards of the state. You can't take over and—"

"The state didn't do a very good job of protecting them. I intend to do whatever it takes to keep them from getting hurt."

Her cheeks turned so red they glowed in the dark, and Seth realized she'd misunderstood and taken his criticism personally. Her eyes narrowed and he recognized all the signs of a woman going on the defensive.

"I did the best job I could. I'd like to see you handle children like these. You'd be tearing your hair out within twenty-four hours. And for your information, even if I agreed with your plan, I can't just haul these boys around anywhere I choose. I practically have to have a court order to take them shopping for new shoes. Lyle had a fit because Dillon wandered off when we visited the Rune Stones."

"The Rune Stones. We need to talk about that, too. You say Dillon went into the caves before?"

"I don't know where he went, actually. And he'll never tell you. I wouldn't be surprised if Dillon isn't making up ninety percent of what he said in there. He'd do anything to keep from getting in more trouble with Lyle. He's—"

"I know. A pathological liar." But because of something Seth's brother had told him before he died, Seth was convinced Dillon McCoy was telling the absolute truth.

"But he's not making this up." He hated to frighten her, but it was critical that she understand the danger to the boys, and that time was not on their side. "I doubt you or the camp supervisor can protect these children from the likes of Lonnie and Nelson Slaughter. You need to understand what we are dealing with here. These are dangerous men. I've been tracking them for years. They know these woods like the backs of their hands. They operate well outside the law."

"You're talking about those crimes you didn't want to bring up in front of the boys?" Now she looked worried. "What kind of crimes?"

"Murder."

She gasped. *"Murder?"*

How could he tell her? How could he make her see? In small doses, that's how. "I have reason to believe they killed a lawman years ago."

"They killed a cop?"

"Yes."

"Then what in God's name are they doing running around these hills?" Her anger had exploded like a flare, surprising him. But at the same time he noticed that she shivered again, despite the night heat.

"The death was ruled vehicular homicide. But it was no accident. They've just been released from prison."

"Why do you think it was murder?"

"We really don't have time to go into all that now.

The point is, now the boys are witnesses to the fact that the Slaughter brothers were digging for someone's bones."

"The cop's?" Rainey looked confused.

"No. Look, I'm sorry, but we really have to get going."

"So you believe Dillon's story?"

Seth frowned. "Why wouldn't I?"

Rainey gave him an incredulous stare, as if to say the answer was obvious. She peeked over his shoulder at Jake.

"Jake does, too. Look, Dillon didn't lie about the duct tape. I peeled the stuff off of them myself."

Rainey clamped a hand over her mouth as if she might throw up right there in the dirt. "This whole mess is my fault," she said through whitened knuckles.

"Let's just concentrate on what we have to do now. My job is to catch the Slaughter twins. They've probably already destroyed the…whatever evidence the boys saw, but now that they think the boys can testify about their activities, and to the conversation they heard—"

"You mean what Dillon heard. With his history, do you honestly think a jury would believe his testimony? He's got a poor record. I can imagine a defense attorney effectively discrediting him."

"Don't forget that Aaron heard it, too."

Rainey shook her head. "I'm not sure he'd make a credible witness, either. The doctors tell me it is unlikely Aaron will ever speak again."

Their eyes connected briefly in the darkness, then

hers glanced away. "He saw his stepfather kill his mother."

Seth's jaw tightened. Every time he thought he'd seen it all… "How?"

"With a knife."

"Nevertheless, Lonnie and Nelson don't know Aaron is the way he is. They won't let this go. They will be planning a way to silence these children."

"To silence them? You mean kill them?" He could tell she was struggling to control her fear. He admired that.

"Yes. The boys are in real danger, Rainey." He took her elbows lightly. "Listen. I'm sending my partner back up to the caves and then I'd like to take the boys into protective custody, but we'll have to be careful how we do it. I prefer to take you along with them, since you can communicate with Maddy and since Aaron obviously depends on you. We can clear that with the camp supervisor. He'll keep his mouth shut. He doesn't want this made public, anyway. Is there someone else we need to contact about your absence? Husband? Boyfriend?"

"No. No one. Well, there is Loretta—my mother—I guess. She'll worry if she doesn't hear from me." Her eyes came up to meet his. "How long will we be gone?"

Mesmerized by those eyes, he shook his head slowly. "I honestly don't know." No boyfriend. No husband. How was it that a woman this beautiful was unattached?

"Doesn't matter." She looked away. "My job's my whole life."

"Okay." Seth willed himself to focus back on the urgent business. "So all we need is a place to hide. Is there someplace safe where you can take the boys and hold them for a few days? A hospital, a school, a group home—someplace where no one but you and I will know their whereabouts?"

Rainey looked at him as if he had just asked her to sprout wings and fly. "A safe place? No. There is *not* some handy safe place where I can just disappear with three boys."

Their gazes locked, and the look in Seth's steady blue eyes reminded Rainey of the unflinching one her father had always used on her. "I'm taking them into protective custody, and that's final."

That's final? *That's final?* Rainey felt her Irish temper simmering up like lava from a volcano. *She* was the one who was responsible for these children, and no overbearing cop was going to order her around. "Well, *I'm* responsible for their welfare. And *that's* final."

As quickly as it had hardened, his gaze grew conciliatory. "Look. I don't like this situation any better than you do. But this is no ordinary set of circumstances." He wrapped gentle fingers around her upper arm. "Please. You're going to have to trust me."

Rainey flicked a glance at Seth Whitman's hand gripping her flesh, and she swallowed. The night was hot, but his touch felt hotter.

When she tensed, he released her arm.

Something in her had wanted to resist that touch, the way she'd rebelled against her father that last time she'd seen him. Something in her wanted to turn her back on Seth Whitman and say that she didn't need him or his bossy ways. But something else in her wanted to melt into his arms right then and there and admit that she *did* need him. And the boys surely did, too. But was this…this *abduction* the answer? To just spirit the boys away in the middle of the night? There had to be a better way. "Why can't we go to the authorities with all of this?"

"I'm a cop, Rainey. I *am* the authorities. And something Dillon said—"

"Oh great. Something *Dillon* said."

"Yes. It was significant. You recall he heard them talking about a guy called Howard."

"Howard? You know who that is?"

His expression became veiled. "Yes. But it's a very long story. Let's just say it makes me realize I can't trust anyone, not now. Right now we need a hiding place." He steered her back on track. "Tonight. Can you think of any place at all?" he urged her softly.

"No, I can't. Unless…oh, man." She considered the idea that had begun to worm its way up a moment ago when she'd started thinking about being banished to Gran's farm every summer when she was a kid. But then she shook her head. "No. We couldn't possibly take them up there. They'd go nuts."

"Where? The sooner we act, the better off the boys will be."

"This is too crazy!" Rainey raked a hand through her tangled hair. "But what does it matter if I do something crazy now?" she said in a rush, seeming to be arguing more with herself than with Seth. "My job is history. I won't be able to get any kind of DHS job, not in the entire state, not after this fiasco. No one is going to trust a caseworker that lets her kids wander miles away from camp in the middle of the night, lets them get abducted, no less. I'll have to start my whole life over in a whole new field, or worse, go back to practicing law." She released a visible shudder. "And what about the boys?"

"Yes, ma'am. That's what we have to keep in mind. What about the boys?"

"We can't just hide with them up there—won't it mean we'll be breaking the law?"

"I think I can arrange to make it legal. The local judge is one of my buddies from high school. I can pull some strings, get a piece of paper."

"You mean make me the boys' guardian ad litum?"

He quirked an eyebrow at her use of the legal term. "I forgot. You know the law."

"You can accomplish this tonight?"

"With one phone call." He was already digging a cell phone out of his pocket. "So, where are we taking them?" He was punching in a number.

"My gran's house. She lives way back up in the Winding Stair Mountains. Way, way back. Gran's farm is about as remote as they come. One road in, same road out. A great view in all directions."

"Perfect." She heard Seth leave some guy named Max a message, then he held the cell phone out for Rainey. "Call your gran and see if we can hide the boys there, at least for a few days until I can figure out the Slaughters' next move."

Rainey shook her head. "Gran doesn't have a phone."

His deep-set eyes widened a fraction. "No phone?"

"And no electricity, either."

"You gotta be kiddin' me."

"Nope. But it's not totally primitive. She has a propane tank out back. A gas-powered generator to run a few lights, a tiny refrigerator, an even tinier TV. But nobody ever goes up there, not even the mailman. She picks up her mail at a post office box down in Wister. The only way to talk to Gran is to drive right up to the door of her cabin. I doubt that thing will even work up there." She nodded at his cell phone.

Seth made an annoyed face and flipped the phone shut. "Won't it freak your grandmother out if you show up at her door in the middle of the night with a strange cop and three delinquent boys in tow?"

"Gran? Nah. She raised four sons up on that mountain."

Rainey paused and looked up at him, sizing him up fully for the first time. She couldn't figure this guy out. He was all male and undeniably handsome, that was for sure. But he needed an attitude adjustment in the worst way. That or a boot to the behind, as her gran used to say. Was he just another macho, overbearing cop with the guarded emotions and the love 'em and leave 'em attitude that Rainey had detested all her life, or was he some kind of white knight?

And there was something else. She had sensed it when she had told him about Aaron's past. It was something that put a look so secretive and deep in Seth Whitman's eyes it was hard to look there for long.

Didn't matter. Whatever he was and whatever was eating him, Gran could handle it. Rainey had never seen any man her gran couldn't put in his place. "Nothing could shake up Granny Grace," she said with a note of challenge. "Not three delinquent little boys. And certainly not a strange cop like *you,* Seth Whitman."

CHAPTER FIVE

THE "ROAD" THAT CLIMBED to Rainey Chapman's Gran's house was hardly worthy of such a name. Seth had made it his business to become familiar with every dark, twisting backwoods track in Le Flore County, but he'd never been near the rocky rutted lane that Rainey directed him to, rising to the south off the highway out of Wister. This road was buried deeper in the Winding Stair than even the roughest logging trail.

Despite the light of a full moon and the fact that Rainey assured him she had been here many times, they missed the turn. Seth was forced to switch on the deer lights mounted high on the cab of his Silverado pickup. He'd been driving with only the fog lights out on the highway, and for good reason. Anyone sitting up on a ridge with a set of high-powered binoculars could spot headlights after they left the main road. When Rainey found the turnout on the second pass, Seth slammed on his brakes, turned, and they bumped onto a narrow gravel path that veered sharply upward in the dense underbrush.

"I warned you, it's bad," Rainey said.

"Cool!" Dillon shouted from the rear seat of Seth's double cab pickup.

The boys were crammed shoulder to shoulder, with Aaron and Maddy, predictably silent, looking increasingly anxious. But Dillon was acting loud and boastful enough to make up for the other two.

"I wish *I* could drive *this* road," he shouted in Seth's ear. Seth knew the boy was masking some serious anxiety.

"I wish you could, too," he replied dryly as the pickup bucked up the steep, rocky path. He switched off the high beams.

"Are you crazy?" Rainey clutched the darkened dash as if she could hold them onto the side of the mountain that way. "This trail skirts a hundred-foot dropoff!"

Even by moonlight, Seth could make out the grim downturn of her delicate mouth.

"Unfortunately, the Slaughters know every high point for miles. They could be watching for us right now. You can spot headlights from quite a distance out here. It wouldn't take them long to pin down our location. They know the roads out here as well as I do."

"Well, *you* didn't know about *this* particular road," Rainey challenged.

"This doesn't exactly qualify as a—"

"Road." Dillon finished Seth's sentence as the truck jostled over a sizable slab of buried sandstone. "This is more like a roller coaster!" The boy leaned forward in the seat like a kid on a carnival ride.

"It would be stupid to lead the Slaughters right to us." Seth glanced at Rainey and downshifted. "No headlights."

"I hope you know—ugh!—" Rainey clutched the dash tighter as the pickup bounced down off the slab of rock "—what you're doing."

He hoped so, too. He hoped he was doing the right thing by these vulnerable boys and this delicate woman. He flicked a glance at her, then concentrated on his driving. Rainey Chapman was way, way different from the women he was used to.

The pickup jolted over another mound of rock. "Yeehaw!" Dillon yelled. "Ride 'em, cowboy!"

"Dillon," Rainey snapped. "Be quiet. Officer Whitman is driving."

The boy sat back in a pout, but when the truck bucked again, his cracking young voice erupted, high with excitement. "I'm tellin' ya, Sheriff! I could handle this dude!"

Seth glanced in the rearview mirror and could see that the boy's bravado was phony as a three-dollar bill. The other two looked plainly terrified.

Dillon's expression became defiant when he caught Seth studying him in the mirror. "I can handle a stick shift good as anybody."

"I don't doubt it." Seth downshifted as the tires skidded and ground in the rocky ruts. "But right at the moment—" he shifted one more time "—I'd appreciate it if you'd settle down, pardner." Dillon answered with a resentful squint.

Seth turned his attention back to the treacherous road. "How long does this go on?" he asked Rainey.

"Eight miles."

The place was beyond remote. When they started to climb the narrow track of Granny Grace's rocky drive, Seth spotted the profile of a tiny log cottage tucked high up in the trees. Perched on stilts at the peak of a sheer rocky incline that looked out over a valley, the structure appeared to list to one side, looking like some long-forgotten fairy cottage punctuated by several sagging, steep-pitched gables. All of the tall windows were dark.

"We aren't gonna stay here, are we?" Dillon grumbled. "This place looks creepy."

"'Fraid so," Seth said dryly. "For now this is home sweet home."

"Home sweet home," Dillon echoed sarcastically, as he signed something presumably derogatory to Maddy.

A cacophony of barking broke out as they pulled into the gravel clearing and up to a rickety-looking wooden staircase that rose to the dark house. Before Seth had even braked to a stop a couple of mixed mutts came barreling out from under the stilts.

A light winked on inside the house, followed by a weak bulb flicking awake next to the door on the screened-in front porch.

Seth leaned forward to peer up through the windshield. "So. You want to go up alone and explain things first?"

"No. You guys can come on, but stay behind me. Those stairs can be tricky in spots."

"I hate dogs," Dillon shouted above the barking. "If one of 'em comes near me, I'll kick his teeth in, I swear."

"You will do no such thing. The dogs know me," Rainey explained. "They'll be fine as long as you behave yourself."

The animals had charged the pickup, scratching at Seth's shiny door handles. "Whoa, now," he said.

Rainey rolled down the window and shouted, "Quiet!" When the dogs quieted and touched paws to the ground, she turned to the boys. "These dogs aren't vicious." She got out and threw the passenger seat forward and signaled for the two mute boys to get out of the back seat. "You, Dillon, will be nice to my gran *and* to her dogs."

"Or what?" The boy slumped in the seat defiantly.

"Or you'll answer to me." Seth had come around the rear of the truck. "Come on now."

"Who's out there?" a reedy female voice called.

Rainey turned, leaving the door ajar. She stepped into the ray of the fog beams. "It's me, Gran."

"Rainey? Honey? Is that really you?"

"Yes, Gran. It's really me."

"Lord Almighty, child. I sure wasn't expecting you in the middle of the night."

"I know, Gran. I'm sorry for just showing up this way. It's sort of an emergency."

The screen door creaked and a woman appeared under the faint globe of light. In its glow, Seth could make out a tiny stick figure in a pale robe, with a long gray braid trailing over one shoulder. "An emergency?" she said. "Well, come on up, then. All of you."

As the crew climbed rickety, rotting steps to the screened-in porch, the dogs took up a fresh round of barking.

"Killer! Butch!" the tiny woman hollered. "Hush up!" The dogs trotted up the steps to her side and she said "Stay," pointing one finger at the ground. She braced her feet wide and waited…clutching a shotgun across her middle.

As Seth's eyes adjusted to the darkness, he was gratified to see that the old house had a high upstairs addition that jutted out well above the treetops. He could see the glass of a large window winking in the moonlight, but it was facing east. He would need a place with a clear view of the road at night.

He followed Rainey and the boys up several flights of crude steps that twisted and turned toward the porch, while the little old woman held the shotgun like Moses's staff. Several times Rainey pointed out rotting places in the steps, warning, "Careful. Be careful."

When he got to the landing at the top, Seth found himself staring at the business end of the shotgun. "Who's this strappin' fella?" Gran said with a jerk of the barrel.

"Gran—" Rainey began with a note of exasperation.

"Ma'am," Seth interrupted. "You can put the gun down. I'm with the Tenikah police." He stepped around the boys so she could see the reflection of his badge in the weak light.

The old woman flicked on the safety and the shotgun disappeared into the folds of her robe. "Cain't be too cautious these days. Grace Chapman." She thrust out a knobby hand and Seth gently clasped it.

"Seth Whitman," he said.

"Whitman? A cop? You related to that cop that was killed out near the Rune Stones some years back?"

"Yes, ma'am." He kept his eyes off Rainey, who stood hovering near the boys in the porch shadows. He didn't want to see the look on her face if she added two and two. He didn't want anybody's pity over Lane's death. It was long past. There was nothing he could do about it now except avenge it. And that was exactly what he intended to do.

Gran turned on Rainey. "You look awful, girl. Is everything all right?"

"Not exactly." Rainey sighed.

"What are you doing here with the law at this ungodly hour? And who are these youngsters?"

While Rainey introduced the boys and explained that they were her charges from Big Cedar Camp, and what had happened, Seth took stock of Rainey's Granny Grace.

The old lady was pretty much what he had expected. In his police work, he had often encountered elderly women exactly like her, tucked back into these hills. They tended gardens they'd scratched out in their beloved rocky soil, they babied paltry livestock, they fashioned stunning quilts from the scraps of their lives, and they basically preferred to be left alone.

The ones he'd seen in Tenikah rolled their decrepit cars into town once or twice a week to attend church, visit the post office or buy provisions. They reported trouble to the police like faithful little tattletales, appearing at the station to shout into the microphone in the glass security window. So-and-so was burning leaves despite the burn ban, or a newspaper stand lay facedown in the creek with the cash box pried open, or one of old man Goodner's cows was loose out on the highway again. As the junior officer on the force, Seth often had to follow up on all this nonsense.

"Land sakes! That's awful!" Gran said when Rainey reached a stopping place. "Come inside then, all of you."

"Ma'am?" Seth halted their progress. "What's behind your place?"

Granny turned. "The house sits at the top of the ridge. The backside drops off into the river."

The place might actually work. When he got everybody settled, Seth decided he'd walk the perimeter, check for a lookout.

The two women continued to talk nonstop as Seth and the boys followed the tiny lady inside the house. She lit an antique oil lantern and set it in the middle of a round kitchen table with a red-checked oilcloth spread on it.

Seth felt as if he'd stepped back in time. The boys, he could see, were stunned by these unusual surroundings, or maybe they were just too tired to care. Likely none of them had ever seen a place like this, except in the movies. Even Dillon seemed subdued, taking in the cluttered room with wide-eyed fascination.

But Seth had been in houses like Grace's plenty of times, though never one quite this solidly frozen in time. The kitchen where the six of them stood in an awkward ring, softly lit by the glow of the lantern, was little more than a box lined with crooked white cabinets yellowing with age. Clean but dented pans were stacked on an actual wood-burning, cast-iron cookstove. A home-sewn feedsack curtain concealed the guts of a huge enamel sink where bunches of enormous carrots with the green tops still attached lay at an angle. All manner of dried herbs lined the narrow windowsill, tied in neat bundles or propped up in tiny colored-glass medicine bottles.

Covering every inch of wall space were animal skins and American flags, crosses and family photos, postcards from trips to far-flung places like Eureka Springs, Arkansas. A small refrigerator, run off the gas-powered generator, Seth assumed, was plastered with all manner of cheap magnets. Some were frames with tiny pictures of a little girl in them. Rainey? A bowl of fresh peaches ripened in the corner of the counter next to a large bin that was stamped Bread.

It looked like the kind of place that had produced meal after hearty meal for decades and didn't know how to stop. In fact, Seth imagined there were cookies resting under the embroidered dish towel that covered a plate in the corner.

"So, we have to have a place to hide the boys,"

Rainey said, finishing up her story, "We have to keep them safe until Seth can catch those men. I hate to put you in a fix, Gran, but I couldn't think of anyplace else to go. I hope you can help us."

"You know you can always come to me if you've got trouble, honey," Gran said. "I bet you boys are hungry as horses."

She reached for the towel-covered plate and folded back the corner. Sure enough. Cookies.

"Sit down, then, and eat." Gran encouraged them with a sweeping gesture and the boys tumbled into the dinette chairs. "You should eat, too, Rainey," she said, eyeing her granddaughter's slender frame. "Looks like you're still not eating enough to amount to a hill of beans. You look plumb peaked, matter of fact."

"I'm just tired, Gran. It's been a long night."

Rainey leaned her hips against the counter edge and Seth positioned himself at a distance, one shoulder propped against the doorjamb.

"You're welcome," Gran chirped as she passed the boys the cookies, "you're very welcome," even though none the three had uttered a word of thanks.

When Granny held the platter out to Seth he said, "None for me, thanks." He was impatient to get everybody settled in so he could check over the place and begin his watch.

While the boys ate greedily, Grace poured milk into cut-glass tumblers, then seated herself in the last chair. She and Rainey resumed a carefully worded interchange, back and forth, about the boys, about their various histories, their various problems, about what had happened out there in the woods to land them all up here.

While the women talked, Seth laid his plans. He'd go into town tomorrow, before the sun was up, so there'd be no chance of Lonnie and Nelson tracing his departure from here. There were questions to ask, discrepancies to clear up. The name Howard gnawed at him.

Even as he mulled over the situation, his thoughts, and his eyes, kept straying back to Rainey Chapman. The woman was a surprise. Not because of her stunning good looks. The surprise was how *he* felt in her presence.

In his days as a rodeo champion he'd grown accustomed to women hanging around. And cops, he'd quickly discovered, had to practically beat 'em off with a stick. Women from as far away as Muskogee and Tulsa seemed to gravitate to him. Nice woman with pretty hair and soft voices. Interesting, smart, independent women. Reporters. Politicians. Teachers. Nurses. Other cops. All of them were, as far as Seth was concerned, attractive. As he and Lane used to say, "pretty little things." But none of them had that spark, that something unique enough to hold his heart. He supposed that was because none of them knew the real Seth. He'd never told a single one of them the truth about what tortured him, what kept him awake nights. And he wasn't of a mind to share.

Deep down inside, he harbored the conviction that getting all tangled up with a woman, telling her the truth about what drove him, might even require him to change. What woman would want a man who was driven by vengeance? But Seth had no intention of giving up his quest. Certainly not now, when he was within striking distance.

But even so, as he watched Rainey's movements in the cozy glow of the lantern, he felt the kind of keyed-up fascination that he thought he had left behind with his youth. Not since KayAnn, in fact, had Seth seen a woman this gorgeous. But KayAnn was trouble. Unlike his brother, Seth had had the sense to resist KayAnn's blatantly female charms. And every time he tried to talk sense to Lane, they'd ended up fighting about it, until finally the subject of KayAnn Rawls became sorely off-limits. Only when he'd read the diary he found in Lane's things after his death did Seth begin to understand his brother's obsessive protectiveness of KayAnn. And only now, looking at Rainey Chapman, could he imagine feeling the same way himself.

He refocused his mind on the problem. Before this woman had "turned into his hand" up on Purney's Mountain, he reminded himself ruefully, he had been within inches of realizing a seven-year-old goal—eradicating the Slaughters from the face of the earth.

And it had been a very long seven years.

When his uncle Tack had stopped Seth in the midst of settling atop a big Brahma in the loading chute at Bullnanza, Seth had been a reckless and cocky twenty-two-year-old bull rider, and nothing like his brother. Back then, he had lived a life that was as wild and selfish as the devil. That very night he had been about to take the big prize.

The crowd was already screaming for another breathtaking Seth Whitman ride, so Tack had had to yell directly into his nephew's ear. "Get off!" the old man screamed. "We got trouble!"

While the crowd quieted, muttering in bewilderment, Tack led Seth off into the bowels of the enormous Lazy E Arena. Once they were back in a more or less quiet corridor, Tack turned on him and said, "Brace yourself, son." Tack always called Lane and Seth "son" and the boys had never questioned it. After all, even when they were alive their parents hadn't been their parents. Aunt Junie and Uncle Tack were the people who loved them and fed them and gave them sound advice.

A couple of cowboys eased past with wary glances, but Seth ignored them and focused on his uncle's face. Drama was not Tack's way.

"What is it?" The air in the corridor was thick with dust from the arena floor, and Seth found himself hardly able to croak out the words, hardly able to breathe. Because right now Tack's face looked too much like it had the night Mamma and Daddy died. Way too much.

"Somethin's happened. Somethin' bad." The old man's lips were stiff with emotion.

"What?" Seth said. When Tack didn't answer immediately he repeated, "What?" his voice echoing in the concrete corridor.

"It's your brother."

"Lane?" Seth said senselessly. He only had one brother.

Tack had nodded. "He's come up missing."

Seth stared at the glowing lantern on Grace Chapman's kitchen table, remembering it all for the hundredth time.

While he'd gulped for air in that dusty corridor, Tack had told him what they'd found—Lane's hat, one boot. Blood on each. Lane's blood, it turned out. Which, as far as Seth was concerned, was the same as his own. Whoever killed Lane that night had killed Seth, in a way. Because that night the reckless young cowboy had disappeared for good.

That night, Seth had climbed off his last bull. That night on the long trip down I-40 east to Tenikah, he had started to wonder what had ever made him leave his hometown. He'd wondered why he hadn't stayed to help Lane face down the Slaughters.

When they found Lane's body, the coroner ruled it an accident, but nobody had to tell Seth what really happened. He knew. Getting everybody else to believe him had been the tough part.

Seth told himself that nobody, excepting maybe his uncle Tack, could detect the rage seething beneath his steady exterior in the days, the weeks, the months that followed.

When your dead brother's reputation for honesty and fairness preceded you, the local police force welcomed you with open arms. The few weeks of law enforcement education that followed were just a formality. Lane had already taught Seth nearly every-thing he needed to know. And Lane had already told him more than he needed to know.

That first year, playing the role of the easygoing rookie came naturally. Seth had always been "the younger brother" around town. On the job he made a habit of smiling at people a lot. He went through the motions of performing his mundane duties thoroughly, professionally. It came easy. Most of the time all he had to do was show up and the trouble stopped.

When you were already known as the sharpest of sharpshooters and the toughest of fist fighters before you'd clipped on a badge, even the lowliest perps wouldn't mess with you. Even the suits downtown in government respected you when, ever since you were eighteen years old, you'd been known as the guy who relished subjugating a nineteen-hundred-pound bull.

Seth missed riding the bulls, but that was a life that claimed the whole of a man's days, and the whole of his soul. And seven years ago, while the tires on Tack's old pickup had hummed a relentless rhythm as they carried Seth back toward Tenikah, back to his dead brother's remains, Seth Whitman had made the decision to trade his soul away in the name of vengeance.

The boys started yawning, so Grace pushed herself up from her seat. "I've got my sons' old sleeping bags. You know where I keep them, Rainey? Upstairs?" She pointed toward a narrow enclosed stairway. "We'll bed you boys down on the living room rug."

Rainey pushed off the counter and crossed the room to the stairway door, but Seth grabbed her elbow. "I'd like to talk to you first," he said. "Alone."

CHAPTER SIX

THE WAY RAINEY GLANCED down to where his hand touched her made him let go instantly. Funny. He'd been touching her—holding her hand or her wrist, even clasping her waist—all the way down Purney's Mountain, but now that they were in the confines of her grandmother's kitchen, apparently he had to watch himself.

She covered her discomfort by raking her hair back behind one ear. "Okay. How about out on the porch? I'll be back in a minute, Gran, and I'll bunk with you."

Rainey had volunteered that cheerfully enough, but Seth detected a note of unwillingness in her voice.

"That'll leave the attic room for you, I guess." Grace smiled graciously at Seth. "Nothing fancy. But at least you'll have your privacy up there."

Seth had been wondering where everyone would sleep in this tiny house. He knew he'd want to be as far away from tempting thoughts of Rainey Chapman's slender body as possible.

"Thank you, ma'am, but if it's all the same to you, I'll just stay out in my truck." Sleep wasn't in his game plan, anyway. If despite his precautions the Slaughters had tracked him, they would most likely show before the sun came up. They'd never been much for the daytime hours.

"Whatever you say." Grace turned to the kids. "Boys, around this house we got rules. One is we wash up and brush our teeth before bed." She pointed to a narrow door at the back of the kitchen. "Bathroom's off the back porch."

"The bathroom's on the back *porch?*" Dillon made a face.

"It's real nice, too. Rainey's grampa built it. Got a toilet and a tub. No shower, though."

Maddy signed something to Rainey and raised his shoulders in a shrug.

"What he said." Dillon shrugged as well. "We ain't got no toothbrushes."

"Well, you got fingers, don't ya?" Gran demonstrated, rubbing her own teeth vigorously. "There's a box of baking soda on the shelf. After the tooth brushin' and such, you youngsters can help me haul the sleeping bags down out of the attic. Let's go."

Rainey quickly signed Gran's instructions to Maddy, who shuffled out behind Gran and the other boys. Seth had headed toward the front of the house. Rainey caught up with him on the porch.

The weak light had been doused, but the bright moon cast shadows on the weathered wood planks. Seth's shadow was long and lean as he stood waiting for Rainey with one boot propped on the porch rail, staring out into the dark woods below.

She came up beside him, feeling the slightest twinge of vulnerability. She attributed the sensation to the difference in their sizes. He was an imposing man. "Are you sure you want to sleep in your truck?"

"Who said anything about sleeping?"

"Oh."

"I told you. The Slaughters are treacherous. They like to sneak around at night."

"If they're so bad, why don't you call in reinforcements or something like that?"

He straightened slowly. "This is actually the local county sheriff's territory out here. He's convinced the Slaughters have gone to Mexico. Now I'm wondering if he didn't start the rumor himself."

Rainey frowned. "Why would he do that?"

"Me."

Her frown grew deeper.

"He thinks I've got a personal grudge against the Slaughters that impedes my judgment."

"Are you telling me that if we call the sheriff, he won't help us?"

"I'm telling you things are a little complicated down in Tenikah. Until I can sort a few things out, I prefer to handle this alone. I can take care of this place for the night. Jake's on lookout elsewhere. We can trust him. After sunup we can relax. Lonnie and Nelson seldom show themselves in the daylight.

"I'll explain everything after I clear some things up in town. I'm sorry that I keep having to ask this, but for a little while you'll just have to trust me."

"Trust you?" Rainey shuddered as her eyes searched the dark woods. "How can I trust you when I don't even know you? I'd never even seen your face until you grabbed me a couple hours ago, and now I'm supposed to trust you with my life, with the lives of those three boys?"

"Can you trust me for just one night?" Looking up into his intense dark eyes she thought, *What choice do I have?* What was she going to do? Send their protection away? How could it hurt to have a cop keeping watch in front of Gran's house? Still, without knowing what was going on, how could she gauge the consequences of her actions? Everything she did affected the boys. "Did you clear the way with the judge?"

"Yes."

"I have to wonder what kind of town Tenikah is when you can rip three children out of their environment with a simple phone call."

"Tenikah's a great little place. A pretty little town." He stared off into the dark woods and Rainey detected sarcasm, an edge of anger, in his voice. "It's the kind of town where Main Street gets decorated for the homecoming parade and practically everybody shows up to support the football team on Friday nights. All decked out in Pirates black, no less. The sidewalks are clean, the flags are flying, the flowers are blooming." His expression darkened like a wall cloud about to spawn a tornado. "It's the kind of place where a couple of well-connected thugs can get away with murder."

Whatever was behind Seth Whitman's anger, whatever the secrets or problems in Tenikah were, Rainey had only one concern foremost in her mind. "All I care about is these boys. I don't want them to get hurt because of something that happened in Tenikah a long time ago. Promise me you won't let that happen."

"Nobody's going to get hurt if I have anything to say about it. Not the boys. Not you."

Keeping her gaze firmly on his, she drew a huge breath. "Let's hope not."

Seth studied the green-eyed beauty facing him in the moonlight. The anxiety in her eyes said he hadn't reassured her. He knew nothing about what made Rainey Chapman tick, yet he wanted to. In fact, he very possibly wanted to know everything there was to know. "Are you sure there isn't somebody you need to call? Somebody who'll be wondering what's happened to you, somebody back in Tulsa?"

Rainey frowned. "Like I said, my mother, of course. She'll eventually get wind of the fact that I've taken leave from the camp. But I don't know how I can let her know that I'm safe at Gran's without jeopardizing the boys' whereabouts in the process. Couldn't the Slaughters trace the boys through me, through her?"

Seth shook his head. "Doubt it." Her answer wasn't the one he was angling for. "You said you don't have a boyfriend, but are you dating someone? Someone who might look for you?"

"Dating someone?" She tucked a wisp of her soft, strawberry-blond hair behind one ear, seeming suddenly self-conscious. "No. No, I'm not."

Seth liked that, the fact that he made her just a tad nervous. He nodded and smiled. "Why not?"

"Why not what?"

"Why don't you have a boyfriend?"

"Oh." Rainey crossed the creaky porch and turned her back to him. Standing at the side rail, she looked out over the moonlit mountain, clearly stalling. "There are lots of reasons, I suppose. What about you?"

"What *about* me?"

"Are you…married or…anything like that?" He caught her quick glance at his ring finger. It was empty, but that didn't always signal availability. Some cops removed their rings when they went on duty.

In the dark he smiled, glad to see that she wanted a clear answer, same as he did. "I'm very single."

"What's that mean? *Very* single?"

"It means never married. Never even engaged."

Rainey thought he sounded almost proud of it. She suppressed the urge to say, *Are you gay or something?* But she figured it wouldn't be prudent to antagonize the man who had assigned himself to be her protector.

Still, he had to be at least thirty, and why was a man that age so thoroughly unattached? Especially one this good-looking?

But the times Seth Whitman had touched her, he had sent enough currents through her flesh to convince her that he was definitely the kind of man who was interested in women, maybe even interested in *her,* which she found frankly thrilling…and vaguely threatening.

All the men she'd dated in Tulsa had left her unmoved, unfulfilled. She would have feared there was something wrong with her if her best friend, Kara, hadn't diagnosed her problem as Rainey being just too picky.

The men she dated were fun guys, most of them. Interesting companions. Excellent kissers. Successful, charming men. Polite, kind. Brave, thrifty, clean and reverent. So why hadn't she ever gotten deeply involved? The only way she could avoid the question was to turn it back on him.

"Why not?"

He didn't even pretend to not understand the question. "Obviously I haven't met my soul mate."

Despite his lightly sarcastic tone, she felt there was something more to the story. She glanced back at him. He was watching her steadily, solemnly. Those deepset eyes of his would surely be her undoing. She looked away. She'd certainly never imagined that a man this far out of her element would be the one who finally rang all her bells. And certainly not a cop. No, never a cop.

Her jumble of conflicted thoughts finally trailed into a mumbled, "Really?" and she imagined she sounded like a dolt.

"Really." He smiled indulgently. "You need to get some rest now. It's been a trying night and it's really late. You go on up and take that attic room. I had the feeling you weren't too crazy about the idea of sleeping in your gran's room. Like I said, I'll be fine out here."

She smiled. "Thank you. Gran's bed is a lumpy old bag that creaks every time you breathe, and besides," she lowered her voice to a conspiratorial level, "Gran snores like a freight train."

"Nobody's perfect." Seth grinned down at her, and as she smiled up at him, another charge passed between them, as if the slightest movement on either side might slam them together, like a magnet and steel.

"Anyway…" Rainey subtly backed up and kept her voice light "…the old beds in the attic aren't much better than Gran's—thin cotton mattresses on old hospital cots—so you aren't missing much. I guess you figured out by now that my gran is a pretty simple woman."

"Don't apologize. Simplicity is a quality I admire."

That put her on the defensive. "Don't get me wrong. Just because I grew up in a nice suburb of Tulsa, I don't look down on Gran's simple life. I happen to love it here. The peace and quiet, the sunsets. I even love soaking in that old claw-foot tub out on the back por—"

She bit off her words, and even in the pale moonlight he could see her cheeks coloring over conjuring up that image—herself soaking in a bathtub. Again, her discomfort actually pleased him for some perverse reason, possibly because it betrayed the same rush that had stirred his own core. Or perhaps it was the knowledge that, as spunky as she was, this woman could still be vulnerable.

A wave of heat that had nothing to do with the hot August night rippled between them. Seth couldn't remember when he'd felt this much chemistry emanating

between himself and a woman. This whole situation—
the boys, the old woman, this way-too-attractive female—promised to amount to a giant pain in the neck.

He clamped a palm there and backed up a step. "Ms.
Chapman…" He cleared his throat.

"Rainey."

"Sorry. Rainey. I think it's time we got to bed." To
his consternation, he discovered that the spunky little
blonde wasn't the only one who could blush over poorly
chosen words. He felt his own face heating up.

She smiled graciously. Or was it knowingly? "Good
night, Seth."

CHAPTER SEVEN

AS SHE STOOD AT THE TINY attic window and watched
the first thin light of dawn seep over the ridges of the
Winding Stair, Rainey thought surely she must be the
only person in the household who was awake.

Awake was probably the wrong way to put it, since
she had never actually been asleep. She had tossed and
turned on one of the narrow cots in the stuffy little attic
until she'd wondered if she was suffering from a fever,
on top of everything else. But she knew that the only
fever besetting her was the kind visited upon a woman
by the sudden interest of an overwhelmingly attractive
man.

Seth Whitman's interest was as plain as the badge
on his chest. She could see it in the movement of those
deep-set eyes, constantly watching her. She could sense
it in the set of his broad shoulders, angled toward her
when he wasn't even aware of it. She could feel it in
the gentle protective touch of his hands. Those hands.
She wished to goodness she'd never felt them on her.
All night long she had thought about the way he had
touched her.

The only thing she wanted now was a hot cup of tea and some quiet time to process all the crazy things that had happened last night. But when she opened the stairway door, she heard the banging of pots from down in the kitchen.

As she descended the narrow stairway she smelled the aroma of strong coffee brewing. The door at the bottom of the stairs was ajar and she caught a glimpse of Gran's gingham-robed back. Gran's skinny elbow canted out as she poured coffee from her enormous enamel stovetop pot into a thick white mug.

Rainey came up short as she caught sight of a masculine hand reaching out to take the mug. Great. The cop was already up and at 'em. So much for some quiet ruminating about this predicament…and this man. These two were already yakking their heads off.

"Don't you worry about it, Seth," Gran was saying. "I can handle these youngsters for the day. I got plans for 'em."

"I appreciate your cooperation, Mrs. Chapman. I know it's an imposition, but I'll need you and Rainey to keep them close by today, until I can assess the lay of the land."

"This place is secure. Only that one road up. There's a high outcropping of rock about a hundred yards up the mountain from the house. You can see the whole valley, including the road, from there. The creek starts up on the ridge and becomes a river down in the gorge. Anybody wanting to sneak up on this place without using the road would have to come upstream in a boat from the back, or climb up the rocky ridge in plain sight."

"Yes, ma'am."

"And you just call me Grace, okay? No need for formality in this house. I feel like I know you, anyways. I've been hearing about you for a long time. I remember when you and your brother was the same age as those boys in there." She pointed toward the living room, where the kids were still sacked out in their sleeping bags. "And I remember when you and your brother was young bucks on the Tenikah High football team." Rainey heard Gran hesitate before she said this next. "And I remember when them Slaughter boys went to prison, when your brother was killed."

His brother?

Rainey remained frozen in place on the stairs, listening intently now. So his brother was the lawman the Slaughters had killed? Shamelessly, she eavesdropped, hoping Seth would elaborate about it, but all she heard was, "Yes, ma'am. I sure appreciate you fixing me this breakfast."

Disappointed, Rainey padded down the last few stairs on bare feet. At the bottom of the stairwell, she peeked around the door.

She was not surprised to see that Seth was fully dressed. His shirt was badly wrinkled but tightly tucked in at his tapered waist. It stretched across a back so massive and well-formed that the sight of it made Rainey's breath hitch in her throat. One long, lean leg—clad in denim and a well-worn boot—angled out from Gran's spindly little table. He even had his shoulder radio and holster clipped on.

She pushed a frizz of bangs out of her eyes and eased the creaky door fully open, realizing too late that she was not exactly, as Gran would put it, properly attired. Suddenly she felt exposed, even though she was wearing one of Gran's old high-necked, cotton nightgowns. Maybe Rainey's discomfort stemmed from the fact that material of the gown had become thin with age. Maybe it was the fact that she wore absolutely nothing underneath it.

Or maybe it was the fact that the most masculine man she'd ever seen was sitting with his back to her, not five feet away. A man so solidly built his presence filled Gran's tiny kitchen like a genie in a bottle. Just looking at him made Rainey unconsciously cross one hand over her front and gather the neck of the nightgown tighter with the other.

"Hon!" Gran whirled around from the stove. "What in the world are you doing up at dawn? I thought you'd sleep awhile yet."

"Good morning," Seth said quietly. Thank goodness he didn't look up from his coffee.

"I couldn't sleep." Rainey decided maybe she could sidle around behind Seth, get her tea and get the heck out of there.

Gran was heaping food from the stove onto one of her heavy crockery plates. For Seth, obviously. Gran never had anything for breakfast but a pot of extra-strong coffee and a dab of oatmeal. Why was she insisting on serving this man like a waitress? And why on earth was *he* allowing it? "I figured you'd be all tuckered out," Gran said as she finished up her job, "after having such a scare and gallivanting around until all hours."

"Actually, I don't think I ever got to sleep," Rainey admitted. "Too keyed up, I guess." She hated to tell Gran that she'd forgotten just how uncomfortable the beds in the attic could be. Packed tight with real cotton, those so-called mattresses were as hard as a mortician's slab. And she wasn't about to admit, right in front of the man, that thoughts of Seth Whitman had contributed to her tossing and turning.

"You want some breakfast, hon?" Gran slid the platter in front of Seth and whipped back over to the stove faster than a waitress in a greasy spoon.

"I just want a cup of tea if that's okay."

"Kettle's already hot. Help yourself, though you really should eat something. You are looking far too thin." Gran took a potholder, grabbed a baking pan bursting with steaming biscuits, and ferried them back to Seth at the table.

Rainey slipped over to the stove, hoping to use her grandmother's diminutive frame as cover.

But while Gran eased a steaming biscuit out of the beat-up baking tin, Seth slid his chair back slightly so he could see around her.

Rainey lifted the teakettle, then halted when she realized he was watching her backside. She turned and looked over her shoulder, and a jolt of sexual awareness shot through her the instant their gazes connected. He wasn't smiling or leering or anything like that, but his eyes said he definitely appreciated what he saw.

And for one brief moment, as they stared at each other in the cozy little kitchen touched only by the faintest daylight, it struck her that his eyes were incredibly intense. They were the kind of male eyes a woman wanted—craved—admiration from. As dark and fathomless and alluring as a hidden mountain lake on a hot summer day.

She wasn't sure, but it looked as if they might also be plenty bloodshot. He hadn't slept, either, Rainey suspected. But his hair was damp and he was clean-shaven. How had he managed that? Using Grampa's old straight razor? Gran kept that antiquated thing, with Grampa's shaving brush and mug, on a lone shelf out on the back porch alongside some of Grampa's other "personal effects." The shelf reminded Rainey of some kind of miniature shrine.

"I'm glad you're up," he said, flicking one last glance up and down the length of the gauzy nightgown. "I was planning to wake you before I took off, anyway." He scooted the chair back in and hunched over the table.

Rainey stood suspended, hand on teakettle. "Before you take off? Where are you going?"

"That reminds me." Gran banged the biscuit pan down and shot off toward the porch.

"Into Tenikah. Here's my cell phone number." He dug into his shirt pocket, then handed her a yellow sticky note with a number jotted on it in a bold hand.

Rainey put the teakettle down, took the paper from him and stared at it. "You're leaving us up here?"

"Not for long. I've got to make some arrangements.

Then I'll be back to stay here for as long as it takes."
He started shoveling in the bacon and eggs Gran had
placed before him.

"For as long as *what* takes?"

"Catching those varmints," Gran said with conviction as she rushed back into the kitchen, the shotgun in
her grip. Apparently she was already privy to some
plan they had concocted. She peered down at the gun
through half-glasses with her nose in the air and her
mouth in a pinch. When she was satisfied that the thing
was in working order, she gave Seth a brisk little nod
of approval. "Seth here'll catch 'em."

"That's why I gave you the number." Seth ignored
Gran's flattery. "So you can call me."

"I'm not even sure my cell phone will work up here,"
Rainey countered. She walked around the table to face
Seth and crossed her arms tight over her middle, no
longer concerned about the immodest gown. "And what
if something happens before you can make it back?
What if those creeps show up?"

"I got my shotgun." Gran propped the gun in a corner.

"You cannot leave that thing out around the boys."
Rainey pointed an accusing finger at the weapon.

"We might need it if trouble comes. Those boys are
old enough to know how to mind and keep their hands
off of things when they are told to." Gran directed the
next comment to Seth. "Don't you worry. If worse
comes to worst, I want it handy."

"Oh, for crying out loud!" Rainey threw up her

hands. "This whole thing is getting crazier and crazier!"

"If they didn't show up last night," Seth said, his tone level, reasonable, "the Slaughters won't come around in broad daylight. It's probably going to take something to draw them out now. I have to assume they've gone into hiding up here."

"What do you mean, up here?" Rainey turned disbelieving eyes on Seth now. "Up here in the Winding Stair?"

"Yes. But they won't expose themselves, not in the daylight. I know their habits all too well."

"Oh, that's comforting!"

"Look, I'm sorry, but you'll *have* to trust me on some things."

But Rainey didn't trust him. Many a cop had gotten himself killed because he thought he knew a perp's habits. Or at least one that she knew of had. "I don't like this setup. Are you absolutely sure you have to go into town?"

Seth wiped his mouth with the checkered napkin Gran had folded beside his plate. "Would you mind trying your cell phone now? Let's see if it at least works in Roam."

"Fine." Rainey stalked back upstairs to get her phone from the pocket of her jeans, wondering how the man knew she had it on her. She dug out the phone and had started to march back down when she remembered her attire. She jerked open the old wardrobe in the corner. The threadbare turquoise quilted robe hanging on the hook in there would have to do. She threw the ugly garment on and dashed back down the stairs, flipping the phone open as she went.

Gran was no longer in the room and Seth was standing by the table, digging through the pockets of his jean jacket. He had put on a black Stetson that Rainey hadn't seen in the pickup the night before. Beneath the shadow of its brim, she saw a crease form between his brows as he took in the sight of her in the ugly robe. Like she cared.

"Okay," she said with exasperation as she frowned at her phone's display. "Roam service area. It works."

"Good. I'm also leaving this with you." From the pocket of the jacket Seth produced a compact handgun. He examined it, checking the safety while he asked, "Any idea how to use one of these?"

Rainey stared at the weapon in Seth's hand. A gun, like the foul thing that had killed her father. A gun, like the one that had forever altered her life.

Seth missed her horrified expression. He was too busy explaining how this "piece" was conveniently fitted with a laser sight on the barrel. He aimed at the wall. "Look," he ordered. "The shot will hit whatever that red dot of light touches. And it's got a pretty soft trigger." He squeezed to demonstrate. "And not much kick. Think you can handle that?"

"I will not be handling that thing." She spoke with a clenched jaw. "Or any other gun, for that matter. I am totally opposed to guns."

Seth pushed his hat back on his head. "Well, me too,

lady. But unfortunately the Slaughters don't agree with our ethics."

When her expression remained stubbornly set, Seth lowered the gun, adopting a tone of extreme patience. "Rainey, you've got to understand—"

"No, *you've* got to understand. Many, many of the children I deal with have gotten into trouble because of guns, Dillon included. I'm starting to think it might be best to take the boys back to Tulsa and put them in some form of official protective custody there."

"That is exactly what the Slaughters are hoping we'll do. Blow our cover. As far as they're concerned, the boys have disappeared. They don't know I have them. Last night I secured the legal sanction of a judge. I know what I'm doing."

"And what exactly are you doing, if you don't mind my asking?"

"The Slaughters won't give up until they get what they came back here for. And I am of the opinion—" he lowered his voice because the boys, though sound asleep, were in the next room, but his speech was pressured, urgent "—I am of the opinion that Maddy was telling the truth, even if Dillon tried to cover something up. The Slaughters would have to have a pretty good reason to come back here after they got out of prison—"

"Wait." Rainey put up a palm to stop him. "If the Slaughters served their time, why wouldn't they come back to their hometown?"

"Because I'm here."

Rainey turned on him. Once again she wondered who this guy was, anyway. And what his real agenda was.

"What were you and your partner doing way out here, so far from Tenikah, chasing two men who've already paid their debt to society?"

"We...well, I—my brother, actually. He believed they hid some evidence—"

"Those bones? Whose bones are we talking about?"

Seth looked agitated, frustrated. "I don't have time to go into the whole story. A girl was murdered."

Rainey sucked in a sharp breath.

"And once they have those bones," Seth added, "they'll scour these mountains until they find the boys. They won't rest until they—"

"I know. Silence them."

"That's why, first and foremost, we have to make sure we leave no trace of our whereabouts. Sooner or later, the Slaughters will slip up and expose their movements. And when that happens, my partner and I will be ready to get them *and* that evidence."

"Wait." She put her hand up again. "You're telling me you're endangering these boys, using them as bait, because you want those bones as much as the Slaughters do?" Rainey did not disguise her disgust at this idea.

"No." Seth looked genuinely insulted. "That's not what's going on here at all."

"It isn't? Then you'll have to explain it to me."

She could see that he was reining in his impatience. "Look, the fact is, I would have had those men—and the bones—in my custody right now if you hadn't spooked them last night. But now they're on the loose out there. And since I can't be with you every second, the least you can do is cooperate with me. So take the gun." He thrust it toward her.

"Nothing, no one, can make me touch a gun." Rainey turned on her heel and left the room.

AFTER A MOMENT, Seth heard the screen door out on the porch bang shut.

He sighed, took the clip out of the gun and sauntered out there, holding the weapon loosely at his side.

Grace was in her rocker, slowly gliding back and forth.

He watched Rainey's back as she barreled away from the house and disappeared onto a path that led into the woods.

"Where is she going?" he asked Grace.

"She's got herself a little quiet spot out there. It's not far. I take it you all had words?" Grace studied Seth with her piercing eyes, the same shade of green as Rainey's. It wasn't exactly a question. She'd heard the shouting, Seth was sure. The house was tiny, poorly insulated. Even now, from the living room, the sounds of the boys stirring awake carried clearly out to the porch.

Dillon, sounding cranky, was barking orders at the other two. "You're doing it all wrong!" he shrieked.

Seth could hear Maddy's hoarse, abnormal laugh and then a tussle ensued.

"I'm afraid you'll have to get in there and enforce the peace," Seth said as he pulled his cowboy hat down low over his brow. "I've got to meet a man in town."

Grace rolled her eyes while the racket in the living room increased. "Those boys'll keep."

Seth turned his head toward the commotion and squinted. He stepped to the screen door.

"Dillon! Aaron!" he shouted. "Cool it." He caught Maddy's eye and made a cutting gesture under his chin.

The thumping and bumping ceased.

"Fold up those sleeping bags, and find a way to make yourselves useful to Mrs. Chapman."

Grumbling followed, but stopped short when Seth said, "*Now.*"

He stepped back over to where Grace sat, still slowly rocking. "I really apologize for having to leave them with you. Believe me, I'd like nothing better than to take those kids in hand, but—"

"I know. You've got a few things to tend to in town first." Gran held out a wrinkled hand. "Give me that gun. Push comes to shove, she'll use it."

"You mean she can shoot?"

"With the best of them. Her daddy taught her."

"Her dad…?"

"William was a cop," Gran explained, "like you."

Seth raised an eyebrow, studying the old woman.

"Oh, yes. I understand all about cops. Been livin' with the guys in the white hats most of my life. My husband, Herbert, was a deputy sheriff for a spell, you know."

"Yes, ma'am. Seems like I remember his name." Seth knew of many men, in earlier times, who had taken on the responsibility of deputies out in these remote areas.

He sensed there was something more she was not telling him. Suddenly he realized that whatever Grace was holding back might explain Rainey Chapman's strong reaction to the gun. But right now he didn't have time to get all tangled up in the full story. Max would be waiting on him.

Seth stared at the trailhead in the distance, where Rainey's slender form had disappeared into the woods. He couldn't believe how curious he'd become about this woman. Curious. *Right.* He was just plain hot for her. The sight of her in that thin nightgown had been enough to make him grind his teeth. And now he was going to be stuck up on this mountain, in this house, with her. He made a mental note to swing by his house to pick up his sleeping bag and pillow, along with a few other important things. This porch would have to do. At least it was screened in and would be halfway cool at night.

"Then you'll know what to do with this." He held out the gun and a couple of clips. "Keep it away from the boys."

"Don't you worry about that, Seth. I know how to keep boys in line." Grace pushed herself up from the rocker. She took the gun and examined it with practiced ease. "Laser sight. Nice."

"Yeah. Nice. Let's hope nobody has to use it." With that, he stomped off the porch, down the steps. He got in his truck, slammed the door, fired up the engine and disappeared down the rocky drive.

CHAPTER EIGHT

RAINEY SWIPED BITTER, salty tears from her cheeks as she settled on the slab of rock at the base of a tall waterfall. Fed by a hidden spring, the falls plummeted twenty feet onto a cluster of jagged rocks to create a fine, cooling mist over a natural pool. From this starting point the water slowly drained into one of the many creeks that fed the river below Gran's mountain. This was Rainey's sacred place. The place where she could come and divine the answer to almost any problem.

She stared at the water, always moving, yet so unchanging, and more tears started to flow.

Something about the splashing, gurgling sounds always seemed to make tears flow more copiously. But what on earth was she getting so emotional about?

The boys. The gun. Seth Whitman.

How long had it been since she'd thought about the way her father had died? And what point was there in thinking about it, even now? That wouldn't bring him back. Wouldn't change the adolescent years she had spent feeling abandoned, isolated, alienated in a lonely, perfectionistic household, trying to please her widowed, workaholic stepmother.

And yet Rainey suddenly felt she *had* to think about it all or she'd go crazy. She pressed her fingers to her temples and stared at the swirling water, remembering the last time she'd seen her father alive.

"Rainey, is that you, sweetie?"

She'd stopped on the stairs at the sound of her father's voice.

She frowned now as, for one second, the memory rode along on the music of the tumbling water. That day seemed suddenly important beyond its original significance. Like a foreshadowing. She blinked, rubbed her brow again. Like a premonition.

Maybe that was why she'd felt so weird when she'd stopped on the stairs this morning, listening to the cadence of Seth Whitman's deep voice. And then the sight of the man's back as it strained the seams of a uniform shirt…like her father's. But the look that had flickered across Seth Whitman's face when he saw her in the nightgown had been nothing like the expression on her father's face when he'd come around the corner of the living room and looked up the stairs at her. William's paternalistic smile had slid away like melting wax.

"Where are you going?" her dad had asked mildly. He didn't add, *dressed like that.*

She remembered grudgingly conceding that her dad had *some* cool, more than most dads. But that didn't mean she was going to give in and let him run her life.

"Out."

"With whom?"

"Craig."

"And where are you and Craig going?"

"I dunno. Maybe the video store. Maybe." She was doing her best to tug her halter top down over her exposed midriff and up over her bulging cleavage. There wasn't much hope of hitching the hip-huggers any higher. The jeans fit her slim curves way too tightly for that. She stopped fidgeting and settled her skinny arms in a tight clutch over the bare skin at her waist, not covering nearly enough.

It was a struggle not to look her father in the eye. But she dared not do that. William was a master at detecting a lie. Rainey and her boyfriend weren't going near any video store. They were going to a party down on the river bottom where there was sure to be a keg, and smokes, and a few other items her dad-the-cop wouldn't approve of. Like the rubbers in Craig's pocket, for instance. Rainey wasn't sure she was ready to "do the deed," even at the advanced age of sixteen, but she knew her boyfriend was more than ready. He'd made that plain, and she had to admit she liked it, liked it a lot, when his hands started to roam over her bare skin.

"You're going to the video store," now her dad said it out loud, *"dressed like that?"*

"Dad, everybody dresses like this."

"Not my daughter."

Not my daughter, not my daughter. If she'd heard it once, she'd heard it a million times. Rainey had stormed back up the stairs, hating those words, unaware that only a few hours later she would have given anything to hear him say them, or any words, just one more time.

Something about Seth Whitman brought all these memories vividly to mind.

She thought again of those first seconds after he'd grabbed her outside that cave. Even though he'd taken her by surprise, she hadn't been frightened after she'd looked in his eyes. She'd never seen eyes like that. Eyes that shone with the man's soul. Eyes that expressed how he felt better than words.

The boys. The gun. Seth Whitman. What kind of situation was this turning into? The push-pull kind, that's what. Because here, finally, was a man she was so attracted to she'd already been fantasizing about first kisses. But he was also exactly the kind of man she'd vowed not to give her heart to. A man who would hand her a gun. A man who would use a gun.

She had to guard her heart. She could not let herself feel these things for this man, the kind of man who had tried to hand her a gun. The kind of man who could get himself killed in the line of duty. Like her father.

What had Seth gone into town to do? Too late, she realized that she should have found out before he left, instead of storming off into the woods like a child. She had to stay focused, responsible, alert for the boys. She couldn't afford to be having all of these unwanted emotions.

"Rainey!" It was Gran's voice, jerking her out of her

circular thoughts like a lasso. The old woman's thin figure materialized on the shady path.

"Peaceful out here, ain't it?" Gran said as she came around the pool.

"Yes." Rainey stared into the water. She wondered if Gran was remembering the time they'd sat out on this rock together, after her father was killed, trying to console each other, trying to sort it out.

"I expect you could do with a little peace right about now."

"This whole thing has been pretty stressful, I'll tell you that." Rainey's head came up. "Where are the boys?"

"Eating cereal."

"As long as they're eating they'll stay out of trouble. Sit with me a second." Rainey patted the rock.

Gran settled herself on the rock beside Rainey, adopting the same pose—arms loosely encircling raised knees. Age hadn't stiffened Gran's joints much. Rainey supposed it was from climbing around on these hill paths like a little billy goat all her life. "Them boys are safe up here. I imagine Seth covered his tracks real well."

"Then why'd he try to give me a gun just now?"

"Just being cautious, being a lawman, I suppose."

"A lawman." Rainey couldn't keep the sarcastic edge out of her voice. "You and I both know they're no better than anybody else."

Gran gave her a sharp look. "They're human, like us. You don't think this one's a cut above average?"

"How should I know?"

"Well, I think he's up to the task."

"How can you be so sure of that, after knowing the man less than twenty-four hours?"

"I've known about him a long time."

"What do you mean, you've known *about* him?"

"Rainey, do you remember when your grampa put up that electric fence?" Rainey was used to her grandmother's way. Gran loved to talk in riddles, to sneak up on a subject from the side. "The one that kept Samson from running off?"

Samson. Rainey hadn't thought about Gran's ridiculously spoiled pet llama in years. That stupid animal. For some reason Gran thought he was so pretty, with his extra-long hair. He wasn't like the little goats, who were content to stay within the barbed wire and stand around with the cows…or even on top of the cows when the bovines settled on the ground to rest. Rainey smiled, recalling the silly sight of a goat standing on a cow's back. There were so many sweet memories like that from her summers with Gran and Gramps.

But Samson galloped off down the mountain all the time, which upset Gran. So Gramps, ever indulgent of his dear little wife, had hooked up a string of baling wire to a battery. Rainey had been fascinated and terrified by the electric fence.

"Remember how if you lightly touched the wire, you got shocked, but if you grabbed it good and firm, and held on tight, you didn't get hurt?"

"Yes, Gran. I remember." Rainey gave her a little smile of forbearance. Gran and her parables.

"It was the touching and the letting go that hurt, wasn't it?" Gran's voice grew musing. "The touching and the letting go."

Rainey knew all too well what she was getting at. They'd had this little talk before. Gran believed in commitment. She believed in finding your man and "hanging on tight."

"I'm just saying I see things, is all," she added. "And this one's got potential."

Rainey fixed her gaze on the water below them. "Stop right there, Gran."

"This isn't matchmaking or anything. But I seen the way that man looked at you last night and again this morning."

Rainey's cheeks flamed, remembering her mortification in the thin nightgown. "I don't know what you're talking about. I hardly know him."

"Be that as it may, you two have been thrown together up here. And it's plain to see he's got eyes for you already. And now I see how you are crying. He's stirred you up, too."

"I was crying about Daddy, if you must know."

"That is my point." Gran went on. "This is a strange situation, all right. The Lord works in mysterious ways."

Rainey gave her a sidelong glance. "Don't go dragging the Lord into this."

"It's divine providence, is what it is. Throwing you

together with this man, this way, him being so much like your daddy and all."

Now Rainey gave her grandmother an incredulous look. "Like my daddy? What on earth are you talking about?"

"You can't tell me you haven't noticed how much Seth Whitman resembles William."

Of course Rainey had noticed. She just hadn't wanted to consciously admit it to anyone…especially to herself. It was the most confusing piece in this surreal puzzle, and in Rainey's mind, the most hideous one. While the falls gurgled in counterpoint to her stubborn silence, she kept her gaze riveted on the water. But she could feel her grandmother studying her profile.

"Well, then," Gran said softly. "I can see that you have noticed. But the boy's good looks are just on account of nature. Character is what counts in a man. It's the heart of a man that matters. And this is one man's heart that don't need breaking, Rainey."

"I did not break Craig's heart."

"Oh, I know. You couldn't help yourself, grieving like you were and all. And besides, that was high school. It's all those others that came after Craig that I'm thinking about. You broke their hearts, did you not?"

"No, I did not. None of those guys took me seriously. And I can't say I took them seriously, either."

"Well, this one's not that kind, if I know men. In my opinion he's a rare one, this Seth Whitman is. He's the kind of man who takes just about everything seriously, including possibly you, I'm thinking. I'm telling you, Rainey, this one's different. This is one live wire you'd better not touch lightly."

"How do you know so much about him? And don't start talking about the electric fence again." Rainey had heard all these warnings about men from her before. What could her grandmother possibly know about the complex relationships between men and women these days? She and Gran couldn't agree when it came to men and marriage, and Rainey wasn't about to try. When the woman stayed silent too long, she moved to get up. "I'd better go check on the boys."

Gran grabbed her arm. "Not just yet. The boys are fine, even if they are having to eat oatmeal. I got some things to say."

"Okay." Rainey settled back down beside her grandmother and listened respectfully.

"Whatever happens or doesn't happen between you and this cop, Rainey, I think I'd better tell you some things. Make you see some things, because this one's not like all the others. This one's special, I'm telling you. I didn't think they made men like him anymore."

When Rainey frowned with genuine curiosity, Gran continued, "I suppose I'm letting certain things I know about him color my opinion."

"What things?"

"Things I know. Things about his past. Things I expect I'd best share with you right now."

SETH SLIPPED INTO TOWN well before the business day started, parked his truck behind the police station, went inside and signed the duty roster. He wasn't surprised to find Jake already signed out. Jake had radioed that he was quitting his watch at dawn. At this very moment Seth's partner was probably stretched out on the couch while his little wife, Marcie, fried up one last big, greasy breakfast for him and packed up his provisions—plenty of doughnuts, brownies and chips. This was a lot to ask of a friend, but Jake had gone on long stakeouts before. They'd busted a couple of meth labs back in the sticks that way. One of those labs, a nasty trailer house, had blown sky-high and knocked Jake flat. Seth still couldn't swear to how he had dragged the unconscious giant away from the flames.

They had radioed back and forth last night, while Jake sat up by the caves and Seth sat guard in his pickup.

"Nothing to report," Jake had grumbled, sounding more bored and disgusted each time they talked. "Nothing from the guys at the roadblock, either. How'd they just disappear?"

"In the Winding Stair?"

"Yeah. No big mystery there, I guess. I say the kid's lying, like the Lyle guy claimed, using the news stories about the convicts on the loose to his advantage. Trying to keep his little behind out of trouble with this cock-and-bull story. Managed to get himself hauled out of Big Cedar, out from under Lyle Hicks, didn't he? The Slaughter boys are long gone to Mexico, like the sheriff said."

"Nope. Sorry. I heard them. Saw the rappelling ropes."

"You heard *someone.* You saw *a* rope. It could have been people trying to make off with pieces of the Rune Stones. Weirder stuff has happened out there. If you ask me, this whole case is nothin' but a poot in a whirl-wind."

"I didn't ask you," Seth had countered. "Now are you in or not?" It *was* a lot to ask. Jake hadn't been told about the bones, or the diary, or Coach. All of that was tucked up Seth's sleeve, and that was where it would stay.

"In." Jake sighed. "You will never let me forget the burning meth lab, will ya?"

This was how Jake got when he was on stakeout. Edgy. Grumpy. He always needed fluffing up. But when you had your back to a wall, Jake was the guy you wanted as your backup. He was fearless.

Seth found the cruiser waiting out back. He pulled the sedan out of the gravel lot and studied the down-town buildings, shadowed in a sleepy cluster at the base of the mountain. The lights at the Tote-a-Poke conve-nience store paled in the first glaring rays as the morn-ing sun inched up over the ridgeline. Not a cloud in the sky. It promised to be another scorcher. Already the tires of the cruiser felt as if they were sticking to the black-top as Seth turned out of the gravel alley.

Descendants of outlaws and moonshiners had thrown up the initial structures of Tenikah in a deep fis-sure in the Kiamichi Mountains more than a hundred years earlier. The remote, rocky ridges surrounding the town had once provided a great place to avoid the law. If Seth squinted against the eastern sun, he could easily imagine the town as it had been back then, trapped in time with the crude storefronts and hitching posts of Main Street crammed up against the face of the mountain.

The town had eventually evolved from the kind of place where even the family doctor packed a pistol, into a respectable county seat. It took on all the earmarks of civilization—churches and shops and schools. A place where people not only obeyed the law, they thought it was their business to uphold it.

But these people could also be insular, judgmental. For example, two young Native American boys escaping from the roaring temper of an alcoholic father and the whining self-pity of an equally alcoholic mother might be looked down upon if they showed up at school unwashed and poorly dressed.

These people wouldn't trust a cop with a hidden agenda. Who could blame them? So Seth had learned to keep his peace.

If these good folks knew what he was thinking now, the whole town would undoubtedly assume he was overreacting again because of his past.

Lane Whitman's death was clearly an accident, everyone said, and it was sad now, wasn't it? Really sad, the way his worshipful kid brother couldn't let go of it and let the dead rest.

But Seth knew better. And when he knew something, he was the kind that refused to argue with another living soul, much less the whole town. Lane's death was no accident. He knew.

He knew because he'd read KayAnn's diary, same as Lane had.

Seth steered the cruiser toward the wide central boulevard by way of the narrow back streets, driving slowly, like a boat putt-putting down a tributary of the lake. He came to a full halt at each stop sign, each light, each alley intersection, idling for a minute, thinking. He flipped on his yellow scrolling lights, just for the hell of it, thinking that a cop patrolling Tenikah was no more of a threat than a Wal-Mart security guard. With the lights flashing a matching rhythm to the one drumming in his head, he renewed his old vow of vengeance. It was like a tape he played in his head. An endless mantra. The truth about Lane. The truth about KayAnn.

He turned onto Broadway, which cleaved the town right down the middle, going north and south like a huge sling that bisected two mountain ridges on the east and west. The courthouse lay dead ahead, with Broadway splitting like a forked river into two arcs around it. Except for the landscape lighting, the place was as dark as a tomb at this hour.

Seth looked up to the third floor windows, where the county sheriff kept offices. When the Slaughters had killed Lane, Seth had gone up there, straight to Sheriff Briggs. The man had known Lane since he was a kid, had screamed his fat guts out every Friday night with the rest of the town when Lane consistently ran the ball into the end zone like the champion he was.

But as Seth sat across from him that gray morning, Briggs had acted as if there was nothing he could do. The twins, he explained, would be released on bail, would be given a fair trial, would undoubtedly be sentenced for manslaughter. It was a drunk-driving accident.

"Leave it up to the law." Briggs had been condescending, as if Seth were nothing but a rodeo hobo without a lick of common sense. "The law will take care of it."

When Seth had said, "Oh, you mean the same way the law took care of that girl?" Sam Briggs's face had flamed red as a cherry.

He seemed to know exactly what Seth was talking about. "This ain't got nothin' to do with that Rawls girl."

Seth had gritted his teeth so hard his jaw had hurt. He'd kept it stubbornly set as he glared at the older man. "Lane sure as hell thought it did."

"Seth, son." The sheriff drew out the S's, as if he wanted to make sure Seth understood that he was intentionally softening his tone. "All this old anger is not healthy. I remember Lane's heartache over that little tramp, how he lost his will to play after that and all, but it was a long time ago. The plain truth is, the girl was a wild little thing. She just up and split. She had a big fight with her parents the night before she disappeared. Her dad told us so. The Slaughter boys didn't have nothin' to do with it. And this bad blood between you and the Slaughter twins has gone about far enough when it's got you to thinking your brother's death was anything but an accident."

"They ran his car over the side of that cliff."

"It was an accident, Seth. The twins were drunk and maybe they were driving a little wild. Boys do. I've even seen you drive too fast a time or two." He aimed an index finger at Seth. "But that don't mean they meant to kill somebody, and now that it's been investigated, I want you to forget about it and leave it with the law."

Seth had glared at Briggs's finger, then past it to his lying eyes. Sam Briggs played the role of good old boy convincingly enough. The fat, jovial, middle-aged sheriff cakewalked through the county elections year after year. He was almost as well-connected and well-liked as his buddy, Coach Hollings. Affable, that's what he was. Just a big old Santa Claus.

Seth had wanted to punch Santa right in his fat face at that particular moment.

Lane was dead, and the guy didn't even care. As far as Briggs was concerned, he'd solved the crime, and now he was free to go home and pig out on his old lady's peach cobbler. "It'll be a cold day in hell before I forget about it, Sheriff. You'd best remember that."

"Now see here, you young pup." Briggs had pushed himself up to lean on his beefy arms. "You don't go telling the county sheriff what to remember and what not to." He'd pointed his sausage of a finger in Seth's face again. "You better call your uncle Tack and have him come haul your butt home before I throw it in the slammer."

And now the cold day in hell was here.

And there was no way Seth was going over to the sheriff's department with what he'd discovered. Let them find out on their own what had happened, preferably when it was all over. Preferably when Lonnie and Nelson were locked away for life…or good and dead.

But Seth had to have allies. He needed someone he could trust. He hoped he'd chosen well.

He turned off of Broadway onto the main east-west road, Parnell, named after some old coot politician who would have been long forgotten if not for street signs. Seth rolled up the hill that rose on one side of town, made a U-turn in the hospital parking lot and rolled back down the blacktop strip that crossed Broadway at downtown. Once again, he headed straight past the yellow brick courthouse before the road rose again to the other side of town, where winding streets and pretty houses dotted Kanaly Hill. Locals liked to point out that Kanaly missed the distinction of being a mountain by only a couple of feet. The streets there were steep and picturesque, mostly secluded cul-de-sacs. There was a one-way road up, a one-way road down.

Seth's home was up there, such as it was.

CHAPTER NINE

SETH'S RAMBLING, ranch-style brick house sat in the shadow of the town's massive water tower—the one painted to look like a Tenikah Pirate wearing a black eye patch the size of a tire.

The plainly appointed dwelling looked cold and abandoned in the weak dawn light. His front yard was totally treeless, and the chain-link fence out back enclosed not a stick of vegetation except a manicured expanse of weedless Bermuda grass that had recently turned the color of ripe wheat in the unrelenting August heat. Seth preferred his yard that way—bare as a football field. One less distraction from his true mission.

Somewhere along the route to fulfilling that mission, Seth the wild boy had become Seth the lawman, just like his brother before him. But only on the outside.

Seth had conceded to the fact that clothes really did make the man, at least in some folks' minds. Especially if those clothes happened to be a lawman's uniform.

Once a week Seth tossed a stack of insignia-embossed khaki through the drive-in window over at the Daybreak Cleaners on Main Street. Later, he made a second pass through to pick up the starched and pressed shirts, neatly buttoned onto paper-covered hangers, the front pockets bisected by knife-sharp creases. Then he'd make the same right turn, park the cruiser behind the Mane Man Barbershop and suffer the same weekly trim. Business cut. Short on the sides. Blocked in the back.

Seth swore that once he'd punished the Slaughters for their real crime, once he didn't need the aegis of being a cop, he'd grow his hair into a ponytail, trailing long and native down his back. Something to honor his Indian-ness. But not yet. How would a ponytail sit with the good folks of Tenikah, Oklahoma? Not very damn well, that's how.

Appearances matter, that's what Lane had always told him. From the mirror-bright wax job on his Silverado to the spit shine on his boots, Lane had been big on appearances. And when Seth stepped into his brother's spit-shined boots, he had never looked back.

After his wild life on the rodeo circuit, Seth had been surprised that the straight-arrow ways of a small-town lawman suited him. He consumed a steady diet of home-style cooking at Rita Stewart's Pie Almighty Café, worked out regularly with his buddies at the Powers That Be Gym, occasionally showed his clean-shaven face at the First Baptist Church and afterward devoured the requisite Sunday dinner out at his aunt Junie's house. He ran the cruiser through the car wash at least once a week, more often in inclement weather, had his modest brick home mucked out by his chubby old housekeeper once a month, even got his pearly whites cleaned over at Dr. Moore's office a couple of times a year. Truth was, all the little routines that kept a small-town bachelor clean-cut, militarily fit and morally straight freed up Seth's mind for more important things.

Like solving a decade-old murder.

But as he sat in his driveway with the engine idling he found himself wondering what a woman like Rainey Chapman would think of his life, whether she would think it boring...or maybe even sterile. No other woman he'd ever brought here had complained. They were the type, mostly, who were interested in a few margaritas and a whole lot of Seth.

But Rainey Chapman, he could already tell, was different. She had that indefinable air about her that some guys called class. And a woman like that would probably despise the looks of this place. She wouldn't comprehend, wouldn't understand, that he'd chosen his stripped-down style because he'd wanted only one focus all these years.

He got out of the cruiser and looked out over the view of Tenikah as he walked to the house. There were things he loved about living in this area—fishing on Honobia Creek, the Fourth of July parade, the striped awnings on the storefronts along the main street.

But the downside of his day-to-day life in Tenikah— Seth's mouth formed a grimace as he thought, *excuse me, make that Purgatory*—was that small-town life could be so tame. The upside was that his squeaky-clean lifestyle appealed to women. In Tenikah, Oklahoma, a man with a real job, a shiny pickup, no hangups on porn, cigarettes or booze, fresh breath, and a halfway decent attitude found the ladies fluttering around him like butterflies. Seth smiled briefly. He never had to use a net.

Besides women, he had resorted to motorcycles, horses, four-wheelers, Sea-Doos, camping, hiking and hunting to pass the days of his life while he played cop and waited. Beyond the toys and a few off-and-on relationships with a few pretty women, he intentionally kept his life free of constraints...of any kind.

He opened his front door, disabled the alarm and went straight to a locked box in his bottom desk drawer. He fumbled for the tiny key on his key ring, where it had been kept for seven years.

He opened the metal box, rifled through a pile of yellowed newspaper clippings. From the stack he selected two articles and one front-page photograph. He stared at the picture, and when he saw what he'd never seen before, his heart thudded with new suspicions. From underneath the clippings he carefully removed a dingy pink diary with a cheap brass lock, the kind little girls kept secrets in. He read a few paragraphs of an entry he'd read many times before, but this time its meaning was different. He slammed the box shut.

He debated about gathering provisions, clean clothes, the sleeping bag, those other items he needed. He checked his watch. Later.

When the blinds were drawn and the alarm was

reset, he got back in the cruiser, put it in Reverse and slowly backed out. He circled the cul-de-sac at the end of his street and saluted old Mr. Pryor, who was out hand-spraying his burned-brown grass with a hose before the sun was fully up. Seth studied his house one last time as he cruised by. It occurred to him that he'd really been living in a state of suspension since Lane's death. Mowing the grass. Painting the trim. Keeping things tidy. Going nowhere.

He wound his way farther up the hill. He was going to quit the force now, of that he was sure. It didn't matter, because the way he saw it, he was utterly expendable. The chief had always suspected Seth's motive for becoming a cop—with good reason.

When Seth got to the very top of the hill, Max Drennan was already waiting. His black Chevy TrailBlazer was parked at the end of a secluded, rutted lane they had called the "Road to Heaven" back in high school. This had been the favored spot to take a girl to see how far a guy could go.

Seth looked at his watch again as Max got out of his car and walked toward the cruiser. The judge was always right on time.

Max opened the door and got in. "We gotta quit meeting like this." He drawled their old high school joke.

Seth kept the motor and the AC running, and when he turned on the red-toned interior light, Max's face looked shadowed and tired in the hellish glow. He was Lane's age, or rather, the age Lane would be by now, barely thirty-three. But his wire-rimmed glasses, preppy clothes and receding hairline made him look more dignified, more seasoned than his years. Even so, the older cops had labeled him "that young judge." Max had taken the job on the bench because nobody else with a law degree would condescend to be a judge in a backwoods town on the eastern edge of Oklahoma, except a guy who had wanted to raise his kids in his good old hometown. Max had actually been Lane's buddy in high school, not Seth's. But like so many other aspects of Lane's life, Seth had adopted Max when he'd returned to Tenikah.

"Thanks for coming all the way up here at dark-thirty."

"No problem, Little Brother." Max's nickname for Seth had started in junior high and had stuck even as the years had layered on an unshakable respect between the two men. He eyed Seth. "You look like crap."

"You, too." Seth smiled. "I was on a stakeout up in the mountains last night. What's your excuse?"

"Nothing as exciting as all that. A stakeout? Does this have anything to do with the three kids?"

"Thanks for getting the guardian thing done, by the way."

"Again, no problem. Who's this woman you've got yourself mixed up with, Little Brother?"

Seth gave Max a withering look. "And thanks for not asking a lot of questions."

"You about done thanking me? 'Cause if that's the only reason we're parked up here on lover's lane, I've got a warm woman at my house who's a whole lot better at making me feel appreciated."

Seth gave his friend a sarcastic look that said, *Right.* Max always claimed to have a warm woman waiting. Since his divorce last year the guy had acted like a driven workaholic with an adolescent's appetites. He buzzed through his docket and the courthouse secretaries so fast that behind his back the women called him the banging judge. Seth wasn't sure if that referred to Max's gavel or…other things. Max's only anchor in life seemed to be his two small children.

The divorce had been pitiful. Everybody but the couple themselves saw it coming. Greta had had the babies too close together. Max worked too many hours in a week. Greta had run off with some loser from Muskogee, and Max had fought her tooth and toenail to keep his kids in Tenikah. Seth knew his good friend wasn't all that happy these days. Successful and respected, yes. Happy, no.

"What's up?" The worried frown Max gave Seth said he suspected that whatever it was, it wasn't good.

Seth stared out the windshield, in no hurry to make a tactical mistake. He could feel Max's eyes reading him like a jittery witness on the stand. His old friend undoubtedly saw how keyed up, how anxious he was right now. It was hard to hide your emotions when you hadn't had any sleep. Seth had thought about this all night on his lonely watch, and still he couldn't decide if he could really trust Max or not. Apparently Lane hadn't. But Lane had thought he had other choices, other places he could go. Seth had none. Jake, like any cop, could accept Seth's secrecy. Max would want explanations.

Without saying a word Seth handed the judge an aged newspaper clipping.

"What's this?" As Max took it his frown deepened.

Seth turned his face back toward the windshield. Streaks of pink were showing over the ridges in the east. "It's something, or maybe I should say someone, everybody has forgotten about. Can you read it by the safety lights?"

"Sure."

When he finished reading, Max's frown looked genuinely troubled. "Why are you showing this to me now?"

"I've never let anybody else see that, you know."

"Well, surely lots of people read it at the time." Max turned the newspaper article over and examined the back. "It's from the *Tenikah Register*, isn't it?"

"Yes. I imagine lots of people did read it back then. But that particular copy belonged to Lane. Do you remember reading this?" Seth flipped the newsprint with the backs of his fingers. "Back then?"

"No. We were only seniors in high school. I never read the paper, except to see what they'd said about our performance in the games on the sports page. But of course I remember KayAnn running away and all. That's all Lane talked about."

"Look at the date."

Max did so.

"Now—" Seth handed him another article "—look at this date."

Max examined the second yellowed paper, and his frown returned. "Okay. It was two weeks later."

"You remember that game?"

"Of course I do. It was ridiculous. It was probably the worst game in Tenikah history. We missed our shot at the state championship."

Seth stared out the windshield at the dawning sky. "Lane had been acting so distracted over KayAnn. Coach said he put Lonnie Slaughter in because Lane was off his game, but now I don't think that was it."

"Whatever it was—" Max frowned "—there are more important things in life than football. What's this all about, Seth?"

"Look at one more thing." Seth handed him the front-page photograph.

Max gave it a quick glance. "Lonnie and Nelson on the day they were sentenced for causing Lane's death."

"I cut that one out, of course. But I didn't see something at the time. Look closely at the faces in the crowd in the background."

Max squinted at the paper under the reddish light, then looked up. "You mean Coach?"

Seth nodded.

The glow from the rising sun on Max's face emphasized the fact that he was now truly confused. "Maybe he was there because he was curious, like everybody else."

"Look closer."

Max held the grainy black-and-white photo closer to the light.

"Doesn't he look scared? Worried?"

"I dunno. It's kind of blurry, but he does look…kind of freaked out, I guess. Maybe he was just horrified that a couple of his star players were going to prison."

"They were never his star players." Seth made no effort to keep the venom out of his voice. "*Lane* was his star player. Lonnie and Nelson were screwups that Coach coddled. I never could figure that one out, until now."

"Until now?"

Here was the part Seth had agonized over most of the night. When he'd asked Max to make Rainey the boys' guardian, he had been intentionally vague about the three little runaways. He had revealed only enough to put them in protective custody. But if he was going to enlist Max as an ally, he would have to make him see the stakes…and the need for secrecy. Seth's heart beat a little harder as he started in. "When we found those three boys last night, one of them—the only one that can talk—"

"The one Jake thinks is just making it all up?"

"Yeah, him. Except he's not. The kid heard Lonnie and Nelson talking about somebody they called Howard."

"*Howard?*" Max pointed at the picture of Coach and his tired face suddenly woke up. "*Howard Hollings?*"

"I look at these…." Seth took the yellowed newspaper clippings from Max's hands. "I look at the dates. I look at what happened, the sequence of events, and I see something I never saw before."

Max frowned.

"I don't know what the tie is, but I think Coach is hiding something about Lonnie and Nelson. He's covering for them, always has been. The question is what, and why?"

Max blew out a pressured breath. "Man. That's a real stretch, Little Brother. To make a connection like that you'd need solid proof."

"That's what I intend to get. Proof."

Max shook his head. "I'll go along with hiding the boys if you think that's necessary. But I can't see how dragging Coach into this will accomplish anything, Seth. The twins killed Lane in an accident. They went to jail for it. The fact that they were talking about Coach, the fact that he let them play in the championship game instead of Lane, the fact that KayAnn ran away… I don't see how—"

"There's more."

Max drew a deep breath and waited.

"The deaf boy, he reads lips. He saw the twins talking about bones."

"Bones?"

Seth let a beat pass before he said, "I'm thinking Lane was right all along." He paused again, not for effect, but because saying it out loud seemed so ugly. "She didn't run away." Having made up his mind, Seth pulled the pink diary from under the seat and handed it to Max.

As he took it, Max's eyes flicked from the diary to Seth's face and back. "What's this?"

"KayAnn's diary."

Max's eyebrows shot up. Then the deep crease between his brows got even deeper as he said, "Where in the hell did you get this?"

"She left it in Lane's car." Seth swallowed the lump that formed in his throat as he thought of his brother finding that diary after she was gone. "I found it in his stuff after he died. He had kept it all that time, even after he became a cop."

Max sprung the corroded lock and opened the cracked cover. "Why didn't he turn this over to the sheriff when she disappeared?" He started flipping the pages carefully, one at a time, as if he were looking at a piece of evidence in his courtroom.

"Who knows? Maybe he couldn't bear to part with it. It's full of stuff about him. Maybe he thought Sheriff Briggs would confiscate it or give it back to her parents. Or maybe after he read what she'd written, some instinct told him not to trust the good old boys in this town. Read the part I flagged with the Post-it."

Max flipped to the marked part, then glanced up at Seth. "This is right before she came up missing."

Seth nodded. "Read it."

Max cleared his throat and read aloud. "'Dear Diary, he is at it again. He caught me out in the parking lot by the field house when I was getting into my car. I sneaked in late to hang up Lane's sign and put some cookies I baked for him into his locker. (I can't believe

I drew his number this year!!! It's fate, I'm sure! I made the coolest sign for his front yard!)'"

Max stopped reading and frowned. "I forgot about that. KayAnn was assigned to be Lane's pepster. He always did get the cute ones."

"Right." Seth kept his face emotionless while his gut tightened. "Keep reading."

"'He scares me.'" Max's voice slowed and became somber. "'I mean, I was fumbling with the keys because it was so cold and I didn't have any gloves, and all of a sudden there he was, taking my keys without asking and opening the car door. But not in a nice way, not like he was being a gentleman or anything. I tried to act like he *was* one anyway, and said thank-you and all, even if I thought it was a little weird, him opening the door for me, even if I am a cheerleader and all.

"'But before I could get in the car, he pushed me up against the fender and said that he hoped Lane realized he was the luckiest man in this town. I think he was trying to kiss me, his face got so close. (I could smell some kind of liquor on his breath. *Gross.* Was he drinking it in the field house? If anybody found out about *that,* he might lose his position and wouldn't *that* serve him right?)

"'I told him to let go, that I had to go study, and he just laughed kind of nasty-like. But he finally let me go and said I should be careful, out here alone so late.

"'Mama is right, I guess. That stuff is all guys think about. But if he does one more thing, one more time, I swear on this diary, I am telling. But who would believe me? Lane would, I guess. But I can't tell him because I know how he feels about him. I'm afraid Lane would try to beat him to a pulp, and what would that do to his football career right here before a championship game? What would that do to Lane's chances of getting that big college scholarship and getting us out of this place someday? Then Lonnie Slaughter would end up quarterback for sure. There's more, but I'd better not write it down. Certain things a girl can't even share with her diary. But, oh! I wish I could tell somebody my terrible secret.'"

Max flipped a page. The diary was blank after that. He let out a strained sigh and was quiet for a long time before he said, "This isn't evidence of any kind. There's no indication of who she's writing about. In fact, it sounds like she could be talking about Lonnie."

"True. I think Lane always assumed it was, because Lonnie had a pattern of forcing his attentions on Kay-Ann like that."

"Lane told me about it. He told anybody who would listen that Lonnie had been bothering her. But even if Lonnie did something to her, that still doesn't have anything to do with Coach."

"Read it again, with fresh eyes, the way I did this morning. That part where she says, 'I know how Lane feels about him.' What if she was talking about hero worship instead of hatred?"

Max didn't look at the diary. Instead he stared at Seth with an expression of dawning horror. "Hold on, Little Brother." He put up a palm like a cop stopping traffic.

"Running around making accusations like that about a man like Coach is going to get you nothing but trouble in this town. You are fixing to get your tit in a ringer."

Seth turned off the interior lights. The sun had risen over the ridge now and the town, spread out below, was lit in soft golden relief. From up here it looked like a painting of an all-American hamlet, not the kind of place where young girls were murdered.

"That's why I'm meeting you here, why I didn't even want to talk about this on a cell phone."

"What is this going to accomplish?"

"I think Lane knew, or at least he did later, after he got involved in law enforcement, that for some reason KayAnn's case had not been properly investigated. So he took it upon himself to find out what happened to her. I think he was closing in on the truth—maybe he was even about to find those bones—when Lonnie and Nelson ran him off that road."

"And maybe he had figured out what Coach had to do with—" Max snapped his fingers. "You know, reading this diary reminded me of something Lane said to me back then."

Seth turned to his friend. "What?"

"He said he saw her car at the field house that night."

"The night she disappeared?"

"Yeah. That was a Saturday, remember?"

"Yes." Seth fingered one of the newspaper articles.

"Lane said he wanted to go in and see what she was doing in there, but he'd been out drinking beer and he didn't want Coach to smell it on his breath."

"Coach?" Seth straightened in the seat.

"His car was in the parking lot, too. But Lane didn't think anything about that. Coach was at the field house ninety percent of the time those days, since we had that state championship hanging in the balance. I didn't think anything about it, either, but now that I've read this…" He tapped the diary.

"Why didn't you ever tell me this before?"

"Like I said, I never really thought anything about it. I assumed the sheriff questioned everybody when KayAnn came up missing." Max twisted in the seat. "Lane never told you about it? About Coach's car?"

"He told me about KayAnn's car. Told the sheriff, too. They decided she must have gone by to get her cheerleading stuff from the field house. Her locker was found empty. When they questioned Coach, he said he didn't see anybody that night. And our stupid sheriff just made a note on his clipboard and moseyed on."

"Or not so stupid," Max stated.

Seth waited. It was tricky, getting a judge to talk openly about corruption. Careers imploded over such things, and Max had his kids to think about.

The two friends sat in silence, letting the gravity of this conversation sink in.

At last Max said quietly, "The sheriff's always been real tight with Coach. I think we really are on to something, Little Brother."

At the word *we* Seth felt a rush of relief. "Suppose Lane figured out that someone—"

"The Slaughters?" Max interjected.

"Not long before he died Lane told me that he'd always suspected one of them raped KayAnn, but he couldn't prove which one. Suppose they killed KayAnn and hid her body in those caves?"

"Man." Max rubbed his forehead as he stared at the diary. "It's almost too much to fathom."

"Suppose that for some reason Coach intervened in the Slaughters' case with the sheriff when they killed Lane. That case was in the sheriff's hands, too, since it was on a county road."

"Yeah. I'm seeing it all now, especially with that boy coming up with the name Howard out of the blue like that. He couldn't have just made that up."

Seth nodded. "Right. Coach has got something to do with this. But I can't piece anything together without those bones."

"So what are you planning to do now?"

"I'm not gonna make the same mistakes Lane made, that's for sure."

"You aren't planning to deal with the Slaughters on your own? Without getting any authorities involved?"

"Only you."

Max snorted. "Didn't anybody ever tell you that a judge is the last person you should drag into a conspiracy?"

Seth felt a load shift off his shoulders. Max would make a strong ally. He was smart and tight-lipped, and since the divorce he had ceased caring what the townsfolk thought of him. "So you don't think I'm crazy?"

Max grinned. "You are absolutely certifiable, but what's that got to do with the price of potatoes? You're a long ways from catching the Slaughters and you're a long ways from figuring out how Coach ties into this."

Seth reached forward and plucked the two other aged newspaper articles off the dash, then extracted the diary from Max's hands. "I know I am stumbling in the dark. But I also know that all of this—" he slapped the papers as he pushed them down into the console "—is no coincidence."

He snapped the cover shut, then draped his arms over the steering wheel and hung his head, conveying regret. "I need a couple of favors."

"Here we go." Max crossed his arms over his chest and slumped in the seat. "Conspiracy time."

Seth just waited. He had become good at that over the years.

"Okay." Max sighed. "What?" Seth didn't need to hear a long speech to know that his friend was prepared to go to the wall.

"I'm taking the cruiser back to the station and I'm walking in there and I'm laying down my badge."

"The chief'll never let you do it. You're too good a cop."

"I've got a lot of comp time built up. I'll take a leave of absence. Whatever. The point is, I'm going to disappear. I don't want you to tell anyone I have those boys."

"Done. But wait. What about Jake?"

"He's cool. He's taking some of his own leave time so he can keep a stakeout up by the caves. That reminds me. I need to borrow your old Jeep."

"It's in mothballs in the garage, but if we can get that old donkey fired up, it's all yours."

"I'll be taking it up into the Winding Stair with me. You can keep the Silvarado if you like."

Max waved his hand. "I like my Chevy."

"Another favor. In the next few days, I want you to arrange a phony article in the *Tenikah Register.*"

Max cocked an eyebrow at him. "You don't want much, Little Brother."

"You can get Virginia to do it. The editor's an idiot who never checks anything." Everybody knew the local paper was full of errors.

"I never talk to Virginia anymore."

"She's still stuck on you and you know it."

"I guess." Max shrugged.

Seth had to smile again. Virginia Lewis was a smart, attractive woman, a general assignment reporter who covered the courthouse beat. In Max's words she had "nearly snagged" him before he had "come to and wiggled off the hook."

"We're talking about three young boys here, Max. If the older one is telling the truth, they've seen too much to ever be safe as long as Lonnie and Nelson are on the loose. For these boys' sake, I've got to flush the Slaughters out."

Seth watched the last of Max's reluctance unravel as he stared out over the sleeping town below them. Kids were his weakness. "So what's Virginia supposed to report?" he finally asked.

"Have you heard the rumor that more rune markings have been discovered recently?"

"Yeah."

Seth figured Max would know about this. The judge was fascinated by the Viking markings that had been discovered in eastern Oklahoma in the 1920s. Some estimates said the Norsemen had made their etchings on walls of rock in the Kiamichis almost a thousand years ago.

"Have her write an article about some team of experts coming out here from back East or somewhere to excavate the new rune stone markings soon."

"You gotta be kidding me. Some experts from back East?"

"Or whatever. Virginia's smart. She'll know what to say. Have her make up quotes about how they are going to do extensive digging, blasting, stuff like that, in the caves up on Purney's Mountain. And I mean soon. I don't want to have to keep those boys in hiding forever."

"Anything *else?*" Max asked.

"I've got to stay up in the Winding Stair with Rainey and the boys. But something tells me Lonnie and Nelson will be looking to talk to Coach right away. Probably to tell him about the boys, about the bones. I want to know if they come into town to meet with him. If possible, I want to know what they tell him."

"You don't want much. How in the heck am I supposed to find out something like that?"

"You're a judge. Don't tell me you don't have sources. Put Tack on it. He'll do it for you…and for me. It would easy enough for him to tail Coach. Nobody'd ever suspect anything from Tack."

"True. Least of all Coach. I see them having coffee at the Pie Almighty nearly every morning."

"Don't tell Tack the deal. Not yet."

"He's gonna want to know something, especially when he figures out you've disappeared."

"For now, just tell him it's a personal favor," Seth said. "The lives of three little boys may very well depend on this."

Max chewed his lip. "Right. And the woman's life, too. Don't forget about the woman, Seth. Have you told her, that social worker, any of this?"

"Not yet." Seth turned his head, looking off at the distant mounds of the Winding Stair Mountains. The endless waves of that range hovered like strokes of watercolor, beckoning him. "So far, you're the only one I've trusted."

Out there, somewhere, Rainey Chapman was no doubt anxiously counting the minutes until he returned. Out there, somewhere, Lonnie and Nelson Slaughter, perhaps in collusion with Coach Hollings, were hiding a terrible secret.

"Speaking of the woman. I'd better get going." Seth fired up the engine. There was no way he could forget about Rainey Chapman. And there was no way he could keep this from a sharp woman like her. Not in a million years. "The chief'll be in by now. I'll swing by for the Jeep later."

CHAPTER TEN

RAINEY WAS AMAZED at how quickly and how thoroughly Seth Whitman won the boys' cooperation.

All afternoon, well on into the evening, they had labored liked little Trojans, right alongside the man. Even Dillon followed Seth's orders, though Rainey saw him cast a wary glance at the man's back a time or two.

First, Seth told the boys to carry in the plastic sacks of groceries from Wal-Mart for Rainey and Granny to put away.

While the boys scurried to and fro, Seth stepped into the kitchen and handed Rainey one of the sacks. "Here. I didn't know what else to get. I know women are picky about their shampoo and makeup and stuff."

Rainey peeked inside. Ponytail holders. A large brush. Deodorant. Toothbrush. Toothpaste. A few other feminine necessities. Rainey was amazed. Grateful. A little embarrassed. "Thank you. This wasn't necessary."

"Sure it was. Unfortunately, you're stuck up here."

"I am? Why?" Rainey's eyes searched his. "The Slaughters have never seen me. How would they trace the boys through me?"

"I have reason to believe they have contacts in town, in law enforcement, unfortunately. With the guardian thing on record, we can't take any chances." The boys were flying in and out of the kitchen, still hauling sacks. Seth glanced at Aaron's back. "I'll explain later."

He reached into Rainey's sack and pulled out a ten-pack of disposable razors. "I'll need a couple of those."

When the supplies were situated, Seth took a minute to sit down on the steps of the screened porch with the boys to explain that Jake was watching for Lonnie and Nelson, and that for now they were all safe up here with him. Other men, he said, were helping them, too. Good men. The boys were not to worry.

Rainey wanted to find out what was really going on, who these other *good men* were, but she realized that would have to wait until they could talk out of earshot of the kids.

Next, Seth decreed that they'd all tend to Granny's animals for her before they got started on their "special project."

Off they went to water the goats and feed Killer and Butch. After that—here was the truly amazing part as far as Rainey was concerned—the boys pitched in like day laborers, helping Seth repair Granny's rotting porch boards.

"Now ain't that a blessing?" Gran sighed with satisfaction as she watched them tear into the old porch.

"It's flat miraculous," Rainey muttered.

Back at the camp, she couldn't even get the boys to pick up their dirty socks without enduring a round of grumbling. But with Seth, they never once complained about the heavy lifting, the sawdust, the dirt, the heat.

In fact, a few times she even heard them all laughing. Maddy's usual faulty, hoarse bark was followed by a new sound from Dillon, a high-pitched, silly giggle. He sounded lighthearted, like a kid. The unfamiliar sound tugged at Rainey's heart. But Seth's laugh stirred something else in her. She caught herself listening for his deep-timbered rumble punctuated by the even deeper roll of his voice, which told her Seth was the one cracking the jokes.

She never heard a sound from Aaron, of course. But when they were unloading the Jeep she heard Seth call out, "Aaron! Catch!"

She looked out just in time to see Seth lob a football in a flawless arch. And Aaron actually caught it! She wasn't sure if that was due to Seth's passing ability or Aaron's extraordinary effort to intercept it. She'd never seen the pudgy boy move so fast. She was so astonished she covered her mouth and felt a little sting of tears.

Rainey was amazed at Maddy's transformation, as well. Throughout the long morning and a stifling lunch hour in the little kitchen, the boys had been as mischievous and quarrelsome as caged monkeys. But the minute Seth returned, their attitude changed. Dillon kept grumbling right on cue, of course, though it was obvious that he was having the time of his life out there with Seth on the porch.

Maybe it was the way Seth doled out orders so matter-of-factly. Maybe the boys were trying to impress him. Or simply keep up with him. Whatever the reason, the time seemed to fly once Seth arrived. His very presence imposed a certain order, a direction. The word *leadership* came to Rainey's mind.

After a particularly loud round of laughter, Rainey overheard Seth ask Dillon if he was serious when he claimed he could handle a stick shift. She looked out the window just in time to see the boy's chin go up. "I said I could, didn't I?"

To her astonishment, Seth tossed the thirteen-year-old his keys, instructing him to back the Jeep up close to the bottom step so they could unload the new lumber directly onto the porch.

"What does that man think he's doing?" Rainey mumbled. "Doesn't he realize that driving without a license was one of the things that got Dillon into trouble in the first place?"

She marched to the door to intervene, but Granny grabbed her arm. "Where are you going?"

"To put a stop to this nonsense. Dillon is too young to drive. He'll have a wreck."

"He's only backing that rattletrap of a Jeep up ten feet."

"But the boy is my responsibility!" Rainey countered.

"It's Seth's Jeep, ain't it? Leave it between the two of them."

Rainey went back to the window and inched the lace curtain back. Dillon was already perched in the seat of the vehicle, looking more like eighteen than thirteen.

With one hand on the wheel and one gripping the open door, he leaned around to peer seriously at Seth, who was standing behind, directing him to inch backward until the lowered tailgate made a shelf over the steps.

When the job was done Dillon looked thoroughly pleased with himself. He slammed the car door and pitched the keys to Seth, who snatched them from the air and gave an approving nod.

Seth and the boys threw themselves into the work of unloading the planks of cedar for the porch. Next came measuring and sawing and hammering, the likes of which Rainey'd never seen. The man was a dynamo, whistling the whole time he worked, keeping the boys in line, making those jokes.

Rainey was drawn to the window to peek around that lace curtain several times. After a few trips, she was startled by the sight of Seth's shirtless back. His skin was as tanned as rawhide, and his muscles were as sculpted as any bodybuilder's. Rainey bit her lip while her insides thrummed with acutely feminine urges.

She told herself that this man wasn't right for her, that what she was feeling was pure physical attraction, plain old lust. But still she couldn't stop staring at his biceps. And right then he turned. From under the shadow of his black Stetson, his dark eyes skewered hers, seeming to read her thoughts. She quickly dropped the curtain and didn't return to the window again.

Before they knew it, it was suppertime.

Granny seemed in her element, cooking for a bunch

of guys again, and Rainey helped her dish up enough meat loaf and mashed potatoes and green beans to feed a threshing crew. They topped it all off with a fresh apple pie.

The boys were so excited about their progress on the porch that they wanted to go back out to finish up after supper.

"Too dark now." Seth stretched. "But if you guys help clean up this kitchen, I'll take everybody up the mountain and show you something really cool."

Rainey wondered how the man was able to sit guard all night in the cab of a pickup and still have endless energy for shopping and animal husbandry and carpentry and mountain climbing and God knew what else. Didn't he ever sleep?

"What's up there?" Dillon was signing for Maddy to hurry with one hand, and clearing his plate with the other.

"How do you sign the word for stars?" Seth asked.

Dillon showed him.

Seth pumped his eyebrows and signed *stars* to Maddy, then surprised Rainey by repeating the sign for her with an inviting smile and some silly pointing and finger walking embellishments.

"So you found Gran's lookout rock?" She smiled back.

"Yep." He stifled a yawn. "Grace, I don't suppose you could fix me some coffee to take up there."

"Coming up!" Gran grabbed the enamel pot.

When the coffee was ready, Grace said, "I will finish up this kitchen. You all go on up the mountain."

They all followed Seth's flashlight up the trail to a large rock that jutted out over a stunning view of the valley, with sparkling glimpses of the river below.

The moon shone as full and lucent as a spotlight.

The dogs had trotted along and threaded underfoot, and the boys were as bad as Granny's billy goats, leaping around on the jagged rocks in the dark. Seth had to grab at a couple of shirt collars and haul them back from the ledge. Finally, they all settled down under the vast night sky for some rapt stargazing.

Up on this rock there were no treetops to disrupt the view. With the lights of civilization far away, thousands of stars shone brilliantly.

"Boys, look," Rainey said. "That's Arcturus." She pointed. "And that's Andromeda. Orion. Granny calls those the Seven Sisters."

While she was speaking a shooting star cut through the dark sky low on the horizon.

"Wow! Did you see that?" Dillon poked Seth's shoulder excitedly. Maddy signed his wonder near Rainey's face in the dark. Even Aaron looked enthralled.

While Rainey was watching Aaron, Seth was watching *her*. At one point they exchanged a glance of protective accord over the boy's head, and Rainey wondered what it would be like, how it would feel, to raise children with the kind of man who would take them up on a mountain to look at the stars.

And what would it be like, she had to wonder as she climbed the narrow stairs to Gran's attic, to keep up with a man with so much energy? She was too tired to think about it for long. She crashed onto the hard cotton mattress like a fallen tree.

The next morning, Seth came down from his lookout, ate the supersize breakfast Granny fixed him, and roused his young crew to work on the porch again.

By the end of the day the job was nearly done, and Granny and Rainey had fried chicken and brownies ready this time.

As the sun set on their third day, the hard labor and Granny's hearty food worked like a powerful soporiphic on the boys. Their eyes glazed over as they finished their brownies. Seth had finally succeeded in wearing them out.

"Certain young men need a bath before they drop in their tracks," Granny announced as she pushed up from the table.

The boys launched into "rock, paper, scissors" to see who had to go first. When Dillon lost, Seth pointed toward the porch. "Fair's fair," he said. The other two boys darted into the living room for some coveted time watching the staticky TV.

"We'll clean up the kitchen," Seth said when Granny started to stack the dishes.

"Yes," Rainey chimed in. "I'm sure you need some rest. Having all this unexpected company must be tiring."

Granny smiled, and Rainey smiled back, but with some effort. She was the one who was tired. Granny had spent much of the day picking and storing apples and canning the ripe tomatoes in fat mason jars, all of which created a horrific mess in the tiny kitchen. And now this bossy cop had volunteered them for KP duty. Rainey normally had energy to spare, but her second night in the airless attic room had taken its toll. She had about had it.

"That's good of you." Granny yawned. "I am about tuckered out. Are you staying in my room, Rainey, or upstairs again, or what?"

The question seemed to charge the air in the tiny kitchen like a high voltage current. Rainey shrugged her shoulders uncomfortably. Seth took up whistling again as he got busy clearing the table.

"I'll, uh, I'll let Seth have the attic," Rainey finally stammered. She wasn't spending another night up in the stuffy house top, anyway, even if she was forced to share Granny's powdery-scented bed.

"I'll be up on that rock." Seth smiled over his shoulder.

"Whatever you want to do is fine with me," Gran offered to Rainey.

"Your room."

"I'll see you in a bit, then. Here you go." Granny held out her pinafore-style apron for Rainey's use.

Rainey took it and kissed her grandmother's withered cheek. "I'll try to be quiet when I come in."

Granny left, but the effects of her question about the sleeping arrangements still lingered. Vaguely uncomfortable at being alone with Seth in the tiny room, Rainey held the gingham apron in a useless wad at her hip.

Seth leaned his backside against the counter and crossed his arms over his broad chest. "Aren't you going to put that thing on?"

"Do I look like the apron-wearing type to you?"

His gaze took in the length of her from head to toe, causing her to frown down at her own tan legs, which tapered to bare feet with toenails painted cherry-red. Suddenly she wished she were a little more covered up. Although she often ran around at Granny's without shoes, the way he was looking at her bare feet made her feel…exposed. She was dressed in a baby-blue scoop-necked, body hugging T-shirt and a pair of white shorts that she'd left here on her last visit—the coolest clothes she could find.

"Definitely not. Better let me have it." He held out his big palm for the apron.

Rainey gave him a smirk as he took it and put his head into the keyhole opening, then tied the sash in a sloppy bow at his back. The waist of the apron hit him just below his well-developed pects. He looked ridiculous.

"What if the boys see you like that?"

He glanced down at himself. "I imagine my reputation will be ruined. Just look at how these little purple flowers clash with my boots."

Rainey noticed the detailing on his black boots for the first time. The fancy white stitching on the vamp created the wings of an eagle. "Custom made?" she asked.

"By elves."

She shook her head, but found herself relieved by his silliness all the same. It was better than overthinking who was sleeping where.

"Why don't you eat that last brownie?" He pointed at the pan. "I hear it calling your name."

He kept up his teasing until the dishes were done—flipping water on her, bumping her hip when they were side by side, showing her the "cowboy method" of sweeping the floor, a kind of two-step with the broom.

By the time he plucked a couple of mint leaves off the plant on the windowsill and handed one to her, Rainey realized she wasn't so tired anymore and that she had never had so much fun cleaning up a messy kitchen.

Seth's expression turned serious. He jerked a thumb toward the front porch, "Once the boys are asleep, we've got to talk."

"I agree."

While Seth and Rainey had been doing the dishes, each boy had taken his turn in Granny's old claw-foot tub out on the back porch. With alert expressions that said they knew something was up between the adults, one by one they trooped through the kitchen, smirking at Seth in the apron, and rolling their eyes at Rainey's giddy laughter. But finally, they settled in for the night with an old wooden crate of Classics Illustrated comic books that Granny had scrounged up from her attic room. Again, Rainey was amazed. She could never get these kids to read anything back at camp.

"Ain't nothin' else to do," Dillon had grumbled. But

Rainey noticed that he became as absorbed in choosing his comic—*Treasure Island*—as the other two boys. The second time she peeked into the living room, all three kids were sacked out.

As Seth and Rainey tiptoed past the bodies sprawled on top of sleeping bags on Gran's threadbare living room rug, none of the kids moved a muscle, and from Gran's bedroom, they could hear the not-so-soft rasp of the elderly woman's rhythmic snoring.

Out on the porch, the nearly full moon seemed to pour down a trough of cooling air with its bluish light.

"Thank God, it's cooling down out here." Rainey ran her fingers over her throat and upper chest.

"It's a hot one, all right." Seth said it lightly, as if they were getting ready to have a normal conversation, which Rainey knew they were not. He drew a deep breath. "But a storm's blowing in. We sure need the rain."

Rainey raised her face to the refreshing night breeze. "Rain *would* be heavenly. Do we need to worry about severe weather?"

"No." He smiled. "I checked with the storm chasers by radio. Nothing but thundershowers tonight."

She turned on him, finished with the niceties. "This has been the hottest, longest, most nerve-wracking… most *trying* three days of my life." Maybe it was the hangover from her sleepless nights, or maybe it was this whole setup, but all day her nerves had felt strained to the point of snapping. She was not going to let this cop act as if hiding three delinquent boys from a pack of murderers was business as usual.

"I'm sorry." His voice was gentle, sincere.

She crossed her arms over her middle defensively. "I don't mean to sound whiney. I know we're in real trouble, and I know the boys' welfare comes first. I know you're trying to protect them. It's just…how long are we going to have to keep this up? The tension is driving me crazy. And the boys—no video games, no pizza or Cokes or ice cream."

Seth put a palm up in defense. "Hey. I bought some ice cream."

She smiled, relaxed, but only a fraction. "You know what I mean. This is no place for three boys, not like these three, anyway." She lowered her voice. "You should have heard Dillon griping when Gran shooed them out to the garden to pull weeds in the heat when you went to town the other day."

"Good for her. Those boys can pull weeds as well as anybody. They aren't physically handicapped, are they? Seems to me they're adjusting okay. Seemed like they had a pretty good time, helping me with this porch."

She eyed him. A virile man with a five o'clock shadow, he looked more movie star hunk than father figure. And was life really so simple for this small-town cop? "They'll rebel sooner or later. This confinement is bound to wear thin." She threw up her hands. "My God. The utter boredom of this place. It was hard enough to manage the boys at the camp, where there were plenty of activities."

"Activities? That's what's wrong with kids these days, if you ask me. They have to be entertained every second of their lives. Whatever happened to playing outside, exploring the out-of-doors?"

"Letting them explore isn't an option when I keep expecting those creeps to jump out of the woods at any second."

He didn't try to tell her that part wasn't so, or that everything was going to be okay, or that Lonnie and Nelson were less of a threat than they actually were. Instead he surprised her by facing her and lightly bracing his big palms on her shoulders. "Listen. I know you're scared." The look in his eyes was tender, concerned. "I know I'm putting you and the boys through a lot. This is going to be tough. I just don't know how else to do it."

"Then at least tell me what's happening." She didn't realize she'd gripped his arm until she felt his warm muscle flex beneath her fingers. Touching him had come too easy. Had felt too right.

She saw his chest expand with a tense breath as she slid her hand away. "What happened in town?" she asked, trying to cover the sudden reaction that touching him had stirred in her. "Did the authorities believe that Lonnie and Nelson tried to kidnap the boys?"

"I didn't tell the authorities anything about it."

She pulled back in surprise and he dropped his hands. "You didn't? Why not? I thought you said you have some good men helping you."

"Look, I've got to explain a few things to you. Let's sit down."

Gran had an ancient porch swing with a fat seat

cushion, and Rainey perched in the corner of it lightly, curling one bare foot beneath her bottom. But when Seth started to lower his muscular frame into it, the thing creaked so miserably she automatically put a finger to her lips.

"How about over here?" he suggested, indicating the first landing of the freshly repaired steps that wound down the hillside. His boots made muffled clunks as he crossed over the new lumber. He sat down on the first step with his arms loosely resting on his widespread knees.

Rainey padded along behind and settled next to him, hugging her own knees to her chest. Though she was careful to keep a respectable distance, she felt a wave of magnetism between them, building momentum as surely as the storm in the sky.

"The Tenikah cops have never been the best in the business," Seth started. "When Lane died—"

"Lane?"

An uncomfortable beat passed as clouds scuttled over the moon, and Rainey stole a look at his profile. A flicker of tension tightened his eyes before he said, "My brother."

"The cop Gran mentioned when she first met you?"

"Yes."

"The cop the Slaughter twins killed?"

"Yes."

She kept her gaze on his profile. He was an extremely handsome man, but something about the way he looked right now broke her heart. Something about his expression made her ask quietly, "Why?"

"Why what?"

"Why are you so convinced it wasn't an accident?"

"I'm not *convinced. I know* they killed him."

The angry edge in his voice made her wonder again what kind of situation she'd gotten herself—and the boys—into with this man. "How can you be so sure?"

"My brother told me some things. And I figured out some other things on my own…after."

"Is that what you wanted to explain to me?"

"No. I can't go into all that right now. It would take all night to tell it. It's too complicated."

But Rainey felt that maybe the truth was it was simply too painful. She suspected he didn't trust her enough to share his story…or his pain. But she figured she had a right to know as much as possible. For the boys' sake, at least. She drew in a deep breath of the woodsy air. "I just happen to have all night."

When he didn't respond, she added, "What else have we got to do out here in the middle of nowhere?"

When he still didn't answer, she prodded, "Gran already told me some stuff, anyway."

That got a reaction. He favored her with a piercing glance.

"The other morning. After you went to town."

"I see. What did your granny have to say?" His tone was guarded and Rainey wondered if there'd been a lot of gossip and speculation about his brother's death and about his reaction to it. Years may have passed, but it was obvious, looking at him now, that Seth Whitman's wounds were far from healed.

"She said that the grudge between the Slaughter brothers and the Whitman brothers goes all the way back to grade school."

"Go on."

"She said you all four ended up playing high school football for the best team the Tenikah Pirates ever had. Expected to win the state championship, faces in the paper all the time, and all that. Said the older three were all slated to play in college. She said the head coach was grooming you for some big scholarships, too, but that you got a nasty chip on your shoulder and quit in your junior year and went off to rodeo around the country the minute you turned eighteen."

"Gran sure knows her history." Again the defensive sarcasm. "How does your grandmother know so much?"

"My grampa was a retired lawman. I guess he heard things."

"I see. And did she tell you how I happened to get that chip?"

"Oh, yes. Gran said the Slaughter boys always played second fiddle to you and Lane on the team, but then suddenly, in Lane's senior year, the coach shifted his favor to the Slaughters. She said everybody claimed it was because Lane went crazy after his pretty little cheerleader girlfriend ran away from town, left him flat. Gran said Lane kept telling the law and anybody else who would listen that he thought Lonnie Slaughter had done something to that girl, or at least that she told him *somebody* had been harassing her, scaring her, right before she disappeared."

To all of this, Seth said nothing. He just stared out over the mountainside as the wind picked up and more clouds scuttled over the face of the moon.

"Seth? Is all of that stuff true? Did the girl claim someone had been harassing her?"

He turned eyes on her that glinted as hard as blue steel. "Yes."

"Did the authorities believe her?"

"She never told the authorities. She never had the chance. But when she disappeared Lane did plenty of talking, and when he wouldn't shut up, Coach claimed his obsession was interfering with his game concentration."

"And then what?"

After a long pause, Seth said, "It was finally decided that Lane's girlfriend was a runaway. She did come from a bad home, after all, but…"

"But Lane couldn't accept that explanation," Rainey guessed.

He kept silent.

"And you couldn't, either."

Again, silence.

"Gran said everybody called her a wild child."

"She wasn't."

"Look, we're stuck in this thing together, so I have a right to know. What finally happened between your brother and the Slaughters?"

Lightning ripped across the night sky, illuminating the landscape. In the flash, Seth's face looked as set as the rocky cliffs that tumbled below them.

"Somehow Lane ended up dead," Rainey stated, "and you blame the Slaughters."

Silence again, but the twitching muscle in his jaw told Rainey all she needed to know.

"Was he going after them when he got killed? Is that it? Was Lane out for vengeance?"

She paused, hating to ask the next question. But she had to know. "And are you?"

He hung his head, staring at his boots again.

"Answer me, Seth. Is that it? Lane's dead, but now you've taken up his cause. Is that what you didn't want to tell me a minute ago?"

She waited while more lightning flickered in the distance.

At last, through clenched teeth, Seth spoke. "That's about the size of it."

Thunder came rumbling over the nearest ridge as Rainey let his admission sink in. She wasn't really prepared for his stark answer. After the things Granny had told her about Seth's history, she was hoping that for once in her life, her wise grandmother had been wrong. But the old lady had nailed it, in her roundabout way. "Ever seen a big cat with a thorn in his paw?" she'd said. "He'll come near to chewing off the whole foot to get shed of the pain."

"I can't be a party to this," Rainey said quietly, firmly.

"Can't be a party to what?" Seth's confusion seemed genuine.

"Using these boys as bait so you can fulfill some sick need for revenge that you've nursed all these years."

The lightning flashed fiercer and the thunder boomed louder, closer, but they ignored it. The threatening storm couldn't compare to the clash of wills building between them.

Seth's lips parted briefly, forming a protest, then he clamped his jaw shut. He jerked a thumb toward the living room as his eyes narrowed and his voice came out low and intense. "Didn't you listen to that boy? Do I have to tell you what kind of animals these men are?" He lowered his voice even further. "They'd as soon kill these boys as look at them. This isn't about me, or Lane, or even a missing girl now. It's about three kids that never even heard of Lonnie and Nelson Slaughter until three days ago."

"And you are hoping that because of the boys the Slaughters will show themselves and you can catch them."

"I'm telling you that no matter what I've felt or haven't felt in the past, the Slaughters have a new agenda now, and I aim to stop them from carrying it out. I believe Dillon…and Maddy."

Rainey was touched that he believed the kids, because, despite every stunt Dillon had pulled in the past, she found herself believing his story, too, even though she couldn't shake the nagging feeling that he was keeping something back. Since they'd gone into hiding, she had questioned the boys on her own. Gently. Firmly. Repeatedly. She kept coming up with the same answers from all three.

"The Slaughters are bound to return to that cave for

those bones sooner or later," Seth said. "I'll catch them when they do. All I ask is your patience," he added softly. "And your trust."

She looked up into his eyes and something in their depths did inspire deeper trust. "Then you've got to come clean with me." She spoke just as softly. "I need to know everything that's going on."

"I understand. I'll tell you everything, at least the parts I know."

He did. He told her about the night Lane had died. How he figured the Slaughters ran Lane's cruiser off a cliff, then left his brother out there after they were sure he was dead. How they'd gotten just drunk enough to make the matching damage to their own vehicle look accidental. He told her about the old grudge between the Whitman brothers and the Slaughter twins, which culminated in their fierce competition for Coach's approval on the football team. He told her about Max, Tack, Jake. About a loyal, quiet country boy named Leonard who knew the woods as well as any man and was watching the river side of Gran's mountain for him.

"But I don't get it," she interrupted at one point. "What is the connection between what the Slaughters are doing now and this Howard Dillon says they were talking about."

"Howard Hollings." Seth shook his head. "The local football coach. He's like a sacred institution in Tenikah. The sheriff is buddies with him."

"So that's why you don't trust the sheriff?"

"Yes, I think he might do whatever Coach asked. I don't know how Coach Hollings fits in here. All I do know is, after KayAnn disappeared, Coach changed. And he moved Lonnie up to quarterback, which didn't make sense. Lonnie could play, but he wasn't nearly as good as Lane, even if Lane *was* upset about KayAnn."

Then Seth told her about the newspaper articles, about the diary that he'd found after his brother's death.

She watched him while he talked, and began to think that maybe her Gran had a point. This man was special. Her respect for him grew as she realized how doggedly he had pursued the truth, and for how long.

He was starting to tell her that Lane had somehow figured out that they had hidden KayAnn's remains, when a horrendous thunderclap split the air as lightning struck in the woods nearby.

Rainey shrieked, cowering back against Seth. He wrapped his arms around her and cradled her head to his shoulder as the rolling thunder rattled the porch.

"Come on." He took her hand, hauling her up. "We'd better get out of this weather."

But before they'd made it up the flights of steps, the sky split open and a torrent of rain crashed down, soaking them. Seth covered Rainey with one arm and they ran to the shelter of the screened-in porch.

She immediately started shivering in her skimpy wet clothes. He wrapped his arms around her tightly and she curled into his chest. This close, the electricity between them became undeniable. Thunder boomed and the sky flared with lightning again as Rainey turned her face up to his. Seth's lips hovered over hers as he looked into her eyes.

Her eyelashes fluttered down and she tilted her head shyly to the side, but he lifted her chin and made her look at him. Again he searched her eyes.

Finally he said, "Yes," as if she'd actually spoken to him. "Yes," he whispered, "I am…" Bringing his mouth closer until his lips were murmuring against hers, "…going to kiss you."

CHAPTER ELEVEN

SETH'S BREATH BECAME Rainey's breath as his mouth lingered over hers. The scent of him—mint, brisk after-shave, even faint traces of sawdust—increased her hunger for a kiss that seemed tortuously slow in coming.

His strong hands clasped her back tighter, pulling her body flush against the muscled length of him. The impact of his hard, hot flesh against her chilled skin melted any control she might have had.

He slid his palms over her cropped shirt, bracketing her ribs and waist as his strong thumbs caressed the undersides of her suddenly needy breasts.

When at last he lowered his head and pressed his firm lips to hers, Rainey moaned at the contact. At the sound, he forced her lips apart and thrust his silky tongue inside her mouth, urgently tasting, and she answered with her own hunger, a desire to have all of him.

They kissed as if they already knew each other's mouths, each other's needs. As if they'd been doing this for weeks, months, years. A lifetime. They kissed in a dizzying give and take that seemed to last forever, but still didn't satisfy.

He broke off and twined his long fingers into her hair, angling her head for a better fit, then he slanted his open mouth over hers to take—and give—some more.

Again, they tasted each other in movements that quickly became ravenous.

Hungry. Demanding.

They broke off, breathless, and stared into each other's eyes as if disbelieving.

"Man," he whispered, then danced her backward as he pressed his lips to her cheek, up to her temple, down to her ear. She clamped her arms around his neck as he lifted her off her feet. He perched her on the porch rail and fitted her thighs high around his hips. Kissing her again, he held the core of her tight against him, holding her up, clasping her small bottom in his big hands. His bold manhandling overwhelmed her senses, but at the same time thrilled her.

"Seth…wait."

"Okay," he whispered. "Okay." He tightened his arms around her back. He held her gently while his muscles quivered and their pulses seemed to beat in sync.

They clung in that entwined position for some seconds, both struggling for control.

Rainey felt small and delicate as he held her against his body with his massive arms. It felt so right. She'd never, ever been held like this before. So possessively. Terrible cravings assailed her. As if, were it physically possible, she would fuse her very being with his. She pressed into him, overcome by this raw need.

"Rainey," he groaned, and lowered his face to her neck, and the feel of his hot, moist breath on her skin made her insides thrum.

"Seth," she groaned in reply, because she had a sudden need to say his name, too. She had to make what they were doing seem more real, somehow, to bring them back to earth. "Seth," she said again. But the spell couldn't be so easily broken. His embrace only tightened at the sound of her voice repeating his name.

He brought his mouth around to hers for another greedy, hot kiss.

When they broke apart, she pressed her forehead to his and said, "This is crazy. What is this?"

"I don't know." He groaned. "All I know is you feel incredible in my arms."

"How can we be kissing like this," she whispered, "when I don't even know you?"

The thunderstorm crashed and boomed around them while they kissed and held fast to each other again, neither one willing to let go, neither one willing to answer that question.

"Ms. Chapman?" Dillon's voice, from just inside the front screen door, made them both jump, as if the lightning had struck their backs.

Rainey instantly dropped to her feet. But Seth didn't fully let go of her. He held her lightly against him, sheltering her body from Dillon's view, cradling her head near his shoulder.

"Is there gonna be a tornado?" the boy asked.

"No, son." Seth turned his head, seeming to have to

collect his thoughts before he could fully answer. "No tornado. It's just a thunderstorm. Now go back to sleep."

"What are you guys doing?" The kid's voice sounded wary.

"We're...just making...plans," Seth answered.

"You okay, Ms. Chapman?" The youth's changing voice cracked.

"I'm fine, Dillon." Rainey swallowed. She was not fine. She was shaken, reeling with this newfound passion. "You do what Seth said now, and go back to bed, okay?" They heard Dillon's footsteps padding away.

Rainey slid out of Seth's arms, putting distance between them, trying to subdue the feelings he'd stirred up in her. She walked to the edge of the porch and stared out at the thundershower, now converging in dark ribbons of water that snaked down the rocky slope.

Seth stepped up next to her and fixed an assessing gaze on her profile. She let herself sink back against the newel post with her head lowered, wondering if she looked as confused as she felt.

"Are you okay?" he said. He seemed to want to touch her, but he didn't.

She folded her arms at her waist in a self-protective hug. "I just wish this were over."

"I've wished that for seven years, Rainey."

"You started to tell me something about your brother, about why he came out here that night."

"I think Lane was convinced the Slaughters buried KayAnn Rawls—"

"She was his girlfriend?"

"Yes."

"Lane had reason to suspect they buried her up in that warren of caves on Purney's Mountain, after Lonnie raped…and killed her."

"Lord." Rainey tightened one arm over her middle and slid the other hand over her mouth. She squeezed her eyes shut, breathed deep.

Seth reached up and stroked her hair. "Are you sure you're okay?"

She nodded. "Give me a minute." After she'd regained her composure, she said, "No wonder you're convinced Dillon's telling the truth. You've suspected the bones were there all along."

"I've been looking for them myself."

"By yourself? For seven years?"

"Just like my brother before me."

"I see. So Lane was trying to find the bones when they killed him?"

Seth nodded. "Or in fact, had found them. Lane's accident fell under the jurisdiction of the county sheriff, since it happened out here in the Winding Stair. The sheriff wrapped the case up pretty tidy, pretty quick. I keep thinking there are four things that have got to be linked somehow."

She nodded in turn, eager to understand.

"One—" he raised his index finger "—Lane played his heart out for Coach Hollings, but then Coach dropped him like a hot rock. Two—" he raised a second finger "—why would Coach suddenly favor Lonnie

Slaughter as his star player when he wasn't nearly as talented as Lane?

"Three—" another finger went up "—the sheriff and Coach are big buddies, always have been."

"And four—" Rainey raised four fingers to match his "—Dillon heard the Slaughters talking about a guy named Howard—Coach."

Seth smiled. It wasn't a glad smile or a happy one. It was the heavy-hearted smile of a man who regrets the truth, but is gratified that someone else sees it. "Like I said, I have no idea what Coach has to do with this, what part he plays in it. But if he did something illegal, if he helped the Slaughters cover something up, I will go after him with everything I've got."

Rainey shook her head. "But why would he do that?"

"That's the part I can't get rounded up. But I've got some leads. Of course, my friend the judge says none of it is solid evidence."

"The judge who appointed me guardian?"

"Max. He says the diary, all the other stuff, is circumstantial."

"You need…the bones."

"And only the Slaughters can show me where those bones are."

"And the boys are the bait for the Slaughters."

"No. That's where you're wrong. I would never do that. Max agreed to plant an article in the local newspaper that'll flush out the bastards—excuse me. Anyway, we think we have a way to draw them out that has nothing to do with the boys."

"How?"

"Are you familiar with the rune markings?"

"Of course." Viking letters carved into a slab of sandstone up in the mountains. Rainey recalled that there was still some debate about how the Vikings made it up the Mississippi all the way to the Poteau River.

"Lately more rune markings have been discovered. In the caves on Purney's Mountain."

Rainey's eyes widened with understanding, and he nodded. "The article in the paper is going to say that some people are coming out from the Smithsonian to do an analysis of the markings. The idea of a bunch of scientists poking around in the caves should give the Slaughters the added incentive they need to come out of hiding. And when the twins make their move, I'll make mine. It's all a matter of timing."

"How will you know when they do it?" Rainey was thinking how he was staying with them twenty-four hours a day.

"My partner's got it covered. I don't want to leave the boys' safety—or yours—up to anybody but me."

"I'm sorry I doubted you." Rainey looked into his eyes. "You know that as long as the boys are safe, I'll help you in any way I can."

"We'll make a good team." His voice grew the slightest bit husky as his gaze strayed down to her mouth.

"Yes." Rainey was suddenly dying to pick up where they'd left off when Dillon interrupted. But at the same time she was afraid. Something told her that once she got started with this man there would be no holding back. "I think…I think I'd better go in now." She turned to go inside.

"No." He caught her wrist and tugged her back. "Please. Don't. Don't go in just yet. Stay here with me for a while."

It was tempting. The storm had cooled the air. The rain settled into a pattering rhythm on the roof. And the man was tempting, as well. Too much so.

"Nothing will happen. I promise. Would it be okay if I just held you for a second?" He drew her into the reassuring hug she so desperately needed. She sank against his chest like a little girl against her daddy.

He stroked her hair. "It was only a kiss," he said, as if reading her thoughts. "I'm sorry I let things go too fast. But surely you're aware that I'm extremely attracted to you."

Rainey could only nod.

He continued stroking her hair. And again, Rainey melted under his touch. Every move he made seemed just right. She had known it would be so before they'd even kissed. For her, the man was as physically perfect as he could be. But he wasn't right in any other way. This was so unfair, so complicated.

"Tell me what you're thinking," he encouraged, while his warm hand found its way under her hair and massaged the back of her neck.

"That I am so scared," she confessed, inhaling the suddenly reassuring fragrance of him—how had she become hooked on his scent so quickly? Usually she had to give herself time to *adapt* to a new man's smell.

But it seemed as if she couldn't fill her lungs deeply enough with the scent of Seth. She let herself be folded deeper into the hug. He smelled the way she vaguely remembered the men in her family smelling. Like leather, cedar wood, clean soap. It was a heady combination that made her feel safe and secure and thrilled to be alive all at once.

"Don't be afraid." His voice was gentle, yet full of resolve. "I'm doing everything I can to protect all of you. This is a great hiding place. There's only that one road up. The route from the river side is impassable except on foot. And I've got a man helping me cover that end."

But Rainey hadn't meant she was afraid of the threat the Slaughters presented. At the moment she was more afraid of her overwhelming attraction to Seth.

"You just take care of yourself," he continued soothingly, "and Granny and the boys. This will all be over soon." The hypnotic rumble of his deep baritone lulled her as nothing else could.

She relaxed in his arms, and he held her gently for a long time. As she listened to the steady rhythm of his heart, the three days of fatigue overcame her. She was about to slip into the twilight of sleep when a light flicked on in the window at the side of the house. Gran. Awakened by the storm. Most likely reading her dog-eared Bible by her little bedside lamp.

Seth studied Rainey's face in the dim glow. "Can I tell you something?" He ran his strong fingers up into her hair again.

"Of course," Rainey murmured, feeling warm and drowsy, feeling safer than she'd ever been, despite their situation.

His voice was quiet, low, sincere. "I think you're very beautiful."

Many men had said similar things to her, many had used those exact words, some almost the instant they met her. But when this man said it, her heart suddenly kicked up with an erratic rhythm.

"I like the sound of your name," Seth said thoughtfully. "Rainey. Where did you get a name like that?"

Slowly, she straightened, staring out into the downpour for a moment, remembering.

"Rainey?" Seth's voice sounded concerned. He curled his fingers under hers, trying to pull her back to the shelter of his warmth. "What's wrong?"

She turned her head and focused on Seth's face, seeing it indistinctly in the dim, watery light.

"My father picked it. Because of a…a whim. It was raining the day I was born." She stood abruptly. "I've got to go in now." Looking down at him, even in the murky light, she could read Seth's disconcerted frown, but still she tugged her hand free.

"Okay." He drew out the word slowly, as if he sensed that something was not quite right. This time he didn't try to grab her wrist or convince her to stay. Slowly, he released her fingers. That last second of contact, as the tips touched and slid away, was pure torture for Rainey. Seth Whitman was going to be very hard to resist.

CHAPTER TWELVE

THE DAYS THAT FOLLOWED were strained for many reasons. Squalls of thunderstorms, atypical for Oklahoma in late August, rose like bad omens over the ridgeline every evening at sunset. The drenching nighttime rains only intensified the next day's heat with cloying humidity.

Without the porch to keep them busy or the mystical and spectacular stargazing to look forward to, the boys grew restless, constantly complaining to Rainey and picking fights with each other over Granny's cache of old comic books.

"Oh Lord," Granny prayed loudly in her best TV preacher's voice one sweltering afternoon. "Help us all get along together. And please yank the corncobs out of certain people's backsides."

Seth grinned at that. He was beginning to appreciate the fact that Granny was a shrewd little imp whose spontaneous "prayers" were often nothing more than thinly disguised lectures. But even when she was being sanctimonious, Seth found Granny an adorable pixie. And he found himself wondering if Rainey would resemble her in another fifty or sixty years.

They all got to know each other as only persons living in close proximity under adverse conditions can.

"Daylight's a'wastin'," Granny would sing out every morning shortly after daybreak. The boys didn't appreciate being roused early. They didn't like the mountain quiet and being cut off from their TV and video games, either. They didn't like Granny poking her pointy little whiskered chin into their business. They didn't like her funny way of talking, her incessant praying, her off-key warbling of church hymns.

Granny did her best to distract one and all with country-style food dished up in ample quantities. Dillon was not shy about making special requests.

"Can we have those mashed potatoes again tonight?" He signed for Maddy's benefit as he spoke.

"The kind with no gravy?" Granny clarified, twirling a finger over an imaginary bowl. "With just a puddle of melted butter at the center?"

"Yeah!"

"Nah," Granny teased. "I was thinking about fixing a big old slimy pot of boiled okra instead."

Dillon signed "slimy okra" to the other two boys and Aaron pinched his nose.

They got into the game, hounding Granny for the potatoes with begging gestures.

"Oh, all right," she huffed. "But I'll need somebody to go out to the root cellar and fetch a big bucket of spuds."

Dillon was already licking his lips…and signing to Maddy that Granny wanted *Maddy* to fetch potatoes.

But Aaron countersigned the truth, for which Dillon punched his biceps.

"Dillon, go get the potatoes," Seth ordered.

Dillon slumped. "Gimme the bucket."

At Gran's encouragement, Maddy chimed in, signing his food preferences—biscuits and fried chicken for dinner again. Even Aaron made his wishes known, when Granny asked him directly, "What are you hankerin' for today, young man?"

He took the scratch pad she held out and scrawled, "rice crispy squares" with a fat exclamation mark.

But when they weren't distracted by food, the boys continued to carp at Rainey, three against one, even though two of them couldn't speak.

"How long are we gonna have to stay up here in this dump?" Dillon whined one morning after breakfast.

"As long as I say so," Seth intervened calmly. "Go roll up your sleeping bags. Then I want to see you out on the back porch."

Rainey couldn't contain her curiosity about that. After Seth and Dillon had been out there awhile, she cracked the back door. They caught her peeking, and Dillon grinned. His upper lip was coated with shave cream. Seth's was, too, and he was holding a disposable razor aloft.

"Is something wrong?" Seth stopped the lesson. Dillon picked up Grampa's old straight razor, idly opening and closing it.

"No." Rainey smiled. "What are you guys doing?" She opened the door fully.

Seth waggled the razor. "Dillon's teaching me how to shave."

Dillon snickered at that, but Rainey rolled her eyes.

"Send out the other two." Seth smiled. "I bought enough razors for them, too, if they want to practice. They're coming along right behind Dillon and will need to shave soon enough."

Dillon winked at Rainey, as if she were dismissed.

Seth knew a lot about handling boys, she conceded. And he knew a lot about the woods, and about animals. He taught the boys so much they took over most of the care of Gran's old horse, her billy goats and llama, the chickens. And of course, the dogs.

From the first day, Killer and Butch had become attached to the boys, inexplicably so to Dillon.

When Killer swiped Dillon's shoe from the porch and ran off with it, Rainey got tense, but Seth's attitude was more amused. "This should be good," he said, as the boy leaped off the porch in pursuit.

The dog dashed into the clearing and waited with the shoe in his mouth, paws down, butt in the air, until Dillon was two feet away. Then the pooch darted off again. Butch charged into the game, barking wildly. Seth laughed his head off while Dillon chased the two dogs in circles and the dogs played keep away with the shoe, finally attempting to bury it. When Dillon dived at the preoccupied animals he hit a mud puddle and slipped, falling on his backside. The dogs leaped on him and a mud fight over the shoe ensued. The other boys had been drawn outside by the commotion. Rainey's heart swelled when she heard the unfamiliar sound of Aaron actually laughing out loud.

"You think that was funny?" Dillon said as he ran up to the porch, dripping mud. He swiped Seth's Stetson off the post and plunked it on Killer's head, pulling it down around the dog's ears.

"Hey!" Seth hollered and took up chase as the dog darted off. And the game became a foursome. Immediately, the other two boys leaped into the wild game. Boys. Dogs. Man. Barking. Yelling. Laughing.

Dressing the dogs became a running joke after that. A dog would come out onto the porch wearing the boys' socks. Or one of Granny's aprons. Seth drew the line when Killer came clumping out in his fancy boots one evening.

"I think you're right, after all," he told Rainey after that incident. "These guys need a little entertainment."

Granny scrounged up some fishing equipment in the attic, and Seth resurrected Grampa's old flat-bottomed johnboat. Seth and Rainey took the kids down to the creek where the waterfall splashed into the natural pool. There, Rainey took the boys out in the boat to fish and swim, although these seemed strange little outings, accompanied by Seth standing guard with a rifle above the falls.

Rainey sometimes felt self-conscious, knowing Seth was watching her from up there. She tried not to think about the picture she made as she helped the boys improve their swimming strokes—a woman without makeup, whose frizzy hair had gone wild with neglect, whose freckled skin had had a bit too much sun. She swam in a pair of baggy, navy-blue jogging shorts and a holey old gray sweatshirt that she'd mutilated by cutting out the sleeves and neckline. Very flattering. But at least it preserved her modesty in front of the boys…and in front of Seth.

Dillon, of course, insisted on taking undue risks.

"Dillon!" Seth bellowed from the top of falls at one point. "Get your can down from there!"

Dillon shot Seth a sheepish grin and immediately backed off the treacherous wet and mossy wall of rock he'd been scaling.

When he got down Seth gave him an offhand salute.

But the happy domesticity ended when Seth came in from the back porch one morning while Rainey was making her tea. The frown on his face told her something was wrong before he spoke. "Have you seen that old straight razor out there?"

Rainey stopped dunking her tea bag. "The one that belonged to Gramps?" Stupid question. There was only one straight razor, Rainey hoped. The presence of the thing had bothered her—it was sharp enough to slice leather—but it was Gran's treasure.

"Dillon?"

"Undoubtedly." Rainey set her mug on the counter. "That explains why he's been wearing those thick socks and hiking boots in this heat. He thinks it's cool to hide contraband on his person. But a knife?"

Seth put up a restraining palm. "We don't know that

for sure. Ask Grace if she put it away. Then let me talk to Dillon."

He did it man to man. Rainey didn't want to eavesdrop, so she simply asked to be present. The three of them sat around the little kitchen table.

"The straight razor is missing." Seth started right in. "We were wondering if you've seen it."

"How should I know what happened to it?"

"Dillon—" Rainey began in exasperation, but Seth put up a palm to silence her. Because she'd given her word not to interfere, she stopped.

"That razor belongs to Grace," Seth explained calmly. "But more importantly, we can't afford to have anybody getting hurt up here over some foolishness like hiding an old straight razor. So don't lie to me." Seth pinned Dillon with a penetrating look and waited.

"Are you accusing *me* of taking it?"

"No. I'm only saying that if you have some idea where that razor is, I want you to bring it to me."

"I sure will, Seth," Dillon vowed sincerely.

But Rainey knew it was a lie. She had been duped by Dillon too often in the past. She couldn't believe Seth let the matter drop there.

And though the razor didn't show up, Seth's trust seemed to inspire a change in Dillon. The boy's attitude began to improve radically after that, but even that made Rainey mistrustful. She wondered if his hero worship of Seth wasn't more manipulation. But Maddy and Aaron followed Dillon's lead so faithfully that she had to admit the results were good either way.

Dillon even took the lead in teaching Seth sign language. Seth seemed eager to learn and practiced with the boys constantly.

While Seth seemed to have a gift for bringing out the best in the boys, he couldn't always give them his full attention. He was often preoccupied. He posted himself up at the top of the mountain at night on the rock lookout, seemed to be always having cryptic conversations on his cell phone with the judge named Max, and often prowled the foot trails on the back side of Granny's mountain, looking for signs of intruders.

IN THE LONG, HOT AFTERNOONS Seth usually slept, stretched out on the fresh porch boards, with one of Granny's sleeping bags underneath as padding. He'd plunk his Stetson over his face and bag out. It was the only way he could keep up his nightly vigil.

Often as Seth drifted to sleep he mulled over what he needed to do next, and how much to tell Rainey.

He had been intending to discuss the latest details he'd learned from Max with her when they got some time together, which wasn't likely to happen, given that Rainey was clearly avoiding being alone with him.

She put her heart and soul into those boys, constantly teaching them, showing them how to get along with each other and with the adults, showing them how to be helpful, how to do new things.

But with him she had been reserved, kind of cool. Even when he'd asked her to train his fingers in the art of signing, she'd punted the task to Dillon.

Ever since the night he'd kissed her Rainey had seemed as uptight and cautious as a jilted spinster. She wouldn't meet his eyes, even when they were all gathered around Granny's little kitchen table for one of her boardinghouse-style meals. Rainey would yak with Gran, fuss over the boys, sign every word spoken to Maddy. But she would never look directly at Seth. It was making him crazy.

Maybe she didn't like the way I kissed her, Seth thought one day when he was secretly watching Rainey pull late summer onions with Granny. But he instantly discarded that notion. He'd felt her passion, as strong as his own. Sure, he'd probably reached for her too soon. Sure, they'd gotten carried away. Rainey, he sensed, wasn't the kind of woman who sold herself short. It would have been nice, he mused, if they could have met under different circumstances. If they could have started out with some normal dates, some low-key courting. But now that they'd acknowledged their fiery attraction, was there any sense in pretending it wasn't there?

Finally, desperate to talk to someone about it, he followed Granny out to her goat pens one evening.

"Why is Rainey avoiding me?" he asked without preamble.

The old lady dumped the scoop of feed she'd been holding. "I figured this was coming. Sit down."

They sat on two tree stumps by the fence. From their perch, they could see Rainey and the boys in the meadow below, engaged in a spirited competition over an old soccer ball Rainey had found in the attic. The sinking sun lit their tan arms and legs, making them look golden, like beautiful figures in a pastoral painting.

In her usual manner, Granny approached the topic sideways. "A while back, I heard you ask her how she came to have the name Rainey. What did she tell you?"

"You didn't hear that part as well?" Seth had suspected Granny might have been eavesdropping that night. Sound carried around the old house like echoes down a well. He wondered what else she'd overheard.

Granny was giving him the eye for his impertinence and so he relented. "She said her father named her on a whim because it was raining the day she was born."

"Did she now? A whim? Well, she left out a few little details." Gran's eyes smoldered with something that looked for all the world like thinly veiled anger, as if some bitter memory had risen up behind them.

"Details?" He flicked Gran a glance. "What are you talking about?"

"It was raining the day she was born, all right. A thunderstorm. And Rainey's mother died during that storm."

Seth frowned. "I don't understand. Rainey said her mother is a lawyer in Tulsa."

"She calls that woman her mother, but Loretta's her stepmother. Her real mother came up here to check on her ailing mother-in-law. Me." Granny poked the bib of her overalls. "I was laid up with a silly little cold. Lisa was in her seventh month of pregnancy. While she was up here she started to bleed. Placenta previa, you know what that means?"

Saddened, Seth shook his head.

"Mother and baby can bleed to death if they don't get help fast, that's what that means. I drove her down, but even when you're so scared to death you're driving like a bat out of hell, you can only make it down out of these mountains so fast, you know?"

This time Seth nodded.

"By the grace of God Lisa stayed alive long enough for Rainey to be delivered by Cesarean section."

Seth could only stare at the old woman in dismay as she went on with the horrible story of Rainey's beginnings.

"Her daddy, Rainey's daddy, was my youngest, born a good number of years after the other three. The older boys were closer than a stand of saplings." She twisted three fingers together tightly, as if they were intertwined tree trunks. Then she looked down the slope to her ramshackle house. "Seeing them three boys at the breakfast table—" she gave a brisk nod "—reminds me of my Roy and Charlie and Bobby. But William, Rainey's daddy, he came to us later in life. I was past the age when a woman oughtta be having a baby. We were glad, though, even though he turned out to be another boy." She gave Seth a wry smile.

"I always figured if the Lord was going to make me keep on being a mamma all the way into my old age, then the least he could have done was give me a girl."

Seth smiled back. "Seems reasonable."

"Well, anyway, I kept him. He was cute as the devil. And he was a smart boy, William was. A good boy. But he was always trying to prove his mettle to his big brothers, always taking wild risks, out there in those hills. When the other boys left for college one after the other, William got so lonely, so bored and restless. He hated being stuck up here on this mountain with just me and his daddy. He left for the city when he was real young. Became a cop, like you."

Seth jerked his head around, staring at the woman. "Rainey's father was a cop?"

"After a fashion. When his pretty wife died like that, William, he went a little crazy. He took off. Just disappeared. So, long story short, it was me that took Rainey home from the hospital. William wasn't fit to nurture no premature infant, anyway. He set about becoming the kind of badass lawman that goes after the worst of the criminals. The drug dealers and such, you know?"

Seth frowned. "Her dad was a cop who worked vice control?"

"Undercover. Rainey don't know that part. Well, she's smart. I expect she's dug around and got the truth by now.

"Anyway, he was living a dangerous life, a rough life up there in Tulsa. I kept that baby until she was three years old. Oh, William, he done right by his child, eventually. He come and got his little girl. Then he swung too far the other way. Made Rainey his whole world. Spoiled her rotten. He finally married himself a high-toned woman, a Tulsa socialite who'd gone to law school. I expect she cottoned to having a man like William at her side. He was a strapping man, real good-looking." Gran shot him a wicked little glance. "Kinda like you."

"God knows I try," Seth quipped, but underneath the joking, he worried. It disturbed him to think that the fact that he resembled her father in more ways than one might have something to do with Rainey's resistance to him.

Granny surprised him, reading his thoughts. "Yes, that is the problem, I expect. I expect she thinks she don't want a man who's so much like her daddy, but that's exactly what Rainey needs, if you ask me."

Seth lowered his brow and cleared his throat.

"Oh, I know. You didn't ask me," Granny chirped, "but I'm telling you anyway. Rainey needs herself a real man, whether she realizes it or not. If the Lord would be so merciful—" the old woman suddenly raised her hands "—he would heal certain hearts and show certain people what they truly need for real happiness. I have always believed there is nothing more beautiful than a committed relationship between two equally yoked people. I don't care how it happens—"

Seth cleared his throat loudly. "Tell me more about Rainey's childhood," he urged, because he was in no mood to listen to one of Granny's lectures. And he imagined the last thing Rainey wanted her grandmother to talk about was how badly her granddaughter needed a real man.

"Well, William and his new wife, they tried to act like they was a family, but that woman never really took to Rainey. She threw even more money at the child than William did, but very little love. And neither one of them knew anything about raising a child up right."

"Rainy became a child caught betwixt and between, kinda like those boys out there." Grace nodded at the meadow again. "She'd come out here of a summer or when those two took one of their cruises—they even left town at Christmastime once. I knew it wasn't ideal, a young girl comin' up here on this mountain to live with her eccentric grandmother...." She cut Seth a censoring look, as if he'd said something judgmental, which he hadn't. "And don't you tell me I'm not eccentric."

"No, ma'am. I won't."

Gran grinned at him. Then her expression sobered as she continued her story. "I know that I am different and I never cared one bit. Except when it came to Rainey. Then I cared. But what could I do? I'm too old to change. I was too old to change way before Rainey was even born. I could no more live in a Tulsa suburb than my prissy daughter-in-law could come live out here on this mountain."

Granny planted her palms on the thighs of her overalls. "So here she was, this precious child. My only granddaughter. A smart little girl, a high-spirited child, full of vim and vinegar, being neglected up in Tulsa or being bored to death down here in these parts with her old gran. Betwixt and between.

"All the while William kept up his dangerous work.

I guess it was in his blood by then. It seemed like the man was living two lives."

Seth kept his steady gaze on the old woman, who, for some reason, would not look at him now.

"Rainey's daddy, the daddy that child adored, my youngest son, was shot. Killed in the line of duty when Rainey was barely sixteen years old."

A long silence passed while Granny Grace gazed out over the panoramic view of the meadow, lost in the memory of her great sorrow. Seth stared at her profile, absorbing the implications of this. The old woman, in a roundabout way, had explained much to him. Rainey's stubborn refusal to take the gun. Her withdrawal after they'd kissed.

"After my son died, my daughter-in-law, Rainey's stepmother, wouldn't let me take Rainey back here to live with me permanently. I thought she needed to be with her people. Loretta wanted to keep Rainey with her. Claimed she wanted a living reminder of Bill— Loretta always called my William that—Bill. But some-times I have wondered if what she really wanted was to appear all noble to her fancy friends in Tulsa. Rainey still visited me, of course, and she always seemed glad to be back up here in the Winding Stair, visiting her cousins and all. Her heart, I reckon, had taken root on this mountain when she was a tiny little thing. But the truth is, that poor child's life ain't never had no center. Not even now, I guess."

Seth was staring down at the meadow, watching the scene that looked so much like a family at play. "Maybe her life will have a center," he said quietly, "someday. And for now, she has those boys." He intended that there be no mistaking his meaning as he added, "And for now, she has me."

Seth turned in time to see the old woman's eyes widen. "So she has you, does she?" Granny Grace didn't wait for him to explain. She studied his face and, in a voice softened by wonder, murmured, "Well, I'll be. Yes, it looks like she does have you, Seth Whitman."

CHAPTER THIRTEEN

WHILE SETH AND GRAN and the boys were getting along better and better, Rainey found that her own patience was being strained tighter than the loop of elastic around her ponytail. Her grandmother's impromptu talks with God had never bothered her before, but these days it felt as if the words were all directed at her.

Rainey knew Gran was of the opinion that her granddaughter was stubborn, hardheaded even. But hardheaded wasn't what she was feeling these days. The real trouble was she was feeling plenty confused. And Rainey didn't like confusion, uncertainty. It made her edgy. It was all she could do to be civil with her grandmother, or with the boys, or with Seth Whitman.

Being around Seth in the close quarters of the house was driving her crazy. She felt like a blushing, babbling idiot every time he got within two feet of her. She wished she could end this torture somehow. She wished she could at least claim to have a boyfriend back in Tulsa. Instead, she felt as if her long dry spell in the love department was written all over her blushing face whenever Seth got too close to her.

Why had she acted like a love-starved fool that night out on the porch? She must have been out of her mind—kissing a man that way when she'd known him only a few days. She stole a glance at the object of her insanity right now. He was down at the bottom of the porch steps, pacing and talking on his cell phone again. He stopped to bend one long leg and prop his boot on the bottom step. The movement emphasized his physique, specifically his backside. She sighed, trying to practice restraint, but ending up with frustration.

Okay, so the guy was cute. That didn't mean she had to make an idiot of herself. And it didn't mean they were getting involved. This man was the least of her problems, she reminded herself on a daily basis. She probably didn't have a job anymore. There were three needy boys to worry about. Murderers in the woods. It was all a bit much.

THE BACK OF SETH'S NECK itched with some instinct that made him turn and look up the rambling steps toward the house. He was rewarded with the sight of Rainey's shadowed face peeking around that lace curtain, watching him. Again.

He was a little sick of this cat and mouse stuff. Maybe the woman didn't realize it, but in his own way he was just as reluctant to get involved with her as she was with him, perhaps more so. He wasn't going to deny what he felt, however. Yet there was never an opportunity to talk these things out, what with the boys underfoot all the time.

"No sign of the Slaughters in town," Max was saying in his ear, "at least, not in contact with Coach. But I figure Coach knows something's up. When Tack made a point yesterday of telling him you took a leave of absence and left town, he commented that it was strange that Jake took some leave time as well. Then he proceeded to make all kinds of loud noises, right there in the Pie Almighty, about how the two of you had always been loose cannons."

"If he's not careful, he's liable to damage my pristine reputation." Seth brushed it off. "Did the article come out in the paper yet?"

"Today. Got it right here. I'll save it for you and you can add it to your little clipping collection." Max's tone grew worried. "I hope this doesn't cause trouble for Virginia. She kept it really short, really vague."

"Read it to me."

Seth heard the rustling of a newspaper in the background. "I'll have you know I had to sweet-talk that girl all night to get this done. She said she could get her butt in a crack for factual error, maybe even for libel. I said, how can somebody sue you for libel when it's not about a real person? She didn't think that was funny. I ended up having to tell old Virginia this was a matter of life or death."

"Old Virginia?" Seth scoffed. Virginia was all of twenty-five. "I owe her—and you—big time. In fact, I'll sing at your wedding."

"Won't be no wedding. And none of your so-called singing, either."

"After getting her in all this trouble, you're not even gonna marry the girl?"

"Marry?" Max emitted a rude curse. "You are one to talk. I haven't seen you forming any lifelong commitments to your one true love lately."

"That could be because my one true love doesn't exist." In his mind he added *yet*. His fascination with Rainey was one of those gut-level things that defied explanation. It had probably started when he'd first looked in her eyes. He'd always been a sucker for pretty green eyes.

"Oh, she exists, all right," Max was saying. "You are just too dumb to find her."

"I don't need any more of your advice for the love-lorn." For some reason, Seth looked back up at the narrow window. The curtain was closed. "So, what does the article say?"

"It says a team from the Smithsonian is continuing to examine claims that markings found in the caves on Purney's Mountain are authentic runic letters. That part's true. Then she goes on to say that experts are expected to begin excavating the stones and exploring the caves for additional markings by early fall. That part's a whopper."

"That should light a fire under them."

"Tack is going to put the paper right under Coach's nose at his usual table over at the Pie Almighty, folded nice and neat with this page faceup. If he doesn't pick it up on his own, Tack has been instructed to *notice* the article and comment about it."

Uncle Tack. Seth hoped the old guy didn't blow it. Not for the first time he wished he could be in two places—three, *four* places—at once.

"YOU DO NOT UNDERSTAND, old man." Lonnie Slaughter slammed his bacon-and-tomato sandwich onto a paper plate and pushed his folding chair away from the wobbly card table. The cramped trailer house, even at eight in the morning, felt hotter than the giant ovens in the kitchen at the pen. Lonnie was sick of this tin can, sick of hiding like this. He was supposed to be a free man now. Living it up on the Yucatan Peninsula in Mexico, with Coach paying the tab.

He stomped to the picture window of the run-down trailer. The glass was so scratched and fogged he could hardly see out of it. Staying in all day. Sneaking around all night. He and his brother lived like the vampires of the Winding Stair.

Nelson stood near the table, slumping like a drudge before his former football coach. He had pulled overalls on over the wrinkled muscle shirt and athletic shorts he'd slept in, same as Lonnie. It had always been like that. Nelson couldn't take a poot without checking in to see what Lonnie was doing first.

"There is only one way up to those caves, Coach." Nelson's voice always registered as slightly whining, placating. "Unless you want to drop down the cliffs. And either way, where he's got himself situated, Jake is gonna spot us. We got to wait."

Coach hunched forward and waved the newspaper

in Nelson's face. "If we *wait,* those caves will be crawling with these experts and the press won't be far behind. He can't camp up there forever," he insisted. "There's got to be some way to get rid of him pretty soon."

"That was our thinking." Nelson's voice wavered.

"Since when have you two been capable of thinking?"

Lonnie turned from the window, sneering. "Oh, we've had plenty of time to think—in prison, remember?" He stepped closer to the card table, balling his hands into fists. He'd had about enough of this old man.

Coach was still fit in an aging football coach sort of way. He still had imposing shoulders, muscled forearms. But his full head of hair was ribboned with gray now and Lonnie figured he could bring the old buck to his knees any time he wanted to.

Coach stared up at the threatening hulk of an older, larger, prison-hardened Lonnie Slaughter and for the first time since that horrible incident with the Rawls girl, he felt the adrenaline rush of genuine fear. A sense of unreality passed over him. How had he, Howard Hollings, the coach who'd taken his 4-A football team to the state championship nine times, ended up in this stinking trailer facing down this churlish brute?

All because of one foolish mistake. But after they'd gotten that girl's body safely out of the field house, he had managed to calm down. And he had to make himself calm down now. *You are going to give yourself a heart attack,* he thought, the same as he remembered thinking back then. And ever since, all this time, through all the years, he had managed to maintain his cool. He had managed to blot out the images. The way she'd screamed, "Lane will kill you!" The way her head had smashed into the tile wall when he'd hit her. One foolish mistake.

Even back when Lane Whitman had been closing in, Coach had remained calm. Nerves of steel, that's what he had. That's what it took to coach a bunch of thick-necked hillbillies to a statewide championship nine times. Why had he ever come to Tenikah in the first place?

Certainly the town fathers had been willing to fork over a handsome salary, which they gladly raised every year when he brought the trophy home. They added cars, vacations, lawn care—so many perks that Coach and his family lost track. It was as if the town faithful couldn't believe the good fortune that had brought this powerhouse of a coach to their little corner of the world, transforming their ragtag team into a winning machine.

But the move to Tenikah didn't have anything to do with Howard's love of football, or with the town's good fortune, either. Howard Hollings had come to this corner of the world running from a dark past down in Texas. That little strumpet of a girl had nearly cost him his marriage. And she could have landed him in jail for statutory rape. He'd sworn to Annette that it would never happen again.

But it did.

No matter how often he told himself to stay away from little strumpets, sooner or later he found himself backing another tiny cheerleader up against the lockers. In Tenikah his godlike status had kept them quiet. Until KayAnn Rawls. Until that night.

He had thought she, of all the girls at Tenikah High, would never tell. After all, she didn't tell when Lonnie forced himself on her. Though Lonnie had told *him.* The players knew to report to him when they had trouble, and Coach would always bail them out. He'd called the girl in and convinced her that she couldn't say for sure which twin had pulled her into a car that night. He convinced her to drop it, for the sake of the team, for the sake of her boyfriend. But later the little slut turned around and had the nerve to threaten to expose him for trying the same thing she'd let Lonnie get away with. *Him,* the coach.

Using what Lonnie had done to the girl as blackmail, Howard had found it easy to coerce the twins into taking care of the body, and in turn he'd taken care of them. His secret would have stayed buried in those caves if not for Lane Whitman's obsession with that silly girl. And now the younger brother, Seth. Why couldn't the man let the dead be dead?

"I think about this all the time." Lonnie was still glaring at him.

Coach squinted up at him. He was even bigger than he had been in high school. If he was of a mind to, Lonnie could crush Coach like a bug. But Coach still had one thing going for him: a history of dominance. "Getting pissed off isn't going to solve anything, boy. Sit down."

Lonnie jerked a chair out from the table and slammed it down so hard it made the trailer floor rattle. But still he sat, and that let Coach regain the upper hand.

He let out a controlled breath. "If Jake's on lookout at the caves, where is Whitman?"

"We don't have any idea." Nelson shrugged. "Plumb disappeared."

"And those three kids? Any sign of them?"

"We were hoping you'd know by now." Lonnie eyed him defiantly. "You've got all the connections. What did your buddy the sheriff say?"

"He says the camp supervisor sent them off to some kind of protective custody with the woman. He says there's a confidentiality issue because they are wards of the state. Apparently Max Drennan pushed the paperwork through to make the woman their guardian."

"That same woman we heard yelling for the boys?" Nelson's voice was so wheedling it made Coach want to cuff him.

"Yeah. Anyway, the boys aren't in the area. And why do we even have to mess with them? I want you to get those bones."

"Whitman is behind this somehow. And if he *found* the boys, you can bet he *has* the boys." Lonnie seemed to be mulling this over more for his own benefit than Coach's. "And you can bet he knows the boys have seen the cave…and what's in it."

"And you can bet he knows those little devils got the skull," Nelson's whiney voice interjected.

"What?" Hollings's head snapped up.

"Calm down, *Howard.*" Lonnie splayed a beefy paw on the table.

"The biggest boy, the Mexican-looking kid, he claimed he had found her skull," Nelson related anxiously, "and that he would show us where he hid it if we untied him. That's how they got loose."

"My God. Is that true?" Coach reared up and took a threatening step toward Lonnie.

"Yes, but if the boy wouldn't tell us where he hid that skull, even after the way we threatened him and his little buddies, do you think he'd lead a cop to it? A kid like that isn't gonna suddenly trust the law. Didn't the sheriff tell you he's already got a rap sheet a mile long?"

Coach nodded. "He also said he's a pathological liar. Could it be the kid is making up the part about the skull?"

"Nope. We were looking for it when they showed up. It's gone all right."

Coach sat down and scrubbed a hand down his face. "You should have told me this sooner."

"Over the cell phone?" Lonnie argued. "The way the signals work—or should I say don't work—up in these mountains? Anybody can pick up somebody else's signal. Happens all the time. You should have come to see us sooner, Coach. You really should have."

Now Coach felt like he might be having an actual heart attack. He drew an agonized breath and muttered, "How in the hell did this happen?"

"She surely was a foxy little thing." Lonnie smiled.

Coach glared at him and fervently wished there were some way to slam these two back into prison without jeopardizing his own future.

As if reading the malice in the older man's eyes, Lonnie sobered and said, "Maybe me and Nelson should just go on and head to Mexico."

Coach stood up again and planted his feet wide. "Seth Whitman will never let you see the sunny side of Juarez. Find him. Find those kids. Get that skull, get rid of those bones and clean up this mess once and for all."

CHAPTER FOURTEEN

SETH ALWAYS LEFT for his outpost up on the rock right after dinner, before the sun had fully set.

Rainey usually helped Granny tidy up the kitchen. When the boys had finished getting cleaned up, she went to take a bath in the claw-foot tub on the enclosed back porch. This was the only time she could be assured of complete privacy, with Seth up on the mountain and the boys glued to Gran's tiny TV for the one-hour fix Gran allowed them each night.

When Rainey came back in her jammies with a towel around her head, Gran was standing at the sink, washing some onions the boys had pulled that morning. "Oh shoot," she said, "I plumb forgot."

To Rainey's ears Gran's tone rang false, but even so she decided to take the bait. "Forgot what?"

"To send the coffee thermos with Seth."

Rainey glanced over at the trusty scratched green thermos that her grandfather had carried to work for years. It was already filled with steaming coffee.

"Why don't you take it on up to him?" Gran had her back turned, but Rainey didn't need to see her grandmother's impish face to know she was being manipulated.

"What the heck is this?" Rainey flipped a palm at the thermos, peeved.

Gran peeked over her shoulder. "Coffee," she said innocently.

"You know what I mean. Seth wouldn't forget his coffee. What are you two trying to pull?"

Gran faced her and planted sudsy fists on her hips. "He's a nice man, Rainey. A good man. It wouldn't hurt you to keep company with such a man. To just talk to him." Gran grabbed the thermos and pushed it into her hands.

"There's nothing to talk about." Rainey shoved the thermos away.

"There's plenty to talk about." Granny thrust it back.

"Oh?" Rainey crossed her arms, refusing to take it. "Like what?"

"Like what are you all gonna do with these boys?"

Rainey had been thinking about nothing but that, and Seth, all week.

"Look here." Granny held out the thermos again. "The moon is rising. The stars are out. It's boring up there all by himself, night after night. He's been keeping watch over us all this time, even in the rain. Put on some jeans, fix your hair and go on up." Granny reached for the heavy-duty flashlight on the windowsill. "Here. You can take this."

As RAINEY CLIMBED the path through the dense trees, she tried to will her pulse not to race. But it didn't work. What was she getting all fluttery and upset about? She was a grown woman, a sophisticated woman. This physical attraction—okay, it was more than physical. It was a gut level thing, something she couldn't explain even to herself, the likes of which she'd never experienced before. But even if there was a strong attraction, even if the man had gotten a hold on her heart, she didn't have to *do* anything about it. She vowed to simply not touch him. Nothing stupid could happen if she kept her hands to herself.

For extra insurance she'd intentionally chosen frumpy clothes. The wardrobe pickings were slim because she'd come up here under duress. Rainey's apparel was limited to what she had been wearing that first night, plus a few outdated, too-snug items that she'd left here back in high school. But tonight she'd rummaged around and found one of Grampa's old boxy denim shirts to button over one of Gran's long flowered "church" skirts. Rainey had braided her wet hair and put on her sneakers with some of Gran's white anklets to complete the dowdy effect. She might smother, but she'd look modest, untouchable.

The trees parted to reveal glimpses of a half moon glowing in a vast, starry sky. At the top of the path, the craggy silhouette of the rock outcropping came into view. She could make out Seth's broad back, glowing in a plain white T-shirt.

"Seth?" she called up to him.

She saw his shoulder turn. "Rainey?" His voice carried down, rich and deep, reaching out to her in the darkness. "Is something wrong?"

"No. I just came to bring you your coffee."

When she got to the rock he was waiting with his hand stretched out to pull her up. She took it and let him help her, feeling the familiarity of the gesture, the warmth of him, thinking that her vow not to touch him hadn't lasted long.

"When I spotted the flashlight down below, I didn't hear the dogs barking, so I figured it was Grace, out checking on her animals or something."

When Rainey finished climbing up onto the rock, he took the light from her hand and flicked it off.

"We can see the stars better without the light," he explained, but he was gazing at Rainey's face, not the sky. "Look up," he added softly. He was still holding her hand.

Though Rainey had been up here at night many times, she tilted her face up to let herself be amazed afresh. "It's gorgeous! No wonder the boys couldn't stop talking about it after we brought them up here."

Tonight the stars seemed even brighter than they had before, brighter even than Rainey remembered from her own stargazing nights as a child.

"Come over here." Seth led her by the hand. The gesture, again, felt intimate. He'd done it before, on the walk down the mountain, out on the porch, but not like this. "I've got one of Grace's sleeping bags spread out."

"I always forget how magnificent the night sky is up here in the summer." Rainey kept staring up in awe even as she settled on the puffy sleeping bag. *Magnificent and romantic*. His dark silhouette, with the backdrop of stars surrounding it, looked so masculine and handsome that she bit her lip and glanced away.

Gran was a crafty old bird. She knew what it would be like, alone up here with him.

But Rainey was determined to keep her boundaries. She tucked her skirt around her legs and wrapped her arms around her knees, training her eyes straight ahead. In the distance the lights of tiny Wister, and much farther away, the more urban grouping that was Tenikah, twinkled like diamonds tossed onto black velvet.

"This is a great vantage point," Seth said.

"Gran used to bring me up here all the time. She would point out the landmarks. She taught me the names of the major stars, showed me how to pick out the constellations."

"I enjoyed hearing you teach the boys. Tell me some of the names again."

"That's Arcturus." She pointed. "That's Andromeda. Those are the Seven Sisters." She could feel him watching her, and dropped her arm. "I'm sure you already know this stuff." She touched her chin to her knees.

He looked up, toggling his finger as he pointed. "Big Dipper. Little Dipper. North Star." He pointed at himself. "Simple country boy."

She smiled. "Have you seen any more shooting stars?"

"Not yet. It's been cloudy every night since that first one."

"I'm sorry you've had to keep watch in such awful weather."

"I've spent nights out in storms before. At least the rain cooled things down some. I like being outside. It gives me time to think."

"What have you been thinking about?"

He gave her a piercing look, then looked away. "Lots of things, lately. Anyway, even in the rain, I haven't minded being up here all that much, though I like it a lot better now that you're here."

She felt her pulse race and her cheeks heat up at his admission. But she couldn't give in to these feelings. Where would it lead? To lonely nights worrying herself sick over a cop who roamed the countryside. It was simple. She would not touch him. She would not get involved. She'd make a little chit-chat and get out of here. "I'm amazed you can stay awake all night, night after night."

"I've done it for lesser reasons. My brother and I used to do a lot of night hunting."

She nodded. Her dad had gone night hunting with his brothers, too.

"And the coffee helps. Thank you for bringing it."

She kept her eyes down, afraid that even in the starlight he might read her confusion if she looked at him. Her vision had completely adjusted to the darkness now and she could see the outline of his large hand, splayed against the dark plaid of the sleeping bag. He was leaning on one arm...toward her.

When he got too close, she said, "Did you forget the

thermos on purpose?" She couldn't help the catch of emotion in her voice.

"Would you feel better if I told you the whole thing was Grace's idea?" His tone sounded teasing.

"Not much." Rainey tilted her head and smiled up at him nervously. She wondered if he could see, in the dark, the effect he was having on her. Every time she was this close to the man, she felt so keyed up. Would it always be like this with him?

He smiled at her and gave an exaggerated shrug. "We do what we gotta do."

She looked down.

"Okay," he conceded. "Maybe it was a cheap trick." She heard the smile fade from his voice. "I just wanted a little time alone with you."

She didn't know what to say, and when she didn't respond he covered her discomfort by asking, "Did you bring an extra cup with you?"

"No." She realized she should have, so they could have some coffee together.

"Lucky for you, my Aunt Junie taught me how to share." He unscrewed the lid of the thermos and poured steaming coffee into it. "Here." He nudged her hand. "You go first."

Rainey hesitated to take it. She wasn't sure why. Perhaps because drinking from the same cup would seem…intimate. There was that word again.

"Come on," he chided. "I don't have any loathsome diseases. Besides, we've already swapped spit."

To disguise how much being reminded of their kisses

flustered her, Rainey took the cup from his hand and sipped. The hot, aromatic drink contrasted deliciously with the cool night air.

When she returned the cup his fingers caressed hers lightly. Again the effect of his touch sluiced from her core like hot lava.

"We have instructions from Gran to talk," she said, making an effort to sound offhand.

"Talk?" He sipped some coffee. "About anything in particular?"

"How about the boys?"

"Ah." He took a longer sip of the coffee. "The boys. Are they doing better, in your opinion?"

"They've settled in better than I ever thought they would. They're getting along better. Even Dillon seems calmer."

"Why is that, do you think?"

"Honestly? I think you have a lot to do with it."

He looked away, cleared his throat. "Maybe Camp Granny beats Big Cedar."

Rainey smiled.

"What do you think will happen to them when we leave here?" he said.

"I'd hate to see them go back to being wards of the state."

He handed the cup back to her. She took it and sipped.

"I'd like to keep working with them if I can," Rainey murmured. "Aaron, especially, seems to be coming around. He's actually smiling now. And Maddy's doing better. I think they trust me more now."

"They surely know how much you care about them. I know I can see it."

She smiled at him. "Thank you for saying that. But I'm afraid it won't matter, because after all this..."

"I know. You probably won't even have a job.'

"What about you?" She gave him a sharp look, having just thought of something. "What about your job? I mean, how are you free to stay up here night and day like this?" She honestly hadn't thought to ask until now. Although it seemed impossible that the Tenikah Police Department would provide full-time security, even if three children were in jeopardy.

"I took care of it. No problem."

But Rainey persisted. "Did you take a leave of absence? Use vacation time? What?"

He sighed heavily. "I took leave. But if you must know, I told the chief I was laying down my badge when this is over."

"You...you're resigning from the force?"

"It's not as dramatic as it sounds. Number one, I never really fit in as a small-town cop. And secondly, I think the only reason I did it in the first place was to fill Lane's boots. I'm all done with that now."

Rainey swallowed. Suddenly the barrier of him being a cop had vanished. She looked at the imposing man next to her with fresh eyes. His powerful legs were bent at the knees like hers, his muscular arms draped, like hers, across them. There was so much she didn't know about this man, so much she wanted to know.

"What will you do now?"

"Don't know. When I told him that, the chief just shook his head and said I'd be back, said being a cop was in my blood. But it's not."

"It's not? You seem very…skilled at being a cop, very suited to it."

"I liked bull riding much better."

"That's what you did until—" She stopped. Their last conversation about his brother had stirred painful emotions in him. She couldn't forget how he'd shut her out.

"Until Lane was killed, yes. It's okay to go ahead and say it."

"I thought you might not want to talk about him."

"Normally I don't. I'm sorry for the way I acted when we talked about my brother before. It's funny. The truth is, I wouldn't mind talking about him with you. I guess that's because I figure you'll understand. You've experienced a similar loss in your own life."

Rainey's eyebrows went up. "Are you talking about my father?"

"Your grandmother told me what happened to him."

"Ah, Gran." Rainey shook her head. "Ever the busybody."

"It's her right to talk about it. He was her son, after all."

"Yes, of course you're right." Rainey clasped her hands tight around the warm metal cup. "It's not like the whole thing happened to me and me alone. It's kind of ironic, don't you think? The fact that we've both lost somebody who was killed in the line of duty?"

His dark eyes studied hers. "Very."

"How do you cope with the…with the sick feeling that it was all a waste? I mean, the druggies who killed my father are probably out of prison by now, probably right back selling drugs."

"The men who killed my brother are *definitely* out of prison, hiding out—" Seth jabbed an emphatic finger at the ground "—in these very mountains. Look." He touched gentle fingers to her arm as he continued to search her eyes intently. "I miss Lane every day, but I know he wouldn't change a thing he did. Somebody has to stand up for what's right."

"Even if it hurts their family?" Rainey's eyes suddenly filled with tears. The way he was touching her made her feel so vulnerable. He had a way about him that made her open up. What did she hope for from this man? Some magic answer to make it all okay?

He reached up and brushed a stray strand of hair off her cheek. A touch of comfort, of apology. "Yes," he said softly, "even then. Even if it costs a man his life, some things are worth the price."

She hunched her shoulders, recoiling. This was her father's kind of thinking. All the heroics couldn't change the fact that a child might end up left behind…alone.

"If you feel that strongly about it, why don't you want to go on being a cop?" she challenged.

"My decision has nothing to do with right and wrong," he said. His fingers lightly circled in the vicinity of his heart. "I was never…coming from the right place."

"Then you don't agree with your chief? Police work isn't in your blood?"

He gave a huff of contempt. "Hell *no*. Pardon my French."

Despite the recent sting of tears, Rainey smiled. These country boys from southeastern Oklahoma. They could shoot you in the backside for trespassing and never flinch, but at the same time they could apologize for using the mildest profanity.

"What *is* in your blood, Seth?"

"Oh, you don't want to know the answer to that one." His voice had an edge as he stared out into the starlit night.

"Yes, I do," Rainey said solemnly. "I really do want to know."

He turned to her, studying her for a moment, his gaze looked piercing in the reflected starlight. "Okay." He took the cup from her and set it aside, then turned fully on her with one knee propped high like a protective shield between her body and the world below. The other leg pressed into her hip. "I'll tell you one thing that's in my blood." His voice grew suddenly husky. "Probably for good."

An excruciating tick of time passed as he leaned in closer. So close she could smell that intoxicating scent of his. He wrapped one arm around her back as his other hand glided up to gently cup her face. His mouth moving closer to hers. "You," he whispered.

Rainey knew he was going to kiss her again. She just wasn't prepared for the way his lips touched hers so slowly, so softly.

This time he kissed her as if it was happening for the first time. Tentatively, seeking permission with his lips, as if he was taking all of this so, so seriously. She felt the light current of his moist breath as he turned his head and skimmed his warm, firm mouth over hers.

In the midst of this gentle assault, the strangest sensation overcame Rainey. It was a sudden certainty that this kiss was different than any she'd ever had. This kiss under the stars was like something she was watching herself doing from a distance, like something of such import that she would play it over and over in her mind, many times, for years to come. Something she would never forget. For one surreal moment the mingling of their mouths felt like a key unlocking a door to their future.

When he teased her lips open with a flick of his tongue, a fire flared to life in Rainey's middle. She moaned and pressed her breasts to his chest fully, and then their limbs entwined, their hands grasped for purchase, while their tongues chased back and forth, their mouths open again, hungry like before.

He stilled her arms and tipped her to her back on the sleeping bag. Then he held and kissed her face. Rainey wriggled her arms free so she could clasp them around his neck. She let her greedy hands roam over his back, his shoulders, the trim line of his hair at the nape of his neck. Everything about him felt solid and clean and utterly masculine. She couldn't touch him enough. When his mouth captured hers again, a small sound of need escaped her throat.

He responded by kissing her harder.

Something made Rainey open her eyes, and she found that he was watching her through smoldering slits. She was shaken, yet thrilled by the impact when those half-closed eyes connected knowingly with her own, even as their mouths connected.

He broke off. "Yes," he said against her lips, "look at me while I'm kissing you."

She did, in shy fluttering peeks at first, and then boldly, with growing passion. Nothing had ever aroused her quite like this. After a while, it didn't matter if her eyes were open or closed. It felt as if he were inside of her, seeing through her, devouring her with his eyes, with his mouth. Their connection was so intense she found she had to remind herself to breathe.

Suddenly he groaned and stopped. She was dismayed to feel the withdrawal of his tense body. She opened her eyes. He sat up, pulling her along with him. "We can't do this."

"What do you mean?" Even to her own ears, she sounded like some whiney teenager who'd been thwarted from making out with her first boyfriend. She plastered herself against him. Clung. "Why not?"

He smiled and snaked one arm around her. She could feel the restrained lust tensing his muscles. "Because, girl, you're too much of a distraction." He jerked a thumb to the east, where the road wound into the valley below, invisible in the dark.

"Ahh." Rainey released a deflating breath and nodded in understanding. He had to keep watch. He had turned his back to her already, doing just that with the binoculars lifted to his eyes.

She nestled up against him again. "If I promise to be good, can I stay up here with you?"

He lowered the binoculars and smiled over his shoulder, then reached an arm back to scoop her close. "Won't your granny be worried if you don't come back to the house soon?" he chided as he hugged her against his side.

She settled under the shelter of his arm. "I think she'll be sorely disappointed if I do. She engineered this little tryst, remember?"

"Ah, yes, good old Granny the matchmaker."

"Are we?"

"A match?" He tilted his head back, studying her eyes. "We could be." His gaze raked down and then he gave her a sexy little squint. "But you'll have to learn how to dress a whole lot better."

Rainey looked down at her frumpy outfit, remembering her reason for donning it, and burst out laughing. She flapped the baggy flowered skirt. "I was trying to make myself unattractive."

"Didn't work." He gave her an appreciative squeeze. "You can't hide your light under a bushel—or even under one of your grampa's old shirts."

She laughed again.

"I sure like the way you laugh, Rainey. The way you smell. I like just about everything about you."

"Just about everything?" She gave him a mischievous grin. "You mean I'm not totally perfect?"

"Nah. Like I said, look how you dress." He reached up and plucked at the lapel of the enormous denim shirt. Using skilled fingers, he peeled open the first button at the throat. Just one. But the intimate gesture made Rainey's cheeks go hot. "The truth is…" He smiled as if he knew exactly what he was doing to her. "I've always thought this country schoolmarm look was kind of hot."

"Oh, *right!*" Rainey slapped at his shoulder and he tightened his arm around her.

"I'm not kidding! And if you keep kissing me like that, we probably will end up a match someday."

Despite his lighthearted attitude, his words had Rainey's pulse racing. She knew he was already more serious about her than he let on. She could feel it in his touch. Something special was already happening between them and they both knew it. The question was what were they going to do about it? But whatever they decided to do, their plans, their future, would have to wait. Right now they had to worry about keeping the boys safe.

"Maybe I'd better go," she said seriously as she thought about Seth's reason for being up on this rock. "So you can keep a closer eye on that road." She started to rise.

"Stay." He tugged at her wrist. "Just a little longer."

She sat down next to him again and he took her hand. "I like your hands." He kissed the one he was holding. "All week I've been sitting out on this rock in the rain, trying to recall the little details of your person, you know? When the moon was still full earlier in the week, I hated to see it disappear behind the clouds every night, because I finally had somebody I wanted to think about while I looked up at it."

His candor was so unexpected, so disarming. Rainey had never met a man like Seth before. She settled next to his warm side, imagining what it would be like to be with him, feeling this safe, perhaps for a lifetime.

They sat in quiet companionship for a while, then he said, "We really do need to talk about the boys."

"How much longer do you think we'll have to keep them up here?" Rainey wondered.

"Until the Slaughters come out of hiding or make a run for Mexico."

"Jake still hasn't seen anything?"

"No, but they're out there."

"How can you know that?"

"If they killed KayAnn, if those were her bones—"

"Dear God." Rainey touched fingers to her mouth, then said through them, "I can hardly stand to think about that."

"I'm sorry. Even after we recover the bones, unless I can get the Slaughters in custody right then, I don't think we can hope that they'll just disappear and forget about the boys."

"I keep worrying about how this will affect them in the long run."

"They've been pretty resilient so far, haven't they?"

"You can't let children like these fool you. They seem tougher than they actually are." Rainey hated to sound pessimistic, but experience had taught her that these boys needed more than Seth's cowboy common sense. "With children like these, there are always downstream effects that cannot be predicted." She looked down at the pointy roof of Gran's little house, already dark for the night because of her "lights out" rule. "Dillon, especially, is far from predictable."

CHAPTER FIFTEEN

DILLON SIGNALLED FOR the other two boys to be quiet. He peeked around the lace curtain, through the screen, to the porch beyond. The headpiece and spindles at the top of Granny's rocker sat perfectly still.

Over his head, Dillon signed "Asleep."

Maddy tapped his shoulder. He leaned around and signed. "Rainey? Catch us?"

"She won't catch us," Dillon signed back. "Playing kissy face with the sheriff."

"How…do…you…know?" Aaron signed.

"Told you. Saw them doing it before." Dillon's hands flashed emphatically. "Let's go." He pocketed Seth's keys, and the boys crept out onto the porch.

Dillon snapped a hand out in warning when Aaron eased the screen door shut and the hinges creaked. The other two boys froze. But the sound of Granny's snoring continued to saw in an unmistakable rhythm.

The boys crept past, down the solid new steps. At the bottom, Maddy grabbed Dillon's sleeve. "Sure you know how to drive?" he signed.

Dillon waved him off and kept going.

Maddy ran up beside Dillon and grabbed his T-shirt. His hand went up to an imaginary hat brim with his fingers in an *S*—their sign for Seth.

"He'll never know." Dillon stopped and signed impatiently. "He won't come down till dawn. Her neither." He rolled his eyes as he signed, "Grownups."

Back in the bushes twenty paces off the rocky drive, they felt their way along until their hands hit the hood of the Jeep. Dillon got in and fitted the key into the ignition, ready to go when he got far enough away from the house. He yanked the stick shift into neutral. While the other two boys pushed, Dillon steered until the Jeep's hood peeked out of its hiding place, aimed downhill. Dillon stuck a hand out. "Faster!" he signed. One more good shove and the vehicle started rolling down the steep slope, slowly at first, then with the momentum of a runaway train.

Dillon panicked as he realized it was all he could do to wrestle the wheel and keep the Jeep's tires in the ruts. The one frantic glance he spared the rearview mirror revealed the silhouette of Maddy running down the drive, waving his arms, with Aaron coming up behind.

Dillon's eyes snapped back to the road. He could barely see in the dark. His feet fumbled for the brakes. His fingers fumbled for the lights. He found neither. He jerked the wheel in a sharp right as the tires bumped on the ruts. He was momentarily proud of himself, but it didn't last. The Jeep skidded, careening wildly before it banged into the ditch, cracking Dillon's teeth together. His head snapped back and forth like a puppet's as the vehicle lurched down the side of the mountain, crashing and tearing through brush. When the Jeep struck the tree that finally stopped it, Dillon's head banged against the windshield. And that was all he knew.

A LOUD CRACK RICOCHETED up the slope to Seth and Rainey's outlook.

She bolted upright. "What was that?"

Seth sat upright, too, listening.

"A gunshot?" Rainey said.

Seth shook his head. "Shh."

But no other sound came.

"Go back to the house." Seth peered through his binoculars as he spoke. "And make sure Granny and the boys are inside and okay." He dug out his cell phone, punched it. "Leonard?

"Go," he said to Rainey above the mouthpiece. "I'm right behind you."

Rainey encountered only darkness at the house, then she saw Maddy and Aaron running up the steep drive, sweaty and gasping for breath.

"Boys!" she called.

As they ran by in a blind panic, Rainey grabbed at their shirts. She shined her flashlight in their faces. Maddy was crying and Aaron's pudgy face was red as a beet. Both boys looked terrified. "Stop!" she signed. "Calm down! What is wrong?" Her first thought was the Slaughters.

Aaron was making the *S* for Stetson near his temple—Seth's sign.

"He crashed!" Maddy signed.

"Who?" Rainey's hand flashed the question in Maddy's face.

"Dillon took Jeep," Maddy signed as fast as his hands would go. "Lost control and went over...." His hand made a diving motion over his arm while his face crumpled in distress.

Aaron nodded vigorous agreement, pointing downhill.

"Oh, God." Rainey clasped her hand to her heart. "He didn't. I should never have left the house."

"Aaron." Seth came from behind Rainey. "Take me to him." The two took off in a trot, with Rainey and Maddy close behind.

Dillon had already come to and staggered out of the Jeep by the time they found him on the dark mountainside.

"Are you okay?" Rainey shrieked as she skidded down the rocky slope to meet him.

Dillon was shaken, but appeared unhurt. "I'm so sorry, Seth," he repeated over and over, his boyish voice cracking each time.

"It's just a car," Seth reassured him. "The main thing is to make certain you're not hurt."

"I'm okay."

And miraculously, except for a fresh bruise forming on his forehead, he was, though he was short of breath, mortified, near tears. He insisted he could walk up the hill, but Rainey and Seth flanked him, each keeping a hand on him anyway.

"Dillon is fine," Granny declared after she put a cold

pack on his head and checked his eyes with the flash-light. "You got yourself a well-deserved goose egg, young man. And your muscles are gonna be plenty sore. I suggest a hot bath. You others should go on back to bed, where you shoulda been all along." Having spo-ken, she shooed the kids out of the tiny kitchen.

"Thank God he's okay," Rainey said when Granny and the boys were gone.

"Yes." Seth slumped into a dinette chair. "But a wrecked Jeep is another matter." He rubbed his fore-head. "I won't know for sure until morning, but I doubt it's drivable. We can't be stuck up here without a four-wheel drive vehicle. I've got a friend who might loan me his Explorer. No one would associate that vehicle with me, either. And I'll have to get the Jeep out of there somehow. It's perched in a very precarious spot. I don't think it's wise to just leave it, but removal will require a wench and a wrecker…and possible exposure."

"I understand." Rainey sat down in the chair oppo-site him, rubbing the back of her neck. Seth stood up, came around and took over the job for her.

She couldn't help but groan with relief as Seth's hands worked wonders on her stressed muscles. Granny had lit her small lamp and the atmosphere in the little kitchen seemed golden, quiet, intimate. When Rainey turned her head and Seth automatically stroked her cheek with the backs of his fingers, the urge to melt made her decide they'd better focus on the children, where their minds belonged. "Whatever possessed Dil-lon to go and pull a stunt like this?"

"He's a thirteen-year-old. I'll have a talk with him. In the meantime, what's done is done," Seth reasoned. "The main thing now is to get the Jeep out of there without blowing our cover. I have a friend in town who drives a wrecker and can keep his mouth shut."

"You sure do have a lot of friends," Rainey said absently.

He stopped the massage. "Come to think of it, I really do." He pulled at the sleeve of the oversize shirt she wore. "Would you say your grampa was a big guy?"

"Yes."

"See if Grace saved a pair of his overalls. And a hat. The bigger the brim, the better. And some boots."

"Grampa was big, but not that big." Rainey broke her reverie and frowned at his feet. "What do you wear? Size twelve?"

"Fourteen."

She sighed. "I'll do my best."

"I'LL BE." Lonnie nudged his brother. "Look what we have here." He handed Nelson the binoculars.

Nelson peered down on the scene below, shrugged. "All I see is some old boy in overalls, plus that old hairball from that greasy garage down on Broadway, Virgil Platt. I dint know he still had that old wrecker. What do you think they're doin'?"

Lonnie ignored the senseless question and leaned in close to his brother's ear. "That's Whitman," he hissed. "Look at the boots."

Nelson jumped. "I'll be. What's he doin' down there?"

Again, Lonnie ignored the stupid rhetorical question and jerked the binoculars from his brother's hands. They had been watching the wrecker pull out a mangled Jeep for some minutes. But it hadn't occurred to him that the character in the overalls and floppy hat could be their favorite cop until a woman came ambling down the road a moment ago. She was very tiny, thin as a teenager, tan or maybe lightly freckled. She moved like a pixie through the woods. Her blond hair was bunched up on top of her head in a high ponytail that bounced as she walked. Watching the rhythm of her thighs in those short shorts sent dirty urges stalking through his mind.

"Remember how Coach said the boys were in protective custody with some woman?" he observed. "Take a look."

Nelson took the binoculars. "Woo-hoo. Yeah. That's some woman all right."

Lonnie reclaimed the glasses with a jerk. "What's at the top of that road?"

"A ratty old farmhouse."

"An old farmhouse where somebody might hide three boys?"

Nelson backed up a step, shook his head. "Huh-uh. We cain't risk it. If we go up there and Whitman sees us, he'll kill us for sure."

Lonnie raised the glasses to his face. Whitman was climbing in the wrecker with Virgil Platt. "Whitman is occupied."

"Coach told us not to show our faces nowhere in the daylight."

"Daylight or no, we've got to move now, while Whitman's tied up with Virgil. This is our chance to get our hands on those kids. We have got to make that little peckerwood show us where he hid that skull, and then get rid of the little bastards."

GRACE WAS SO TENSE she was of a mind to make the boys get on their knees and pray. Seth had been gone all morning and now Rainey had walked to the bottom of the mountain to check on the progress with the wrecker. They were letting the boys take in some horrid movie on television to keep them occupied. What children were exposed to these days made her just plain sick. She decided to go in the kitchen to cut up some veggies for lunch. Idle hands were the devil's workshop, after all.

Grace was halfway through a cucumber when a red-bearded face materialized above the sill of the window over the sink. She dropped the knife and screamed, then snatched up the knife again. "Boys!" she bellowed at the top of her lungs, afraid the TV was so loud Dillon and Aaron wouldn't hear.

Dillon burst into the kitchen at the same instant that Lonnie Slaughter kicked in the back door. Granny had only time to think *How'd that man get around there so fast?* and then to remember that there were two of them before he grabbed the boy and shoved a knife under the soft part of the child's jaw. "My knife's a lot sharper than yours, old woman."

Granny's dropped her paring knife to the floor. "Please," she begged. "Don't hurt these children."

Another man came in the back door, leering. This one was shorter, not quite as heavyset. He looked like a smaller version of the other one—matted hair, bushy red beard—an ape dressed in overalls.

"Tie her up," the one holding Dillon said to his look-alike. He grabbed a nearby dish towel and tossed it. "Use this to gag the old biddy's mouth."

"No!" Dillon struggled like a wildcat against the huge man. "You leave her alone!"

It all happened so fast and left her so breathless that when Granny came to her senses she was afraid she might have had a stroke right then and there on the kitchen floor. But it came rushing back plainly enough.

Dillon had landed a stomp to the big man's instep, and from somewhere on his person the child had produced a knife—William's razor?—and he'd gashed the big man's arm. Deep. Blood was flung everywhere. She tried to help in the attack but had been knocked to the floor like a rag doll. Now all she could see in her line of vision were Aaron's flip-flops and behind them a pair of filthy running shoes. Apparently Aaron was being restrained just like Dillon, now. He must have heard the yelling and rushed into the fray.

She kept her face pressed to the worn linoleum, trying to decide if it would be wiser to play opossum. But immediately she felt rough hands on the back of her apron, jerking her up.

"Leave her," the injured twin wheezed, and she was dropped like a sack of feed.

She peeked through her skewed glasses again and

saw the hurt man grab another dishtowel and bind his arm with it.

"You little prick." Granny heard a sickening crack as the big man slapped Dillon, sending the boy spinning to his knees beside her. "Don't move," she saw Dillon's fingers sign, right before the boy was jerked up again.

"Get your other little friend." Lonnie dragged Dillon toward the violent sounds of the movie in the living room. The one who had to be Nelson dragged Aaron with him.

The clomp of boots. Maddy's croaky, abnormal cry. The bang of the screen door. That's all she heard.

ALL OF DILLON'S MONSTROUS anger at his sorry stepfather came up and lodged in his chest to assist him now. Anger could be turned into power, Seth had told him once, power that he could channel for good. He kept seeing the straight razor, lying back on Granny's floor. If only he had it now he would cut the nylon cord that bound him and the others. Then he would use it on these two smelly creeps. Cut and slash and cut and slash until there was nothing left but a pile of bones.

Bones. That's what they wanted. Dillon tried to concentrate despite the anger that smoldered, hot as a fuel rod at his core. *Think,* he heard Seth's voice saying in his head. *Think.*

What would Seth do?

The bigger one was swilling whiskey to blunt the pain from the slash wounds. Good. Whenever Dillon's stepfather drank enough he'd ended up blind as a slug, an easy target. Dillon had lifted twenties from his wallet many times when he was like that, and had never once got caught.

How bad was the guy hurt? He had clutched his side, limping through the woods on the way to the boat they were in now. Dillon knew he'd slashed the razor across the guy's arm, maybe his leg, must have gotten a stab at his fat gut, too. It had all happened so fast, just like Seth told him things did when you were a cop.

Dillon twisted around in the boat to look at the other two boys. He'd thought Aaron was going to swallow his tongue when they came across that guy's body on the riverbank. The sight gave Dillon a sinking feeling, too, but only for an instant. So they'd got the Leonard guy that Seth was counting on to guard the river. But Dillon wasn't giving up. *Hold on,* his eyes telegraphed to his friends. *We'll get 'em.* With his tied hands he signed, "I will lie."

He turned around, his mind made up. He'd lead them to the wrong cave, that's what he'd do. And then somehow they'd get away. They'd done it before. It wouldn't be a problem to outrun the drunk one. And the other guy—Dillon glanced his way—was dumb as dirt. Whatever happened, Dillon was going to be cool and smart, like Seth.

The men banked the boat, then dragged the boys out and struggled with their captives to the top of the path, where the rocks got so huge they formed narrow corridors. It was the same path the boys had taken up here before, but it looked different in the daylight. As they squeezed between the boulders, Dillon kept thinking, thinking. *What would Seth do? What would Seth do?* The men carried shovels, black plastic bags. Could he get his hands on those? Use them somehow? Maybe after the big one got enough liquor in him. He kept watching him as he took swig upon swig of Jack Daniels.

By the time they emerged from the high boulders at the top of the mountain, the twins were arguing loudly.

"The old man had better be doing his part," the smaller one snapped as the group inched around the rim of the rock ledge that led to the caves. "All we need is Jake coming around the bend. And even after we get the...you know, then what are we gonna do? Lonnie, I am talking to you!"

Swaying as he looked back, Lonnie slurred, "The old man is scared shitless. He will do it."

"I meant what are we gonna do with these boys...afterward." The smaller one sounded like he was going to be sick.

"We kill 'em." Lonnie steadied himself against the wall of rock.

"And what do we do with the bodies?" It came out as a whine.

"I don't know!" the larger one screamed. His voice echoed in the caves. He scrubbed a hand over his face. "But if we don't get rid of them they'll tell—"

"They already told!" the other's shrieking voice interrupted. "Seth knows everything! No need for killin'."

He lowered his voice and caught Dillon's eye with a guilty glance. "We're heading for Mexico anyway, and besides, that old woman—she seen us, too."

Dillon thanked Granny's God that Maddy couldn't hear what these men were saying. He eyed Aaron. The poor kid was shaking all over. Dillon didn't know why he himself wasn't. Dealing with his stepfather's outbursts had made him kind of tough, he supposed. All he knew was he had to do something or Aaron was going to disintegrate.

"Watch out!" he yelled, though the big one was not that close to the edge.

The one named Lonnie took a menacing step toward Dillon and raised his shovel. Dillon cowered. In his best scaredy-cat voice he said, "I just didn't want you to fall, the way you been staggering around and all."

The other twin looked back at them. He squeezed around the boys to confront his brother. "Are you gettin' drunk again?"

Dillon made a barrier with his body, pushing the other boys up against the rock wall. He inched his friends backward to an indented place.

"For your inforn-mation…" Lonnie stepped around his brother and took another belligerent swallow from his bottle. "I have been stabbed." He drained the bottle dry and tossed it over the cliff.

"I don't really give a crap! I am not the one who killed KayAnn Rawls."

"I diddint kill her, either," Lonnie slurred.

"No, but Howard couldn't of made us do this if you hadn't got her in your car and forced her—"

"Shut *up!*" Lonnie roared as he stepped around and cut off the boys' view.

"I'm gonna get those bones." Nelson's voice turned low and cold now. "And get my cash and hightail it to Mexico without you. I don't give a dang what you do with these boys. Move."

But Lonnie blocked him. "*You're* taking him the bones? *You're* getting *your* cash?" He grabbed his brother's overall straps, spinning him around as he shook him. "*You're* headed to Mexico?"

Nelson jerked free, knocking Lonnie off balance as he stumbled backward on the narrow ledge. "I can't have some cut-up drunk slowing me down."

"Don't you talk to me like that, little brother!" Lonnie yelled as he regained his footing.

Nelson cuffed the side of his twin's face and for one instant Lonnie looked genuinely stunned.

"You were the one who got to be the big shot quarterback. What did I get?" Nelson jabbed at Lonnie's chest. "Time in prison, that's what!" He waved his shovel. "I am done with you!"

Lonnie swung his own shovel, but Nelson used his to block it with a clank. Lonnie dropped the implement and charged forward, roaring as he snatched the overall straps of his twin in both hands. Nelson dropped his shovel and grabbed back.

Locked in combat, the twins snarled and fought like vicious dogs. As their feet slid on the crumbling rock and dirt on the dangerous ledge, Dillon saw his chance. He twisted his body until he could grab the nearest shovel handle. With all his might, he swung it like an ax at the back of Lonnie's knees. The top-heavy men teetered for one horrific instant before plunging over the cliff, seventy-five feet to the sharp rocks at the bottom.

CHAPTER SIXTEEN

SETH AND JAKE HEARD THE SCREAMS when the twins fell.

"The boys." Seth looked back at his partner in terror, as they scrambled up the rocks as fast as they could. But near the top they found the three youngsters sliding down on their backsides, with Dillon in the lead.

"They fell off the cliff!" Dillon pointed behind him.

"I'll go." Jake climbed ahead to skirt the ledge in order to have a look, while Seth grabbed for the boys, pulling them toward him by their shirts, hugging them all fiercely, even Dillon.

The boys looked as if they wanted to cry, so to bolster their courage, he said, "How many times am I gonna have to untie you guys?" while he unbound their hands.

"They're goners," Jake announced as he hurried back down to the shell-shocked group.

"I didn't mean to kill 'em!" Dillon cried. "I had to do something!"

"Son." Seth squeezed the boy's shoulders, his heart twisting as he looked into Dillon's dirt and tear-streaked face. "Whatever happened, it wasn't your fault."

Dillon eyed Jake's filthy jeans, ratty muscle shirt and grown-out beard. "Is this the other cop?"

"My partner. Jake. The one who's been on lookout."

"What about the other guy?"

Seth glanced at Aaron and shook his head.

Dillon shuddered. "The big one down there is cut up. I'm the one who did that, too. Back at the house…with the straight razor." Suddenly Dillon couldn't seem to get his words out fast enough. "I'm the one who stole it, Seth. I did it." His dark eyes searched Seth's, and for once there was no trace of a lie in them. "But I only used it 'cause he was going to hurt Granny." His voice choked off.

"Dillon. You did what you had to do. They were murderers." Seth clamped a hand on the boy's neck and pulled his tousled head to his shoulder. Seth was struggling with his own guilt. How many times had he wished for Lonnie and Nelson's deaths? But now that it had happened, he found himself feeling as shocked and repulsed as these kids.

"We got to get back to Granny," Dillon said urgently. "They pushed her down, and she hit the floor hard." He swiped at his eyes.

"Rainey's with Granny. She told us everything. She said you were very brave. All of you." He signed this for Maddy's sake.

"She did?" Dillon looked up at Seth. His tears dried up and his muscled young shoulders straightened. His mouth grew set with determination. "Well, those bastards deserved it."

Seth didn't correct the bad language.

Dillon's expression grew genuinely concerned then. "Is she okay?" He wiped his nose.

Seth was touched that the boy had learned to care so deeply for the old woman. Grace had gotten to Dillon, the same way her granddaughter had gotten to Seth. With her heart. "She twisted her knee pretty bad. Got a bruise. Granny's family doctor came out from Wister and he's tending to her."

"I'm sorry about the razor, Seth. I'm sorry I lied. Real sorry."

Maddy started signing. Seth had learned enough sign language by now to pick up the essentials. Maddy was attempting to take some of the blame. He told Seth that he knew Dillon had the knife all along and he didn't tell. If matters hadn't been so grave, Seth might have smiled. Loyalty. Didn't he know all about that?

"It's okay," Seth signed to Maddy.

But Maddy couldn't seem to stop his hands, a tensional outlet for pent-up emotions, Seth figured. Aaron was biting his nails and looking from one boy to the other as Maddy signed and Dillon interpreted for Seth and Jake.

"He's saying how they fought each other. He's—" Dillon halted abruptly and signed something. Maddy's hands stopped.

"What did he say?" Seth said. He knew these boys by now. Knew when they were hiding something.

"Nothin'," Dillon said.

But when Maddy started signing again, his face

clearly showed anger at Dillon. Aaron's hands suddenly started flying, too.

"Tell me what they're saying," Seth ordered.

Dillon watched their hands for a minute before he interpreted, telling only the story of Lonnie and Nelson's fight and their fall off the cliff. But Seth couldn't shake the feeling that there was more to the story. When Dillon coughed hoarsely, Seth said to let it go, that he'd piece together the rest of what happened later. "Let's get you guys back down the mountain now and get you some water and tend to your scrapes."

But Aaron stepped in front of Seth, waving his hands, more bold and agitated than Seth had ever seen him. He looked into Seth's eyes, urgently signing something Seth couldn't decipher because it was in that flitting telegraphic form the boys had developed.

"Oh, right!" Dillon coughed. "Man. How could I forget that? There's something else. Something Maddy don't know. But both of us—" he wagged a finger between himself and Aaron "—heard it loud and clear."

"What's that?"

"Those twins…" Dillon nodded as his eyes followed Aaron's frantic signing "…they said that the old man, they kept calling him that—the old man—had better do his part. They said he was scared shitless—that ain't me saying that word, Seth, that's what *they* said."

Seth nodded in understanding. "Go on."

"And they said they were gonna get money from him to go to Mexico."

"His part?" Seth gave Jake a meaningful look. "I expect they meant the guy you saw running through the woods."

"Undoubtedly." Jake looked disgusted. "And I let him lead me right off on a wild-goose chase."

"Coach?"

"Stands to reason. Did you get a look at him?"

Jake shook his head, looking thoroughly put out. "Just overalls and a bill cap. Obviously, that's all I was supposed to see."

"We'd better not wait then."

"Nope."

Seth turned to the boys. "You guys will have to be strong just a little while longer. I promise I'm taking you back to Granny's, where Rainey is waiting. But first we've got to take care of something important. Then everything will be all right." Seth clasped a hand on Maddy's shoulder and signed what he'd said as best he could.

"So you're not mad at us?" Dillon would always suffer from this sort of residual insecurity, Seth feared.

"Absolutely not. I'm proud of you. All of you." He clasped the boys' shoulders again. Then, signing at Maddy, he said, "You guys acted like real men out here today."

Dillon gave his friends a satisfied glance. "What do you need us to do, Seth?"

"We have to get those bones."

"Come on!" Dillon swept an arm over his head. "They dropped shovels up there and I remember the exact cave!"

"Got your penlight on you?" Seth asked Jake. The Slaughters' flashlights were with them at the bottom of the cliff.

"Always." Jake handed it over. "You okay with this?" he said under his breath.

Seth nodded. "This is for Lane."

"Right. I'll take care of Leonard…and Tweedledum and Tweedledee." Jake pulled his cell phone out of the hip pocket of his jeans. "Hope this thing gets a signal."

Following the boys, Seth had to wonder about the Slaughters. They had known where the bones were, so why had they brought the boys all the way up here with them? Why hadn't they killed them at the house? Something wasn't adding up. Pieces were still missing. And the way Dillon was acting, Seth wondered if the boy knew what those pieces were.

When they got to the cave, Maddy and Aaron hung back at the entrance. Dillon led Seth on.

Far back in the warren of passages, they found the half-exhumed grave site. "Hold the light," he told Dillon.

As Seth worked steadily, transferring soil and bones to the bags, the belief niggled that Dillon was still lying to him. In the first place, there was no way the boy could have seen this far back if he was standing just inside the entrance of the cave, as he'd claimed on that first night. The second thing that bothered Seth was the missing skull.

"IT SOUNDS LIKE the Slaughters admitted in front of the boys," Seth told Rainey later at the house, "that Lonnie raped KayAnn but he didn't kill her. They kept talking about an old man who was cooperating with them. Later they used the name Howard again. Dillon got the impression this old man was KayAnn's real killer."

Rainey looked over at him. They were sitting at the little table in the kitchen. Seth's expression was set like stone. "Are you thinking what I'm thinking?" she said.

"I'm afraid so."

"But why would this coach do such a thing? I mean, you know the man. Did he ever strike you as the kind who would commit murder?"

"Never in a million years. Coach took me and my brother under his wing and gave us a place in that school, a way to fit in that community. He whipped us into shape, gave us hope for a future." Seth grew so quiet and sat so still that Rainey wondered what he must be thinking, what he must be remembering. He seemed so alone. Was there nothing, no one in life that Seth Whitman could count on? But he had her. And she would help him face this.

"I guess you'll have to set all of that aside now, won't you? What matters now is the truth."

He nodded. "And seeing that justice is done. I'm thinking about what KayAnn told Lane right before she disappeared."

"About someone…that someone was putting a lot of…a lot of sexual pressure on her? But now you don't think it was Lonnie?"

"No. I think Coach ordered Lonnie to steer clear of KayAnn after she went to Coach and told him what the guy had done. Trouble was, Coach was a predator himself."

"But we still don't know exactly what happened the night she disappeared."

"No, but in that diary, if you read between the lines, you see that she was definitely scared of someone."

"Did the boys hear enough to give a statement that would let you arrest Coach?"

"Dillon's the only one who can, and his story is jumbled."

"Not surprising. The poor kid must have been scared to death."

"And with his history…"

Rainey slumped. "Dear Lord. It's like some horrible chain reaction. Now four people are dead."

"Five."

"Five?"

"They killed Leonard, my friend who was guarding the back side of the mountain."

Rainey closed her eyes. "When will this ever end?"

"I intend to see that it ends." The resolve in Seth's voice sent a chill through Rainey.

She turned to look him directly in the eyes. They were as deep-set, as dark, as beautiful, as any she'd ever seen, but something in the depths of those eyes made her blood run cold.

"I want to move the boys to town," he said, "to my house."

"To your house? What for?"

"No one knows I have the bones in my possession

now. I'm not telling anyone. No one. Jake knows I have them because he was there, but he's a rock. Even Max and Tack won't know."

Rainey shook her head. "I don't understand."

"If Coach killed KayAnn, he'll have to make a move to finish what Lonnie and Nelson started."

Rainey looked down at her hands with a sick feeling in her core. Seth was still bent on his vengeful mission. He'd just changed targets, that's all.

"As far as Coach is concerned, with the twins out of the way," Seth continued, "he's only got one problem. The bones. And I'm going make sure he thinks he needs those boys to find them."

Rainey looked up. "How so?"

"I'll have Max run another fake article to increase the time pressure, and we'll make the boys visible."

"Aren't you afraid the boys will blow this plan of yours?" she argued. "Aren't you afraid they'll tell what they heard? Or slip and tell somebody that you already have the bones?"

"Dillon's the only one who can talk, and he's certainly proven he's capable of maintaining a lie. In fact, I want to use Dillon's tendency to lie and brag—"

"No! I won't let you do that! He's come so far."

"Yes, he has. And now he understands the difference between right and wrong. Look how he confessed about the razor. Dillon's smart. He can talk about how—"

"I won't let you use these boys as bait," Rainey insisted.

Seth's lips compressed into a firm line, while at the

same time something in his eyes looked wounded. "You've got to trust me," he stated flatly.

"Trust you? I only met you three weeks ago! All I know about you for sure is that you're a great kisser."

His gaze flicked to her mouth. "Rainey," he chastised. "We have to do something. The bones are the only way to trap Coach. I want him to believe that I'm satisfied now that Lonnie and Nelson are dead. Case closed. As far as he's concerned those bones are still up there, and he's got to suspect that the boys know where the cave is. We can use Dillon's record, his tendency not to trust the law, his lying, all of it together, to get at Coach."

"How?"

"Coach has plenty of contacts at the school. I want to enroll the boys when school starts next week."

"That's crazy! These boys are in worse shape than they ever were before. Now they've seen two men plunge to their deaths. You can't take three boys with their needs and plunk them down in a public school setting."

"That's why I'm going to need you."

"Me?"

"I want you to go to school as the boys' interpreter. That way Maddy and Aaron will be communicating through you. Like I said, Dillon's smart enough to work with me on this."

"Me? In Tenikah? How will I live? My furniture is all in storage in Tulsa. My administrative leave is almost up. Unfortunately, I'm practically broke."

"You can come with the boys…and stay with me."

"With you?"

He nodded. "We can pretend we fell in love while we were stuck up here." His eyes connected with hers. Maybe they really had, and they both knew it. But Rainey wanted him to say it first, and she wanted it to be the real thing, not a ruse. And she wanted it under the right circumstances. At the moment, they had too many blades hanging over their heads to even think about whether their love was real or not.

"What will the people in your small town think about that?" she challenged. "About your moving a woman into your house?"

He actually smiled. "They'll think it's high time. Look, I know I'm asking a lot. And of course there'll be talk. That's the general idea. Coach will hear the talk. Beyond that I don't care what the good people of Tenikah think, anyway. Never have. Never will. But I do care about you. If it'll make it any easier…" Rainey could have sworn he had a perverse glint in his eye when he said this next "…we'll take Granny along as a chaperon."

GRANNY, IT TURNED OUT, had stretched some ligaments in her knee when she fell. The doctor said she would need mobility assistance and several weeks of physical therapy, which would be easier to obtain down in Tenikah. Rainey contacted her father's brothers and a deal was struck—Rainey would continue to take care of Granny, if the uncles would make arrangements for the care of her animals. Once she knew that her place and her animals were in good hands, Granny was uncharacteristically cheerful about leaving her mountain.

"Why," the old woman declared, "the Lord's so good to me. Imagine, getting to recuperate in a big air-conditioned house in Tenikah with my favorite granddaughter tending to me. Sounds kinda like a vacation."

Rainey wasn't so sure. She tried to imagine what it was going to be like "pretending" to be in love with a man that she was, in fact, already falling in love with. Would the *pretending* make it too easy to give over her heart? She wasn't ready for that yet. There were too many unsettled questions about the future. But how could she protect her emotions while she was playing house with Seth? And what would playing house with him really be like?

She was surprised to find Seth's long, low, L-shaped ranch-style home in squeaky clean, functional order, though it was starkly unembellished. The boys immediately gravitated to his giant TV as if it were a golden calf.

"Cool!" Dillon snatched the remote.

"Help with the unloading first!" Seth commanded, both in his no-nonsense baritone and in the sign language he was quickly mastering.

The boys trooped out to Seth's pickup, grumbling about this latest change, but obeying nonetheless.

Granny and Rainey were given a large, airy room with twin beds. It was plain, but functional, as was the spotlessly clean, blue-tiled bathroom adjacent to it. The boys were to share a long, narrow back room that resembled a dormitory. The bathroom back there was immaculately clean also, though Spartan with its brown-toned 1980s decor. This dorm-style room was across from a fourth bedroom, which Seth used as an office.

"A bachelor with four bedrooms?" Rainey teased Seth as she peeked around the corners of his rambling house.

"And six sinks," he said cheerfully as he threw open a window in the musty back room. "I always wondered what I'd do with all this space. It was the only decent house on the market when I moved back to Tenikah. I had some rodeo prize money and didn't care to pay rent. I'd had enough of living in shabby rentals as a kid. So I bought this monstrosity." He stepped back into the hall and she followed. "I've wondered what in the world I was thinking ever since. I've basically been paying to have the spare rooms cleaned for the last seven years." He gestured with an arm. "My office and the master suite are the only rooms I use back here."

Rainey looked down to the end of the hall, where a closed door led to the only unexplored space.

"The master bedroom," Seth said matter-of-factly from behind her.

But she turned to find his eyes studying her with too much meaning in their depths.

"I don't need to see that. Well, there's more stuff to unload."

She scooted past him and told herself to just steer well clear of that master suite. She had no idea where she stood with Seth Whitman, except that whenever he touched her, she melted. She had to wonder what was to become of their relationship, and what would ultimately happen to these boys she'd come to love, once the real killer was finally caught and dealt with. If Seth wasn't going to be a cop anymore, would he want to go back to the rodeo circuit? What kind of life was that? She had no idea. Too many questions.

The first week passed quickly enough, with all the settling in and all the decisions that had to be made. Rainey, as Granny would say, was busier than a mother hen.

She went to Big Cedar to get her Honda and, without telling Lyle the full details of the situation, reassured her former boss that the boys were safe. Lyle made it clear that he thought the boys should return to the camp and that he didn't like the idea of a former child-care worker taking custody of wards of the state, but Rainey refused to give in.

"They're better off with me," she insisted. "And with Seth willing to act as the boys' foster father," she added, "the Department of Human Services will favor foster care over warehousing."

She arranged for home health visits from a nurse and a physical therapist for Granny. Then she went up to the massive combined high school and junior high to talk to the principal about mainstreaming the boys and coming on board as Maddy's interpreter. She arranged for intensive counseling for Aaron, and academic testing for Dillon to get him in the advanced classes he desperately needed to satisfy his mind.

In the meantime, Seth was busy, too. He reminded

Rainey of an efficient innkeeper—clearing space in drawers, finding extra sheets and towels, laying in huge quantities of groceries. He saw that Max pulled all the necessary legal strings to make him a foster dad, and he went down to the police station to return to duty.

He took the boys shopping for school supplies and new clothes while Rainey bought necessities for herself and Granny. Seth and Rainey made a great team.

So all was well in the newly formed Whitman household in Tenikah, Oklahoma, that first week. At least on the outside.

But on the inside an air of tension had taken hold.

Rainey bristled when she overheard Seth telling Dillon that he would have to lie one more time. He prepped the boy nightly—what to say when he went to school next week, who to say it to, how to act. He had covert phone conversations with Max and Jake and his uncle all the time. And he kept strange hours. Cop's hours.

By the end of that first week, Rainey could hardly stand the sight of Seth in his uniform shirts with the knife-sharp creases over the breast pockets. Was he finished with being a cop or not? Was this permanent? Did she even have the right to tell him her feelings about that? Too many questions.

When they came upon each other in the kitchen late one night after everybody else was asleep, Rainey could feel her frustration coming to a head. Seth, shirtless and barefoot, was wearing baggy black exercise shorts and, Rainey suspected, nothing underneath.

She was more covered up in a white stretch T,

cropped pink yoga pants, flip-flops. Because of the boys, she normally went about the house dressed modestly. But tonight she, too, had nothing on underneath her loose clothes.

Someone had left the light above the stove hood on, and Seth and Rainey stared at each other in the oblique glow before they both said hi, then danced around one another to get what they'd come for.

Rainey opened the pantry door and stared. She wasn't really hungry, not for food, anyway. She shut the door and crossed to the fridge, bumping into Seth on his way there.

Rainey jumped back and clamped her arms over her middle. "I do not like this," she hissed.

"You don't like this?" he repeated very quietly. They always made an effort to keep their tense conversations subdued because of the boys…and for Granny's sake.

He left her in her tight pose and continued on to the fridge. "Which part don't you like?" He didn't even pretend not to know what she was talking about. He jerked open the door and peered in as if he were angry at the butter or something. The light reflected harshly on his profile, making him look strained, tired, older than his thirty-one years. "The part where we make the kid lie? Or is it this business of playing house? Or—" he gave her a challenging glare "—is it my going back on the force?"

Rainey turned away from him. "None of it. All of it. You know what I mean." She stalked over, reached around him and snatched a bottled of water from the door.

Seth lifted the plastic pitcher of orange juice and took it to the center island. He turned his back on her and reached into a cabinet for a glass.

They had discussed the first two so thoroughly that there was little left to say about this incredible charade they'd set up. The third thing, though, they hadn't even touched on.

"You think *I* like any of it?" Seth said as he poured his juice.

"I think you like the idea of being a cop again." Her voice was laced with accusation and hurt. She hated that. She tried to tell herself that it was none of her business what he did with his life. That they had no commitments. They hadn't even been on a real date, for crying out loud. But those arguments were no match for her feelings. She screwed the cap off her water with a vicious little twist.

"That's it, isn't it?" he said quietly, but with a bitter edge that Rainey hadn't heard before. "That's what's been eating you today, and yesterday, and the day before, and the day before that."

Rainey took a long draw on the water. "You want to know what's eating me? Like I said, all of it. Pretending we're a couple with the whole town watching. Seeing Gran's eyes get all sparkly every time one of your old crushes mentions your name. Seeing the boys getting settled in here like it might really be their home."

"One of my old crushes?" Seth said.

Rainey couldn't believe he could focus on the one thing she'd said that was patently irrelevant. "Carrie Melton, if you must know. The physical therapist. She came out to do an evaluation on Gran and one would have thought you were a living god the way those two were talking about you."

"Carrie Melton?" He downed the orange juice. "She didn't have a crush on *me*. I always had the impression she was involved with some older guy."

"I don't want to talk about her. Some other woman isn't the trouble between us."

"Then what is the trouble?" He picked up the pitcher and calmly poured more juice. "Because I can sure tell something's wrong. You've hardly looked me in the eye since I started back—" He slammed the plastic pitcher down on the counter and juice sloshed all over the place. "That really *is* it, isn't it?"

She pressed her lips together and kept her eyes on the spray of yellow juice across his shiny linoleum floor.

"Oh, come on, Rainey! Be fair!" He shook the juice from his fingers and ripped a string of paper towels from the roll. "With three kids in the house, somebody has got to earn a living here. Even that stuff costs money." He aimed the wadded towels at her bottled water.

Here it comes, Rainey thought. She'd wondered when this setup would become too much for Seth, when he would start to resent the intrusion on his space, on his time, his money. "It was your idea to do this," she reminded him, "not mine. None of this was my idea."

"What do you suggest?" He bent and swiped up the spilled juice with muscular force. "What do you expect me to do?" He picked up a dishrag and ran water on it. While he waited for her to answer he wrung it out as if he were strangling someone. When she didn't reply he turned on her. "Should we just let good old Coach go on about his merry way now that the Slaughters are nice and dead?" he challenged. "Should we just let Lane and KayAnn...rest in *peace?*" He spat the last word as if it were a foul curse. He started wiping up the mess on the counter with a vengeance.

"No! Of course not! The man has to be brought to justice." But she didn't like the way Seth was going about it, and she was genuinely upset because he'd blithely returned to playing cop without even discussing it with her. Didn't he understand how much his original decision to quit had meant to her?

"I thought you said being a cop wasn't in your blood," she accused. "I thought you said your heart wasn't in it and all that."

The anger seemed to drain from him as he stopped cleaning and looked at her. His eyes betrayed his regret, his confusion. He took a step toward her. "Everything I told you that night was true," he said. "But I can't just come back to town and hang out. I've got to keep up appearances. Being a cop is the only thing I know how to do in this town. And frankly, I'm damn good at it. And we've got to maintain some kind of normal framework for these kids. We've got to pay the bills." He looked around the kitchen. Evidence of the boys' needs was scattered everywhere. Folded clean T-shirts on the table. Checks attached to school notes. Fresh fruit overflowing in a bowl. "I've gotta tell you, the money's getting a little tight around here."

Rainey sank back against the island. "That's partly my fault. I'm sorry I'm not bringing in much income right now. Unfortunately, administrative leave doesn't pay very well."

"No. Listen, I don't want you to worry about that." He breached the last step between them. "But I have to work, don't you see that?"

She nodded.

"Look." He reached up and smoothed her hair. "Everything will be all right." He pulled her to him and wrapped his arms around her. "We're both just a little tired. This whole mess has been a strain. Let's just hang in there a little longer. Maybe you'll get your job back when this is all over. Who knows? Nobody knows the future. Sometimes life is about timing, waiting for things to pan out."

"Oh, I'd say my future's pretty well set. I'll be unemployed." But there were other things about the future that worried her more.

"To be terminated from a state job, aren't there procedures, protocols?" he asked sensibly. "Surely old what's-his-face can't just up and can you without just cause."

"Lyle thinks he has cause. He's going to call my competence into question, probably already has. I'm not sure I could go back to work for that man, anyway. I think I was only sticking it out there because of the boys."

Seth hugged her to him. "Then if you get fired, you get fired. Rainey, listen." He bracketed her shoulders with his strong hands. "I've gotta be honest. I don't know how I feel about being a cop. The truth is, it does come naturally to me. Maybe it's like the chief said. I'm just cut out for it, you know? But that doesn't mean I'm going to keep on doing it after this is all over. I know how you feel about it and you're a lot more important to me than any job."

His admission stunned her, and the heaviness in Rainey's heart suddenly lifted. "I am?"

In one fluid motion he gathered her close and looked into her eyes. "I don't like arguing with you about stupid stuff," he said urgently, "like who's cut out to be a cop and who's not."

Rainey stared up into his face. "I don't like arguing with you, either,"

Their gazes held, filled with deeper meanings. Seth's eyes fell to her lips and his head tilted.

"Seth," she said when his mouth nearly touched hers. Her voice was quiet, almost a whisper. "Maybe we'd better get to bed before Gran or one of the boys hears us."

He tightened his hands on her arms, lowering his head. "I doubt anyone will hear this." And then he kissed her.

It was the first time they'd kissed since they'd moved into Seth's house. An excruciating week had passed while Rainey had thought she would die if he didn't kiss her again soon. Yet she imagined she'd also die if he did.

And right now it felt as if she just might.

Rainey had thought many times about that night on the porch when she'd lost control, and vowed to practice some reserve with this man if he touched her again.

She could feel him doing the same, trying to go slow, trying to be gentle.

But the more they tried to control the kiss, and both surely did, the more the passion that soared between them took on a life of its own. Their mouths quickly found the rhythm that was uniquely theirs, opening wider until their tongues joined wildly. Both ended up groaning, fitting together tightly, her breasts flattening against his bare chest, his hardness undisguised in the loose shorts. His hands came up under the T, around her waist, his thumbs pressing dangerously close to her breasts. Rainey's hands clasped the heated muscular flesh of his back as a stunning wave of desire tightened her whole body. She tore her mouth free and whispered against his neck, "I can't take this."

"I know." He clasped her to him, breathing hard against her temple. "Believe me, I feel the same." He quickly kissed his way down to her neck and held his lips against her pulse for a heartbeat before he said, "Come to my bed."

If he hadn't said the word *my,* Rainey could have easily let herself imagine that they *were* a couple, coming upon each other late at night in the kitchen, lightly clothed, captured by mutual desire.

But they weren't a real couple. They weren't even close.

"Oh, Seth…" She stretched his name out as she pushed away from him. "You cannot begin to know how badly I want that." She swallowed as she looked up into his dark, vulnerable eyes. "But do you really think that's wise?"

"Why not? I want you. You want me. It's nobody's business but ours."

She shook her head. "That's not how I operate, Seth. I want a real relationship. And we don't have a relationship. We've been playing house, as you said, so convincingly that it feels like we do, but it's just pretend, remember?"

He frowned and shook his head. "You make it sound like I'm into some kind of game, Rainey. I'm not." He splayed a hand on his bare chest. "I know this situation isn't ideal, but I can't help the way I feel about you any more than you—" His appeal got trapped in his throat.

Rainey felt like crying as they stood confronting each other in the night silence of his kitchen, both so vulnerable, both so unsure.

"I do want you." He found his voice again. "More than I've ever wanted any woman in my whole life. I have almost from the start. But I don't want to do anything that will give you regrets…later," he finished quietly.

The way he'd said it made her think that there really

might be a "later" for them. And for that reason, Rainey
gathered her courage, said good night and went straight
to her own bed.

CHAPTER SEVENTEEN

STILL STIFF AND SORE from her fall, Granny was confined to her bed or the sofa for a few days, then she had to use a walker, or lie propped up in Seth's giant recliner. She never complained, but neither was she the energetic force she had been before. She read her Bible a lot. Dozed a lot.

The boys couldn't cater to her enough. They spread covers over her twiggy little body, though the temperature still climbed into the nineties outside. They brought her snacks and hot tea, though she claimed she had no appetite. They tolerated her soap opera every afternoon, though she kept the volume at brain-numbing levels.

A nurse checked on Granny once a day, but the visit was a mere formality; the medical checkups were necessary in order to obtain the in-home physical therapy Granny needed. The treatments started as soon as the swelling went down.

Maddy had seemed fascinated that first day when the physical therapist showed up. The other two boys scooped up the basketball and disappeared outside.

Carrie Melton was petite and curvy in her pink scrubs and snow-white running shoes. She had a twist of spikey blond hair at the crown of her head that bobbed freely when she talked. When she arrived for the first actual treatment, Rainey hovered nearby as she got set up, wanting to be sure the woman didn't get overzealous and push Granny too hard.

"People Grace's age are my specialty." Carrie read Rainey's concerned expression accurately. "I work with the patients over at Rosehill Manor all the time."

"I know. You come highly recommended. And she's a very good patient." Rainey smiled at her grandmother, who gave her a wink.

"You know, I've never been in Seth's house before," Carrie continued conversationally while she put a gait belt around Grace and then herself. Her eyes traveled around the beige-and-brown great room and toward the vanilla-colored kitchen beyond. "Kind of a plain place, isn't it?"

"Plain but clean." Grace defended Seth, as Carrie assisted her to a standing position.

"And actually quite comfortable," Rainey interjected. It was true. She couldn't imagine a better environment for three rowdy tweens. The backyard was as flat as a football field—perfect for soccer and…well, football, which Seth and the boys played nearly every evening now. The driveway was the size of a basketball court, complete with the goal at one end. The ka-thunk-ka-thunk of a basketball could be heard all day as one boy or the other or sometimes all three shot hoops out there. Inside, there was nothing to scratch, nothing to break, nothing to stain. A massive black leather sectional, that big screen TV, a Formica dinette set.

"My sister's been in here—she and Seth used to date—but she never mentioned the...well, I'd hate to even call this decor." Carrie smiled.

Rainey smiled back. This woman, maybe a year or two older than herself, had an engaging way about her. Rainey would bet she was a favorite among the patients over at the nursing home. But her complete lack of makeup and haphazard hair seemed oddly apathetic for a woman who was otherwise pretty. Rainey noticed that she wore no jewelry—including no wedding rings—except for a tiny gold cross that hung from a short chain around her neck.

"Seth dated your sister?" Rainey found that, try as she might, her mouth could not be deflected from asking that question.

"Yeah. My little sister, Amy." Carrie smiled. "She works over at the police department. They only dated for a little while. Lots of women have dated Seth, but no one's ever got her hooks into him. Amy had quite the crush on him, I tell you that. Who hasn't?"

"You included?" Rainey wanted to bite her tongue off. Her mouth definitely seemed to have the upper hand here.

"Me? Oh, I think he's cool. But I don't have time for men. Who needs a man? They're like hamsters. Fun for a little while, but then you get stuck with cleaning up the mess." Carrie let out a squeaky giggle at her joke, but something about the sound made Rainey uneasy. She got the feeling there was nothing funny about this woman's decision to remain alone. What would make a girl this cute so negative about men? There was a sadness about Carrie Melton's eyes as she continued. "I like my life the way it is, thank you very much. No man to clean up after. No man to bow down to."

Carrie walked Granny across the room and when she got her back to the recliner, she eyed Rainey.

"I don't mean to pry," she said softly while she did Granny's range of motion exercises, "but there's been some talk. There's bound to be when a man like Seth finally brings a woman into his house, especially out of the blue like this. Are you and Seth, you know… together for good?"

Granny, who'd been listless all morning, napping like a frail kitten, suddenly snapped alert. Her eyebrows went up and her green eyes focused sharply on Rainey as she waited for her answer.

"Oh. Uh, no. We're not a…we're not getting married yet or anything like that." She felt her cheeks heating up at having to lie, and she smiled at Maddy, who was oblivious to the conversation, thank goodness. Maybe she could pretend that he was the reason she hedged.

But Carrie said, "He's the one who can't hear, right?"

"Yes. How did you know?"

"There's talk about these boys, too. The whole town's horrified by what happened up there." Carrie's spikey treetop hairdo bobbed in the direction of the

Winding Stair. "Nobody liked the Slaughters, ever. They were always mean, always weird."

"Well, that's all over now," Rainey said, hoping to reinforce the illusion that Seth had put the case to rest.

Maddy lifted a disposable cold pack out of Carrie's bag.

"I'm sorry," Rainey said to Carrie, while she signed for Maddy to put it back. "He's just curious."

"It's okay," Carrie said kindly. "Maybe he wants to help." She showed Maddy how to snap the cold pack and activate it.

His eyebrows rose in astonishment. "Cool!" he signed at Rainey, who relayed his pun to Carrie.

Over the next few days, Maddy dogged the heels of the little therapist every time she showed up. Carrie proved to be a kindly young woman who patiently taught Maddy how to do things like muscle massage and gentle manipulation of Granny's kneecap. Carrie told Rainey that the boy had "the touch."

"The boys seem to be thriving here," Carrie commented one morning as she manipulated Granny's knee, while Rainey folded a mountain of laundry nearby. "Everybody is just amazed by the way Seth took on three boys to raise. His life has really changed, hasn't it? But then, Seth has always been different. Look how he up and quit the football team back when his brother got sacked."

"You remember that?"

"Everybody does. You don't play the way Seth did and just up and quit the team in a town that lives for football. Not the way Seth did it, anyway."

Rainey frowned. She had had the impression, from Seth, that his brother Lane had been the star. "What do you mean, the way Seth played? The way he quit?"

"He was the star halfback. He and Lane were magic together. Lane passed to him, time and again, and Seth would snatch that ball out of the air and fly into the end zone. They completed one pass that was sixty-four yards long."

"Wow." Rainey knew Seth was naturally athletic, but she'd no idea he had that kind of talent.

"That's why when Coach put Lonnie Slaughter in for the championship game, people were really confused. Lonnie wasn't getting the ball anywhere near Seth's hands. After the third failed pass, right smack in the middle of the game, Seth had a fit and quit, just bounced his helmet off the turf and stalked off the field." Carrie continued to work on Grace's knee as she told the story with relish. "Lane followed him, trying to convince him to come back. The whole crowd was on their feet. You could have heard a pin drop in that stadium. People were so upset some of them left right then, right behind Lane. I remember how Nelson Slaughter actually threw up over on the sidelines. All us cheerleaders were grossed out by that. But he was always kind of a wee-nie."

"I suppose Coach was more upset than anybody." Rainey knew she had to be careful. Seth had warned that if they talked to people about Coach too much, he might become suspicious.

"*Coach.*" Carrie's sweet countenance suddenly

turned bitter. "I don't suppose anybody'd ever crossed that old goat before. He followed Seth and Lane off the field, screaming so hard at Seth that his face turned blood red. Looked like he was gonna have a heart attack. Wish he had," she muttered under her breath.

Rainey thought she'd misheard the therapist. But Gran's shocked expression told her she hadn't.

"Ouch! Easy, hon!" Gran's hands went out toward the knee Carrie was rubbing, obviously too hard.

"Sorry. You gotta love Seth, though." Carrie covered her outburst with a quick smile. "He did not care one bit what that man thought. Even after the almighty Coach ripped Seth's picture off the field house wall." When Carrie looked up, a flicker of something deeper—pain?—just behind the smile set off warning bells in Rainey. "You got yourself one good man here, Rainey."

"I know I do." At having to perpetuate the lie, she shoved her hair nervously behind one ear and looked at Granny, who was beaming at her with fond agreement.

SCHOOL STARTED. Whenever he got the chance, Dillon told his story, lying and bragging like a pro. He told some kids in his gifted and talented class that the Slaughters had hidden something up in those caves and he was going to go back and find it.

"How do you like living with Seth?" one of his teachers asked him one day after class. She was a pretty woman about Seth's age, and her careful smile made

Dillon wonder if she was interested in Seth the same way Rainey was. Women. Dillon thought the girls at this school were cute, and a couple had already flirted with him, but he had made up his mind to be like Seth and live a bachelor's life. He was never gonna let some silly woman get her hooks into *him.*

"He's cool. Even if he is a cop."

"You don't like police officers?" the teacher asked in that prissy singsong voice some women used with boys his age. He was glad Rainey never talked like that.

"Don't trust 'em."

"Well, Seth's a good guy, and he has taken you in."

"I guess. But he doesn't know everything." *He doesn't know about the skull,* Dillon amended silently. And that was starting to bother him. But if Dillon told now, would it get Aaron and Maddy in trouble with him?

He wished he could come clean with Seth and Rainey about all of this. But his past had taught him not to trust adults. And it had taught him that secrets came in handy. He studied the pretty teacher. She, for example, had no idea about the straight razor tucked into his boot.

"Excuse me, ma'am, I'm gonna be late for algebra." He'd learned that "ma'am" bit from Seth. Older women liked it. Even Rainey smiled when he tacked on a "yes, ma'am" here and there. Dillon could be cool. He could be slick. He could do exactly what Seth wanted and draw this Howard guy out of his hole without giving up any of his own secrets.

But another two weeks dragged on with no move from Coach. Rainey hated the tension of having the boys in plain sight, but the children seemed to be thriving in Seth's world and at the school, doing far better than they ever had out at Big Cedar Camp. Maddy continued to learn things from Carrie, Aaron was becoming more physically fit under Seth's influence, and Dillon was bringing home straight As.

Rainey also continued to worry about finances, though Seth had never mentioned money again.

"Maybe the school district would consider paying me for acting as Maddy's interpreter." She fretted aloud to Seth one night after everyone else was asleep. "My administrative leave is about to run out."

"What happens then?" He patted the couch, his signal that he wanted her to sit down and let him hold her.

"I'm sure I'll be terminated." She sighed as she sank against him.

Seth wrapped his arms around her, and the feeling of being centered and whole washed over him, as it always did when he touched Rainey.

With people coming and going continuously, and the boys constantly underfoot, Seth never had a chance to let his hair down and behave as he normally did, alone in his house. But ever since that fight in the kitchen, he and Rainey had fallen into this pattern, which he treasured far more than his former privacy.

They made time to discuss things, to settle down for some one-on-one adult conversation at the end of the day so they could clear the air and check in with each other. Sometimes they went to sit in the plastic chairs out on his bare concrete patio, holding hands and watching the sun set behind the top of the high hill. Sometimes it happened like this, very late at night after the boys and Granny were in bed and Seth got home from a late shift.

No matter where they ended up, or how much time they spent together, it was never enough. It seemed they had even less privacy here in this rambling ranch house than they'd had up at Granny's cramped little cottage. Sometimes Seth wanted Rainey to himself. He wanted her in his bedroom, and not just for the obvious reasons. He wanted her in there where she belonged, with him. He wanted to be able to tell her things, to romance her and win her over and somehow make her his own.

But romance would have to wait until things settled down. When Coach had been found out, Seth told himself, when he and Max had the evidential link they needed, when the boys were safe, he would find a way to show Rainey Chapman that she could be happy with him. That was what he truly wanted. He'd known it ever since he'd moved this woman into his house.

"For now we've just gotta hold on." He wrapped his arms around her. And for now he'd have to be content to comfort her like this. "Dillon's been playing his part perfectly at school. I'm sure Coach is just looking for a plausible way to make contact. Something's gotta break loose soon."

SURE ENOUGH, something broke loose, but it wasn't at the school.

Tack and Junie popped in for a visit on Sunday.

"You have taken in three young boys, and you didn't even call us?" Seth's aunt upbraided him as she swept into his living room carrying a Bundt cake. "I had to hear of this from Debbie Melton, who heard it from her Carrie. Oh, hello!" Junie sailed across the room with her hand extended. "I'm Seth's Aunt Junetta. This is Tack, Seth's great-uncle. You must be Rainey Chapman."

Rainey took the lady's hand warmly and smiled to cover her surprise. "I am. It's so nice to meet you." Why hadn't Seth told her about his aunt? she wondered. The woman was tall and handsome, like Seth. She had the look of the Cherokees about her. Dark-haired, like Seth, though at her age that rich color had to be coming from a bottle of dye. The man was portly and weathered looking, but his blue eyes were kind. Both were dressed in church attire, as meticulously outfitted as department store manikins.

Why hadn't Seth told her more about his family? When she had asked about his parents he'd muttered, "You don't want to know." Maybe the truth was *he* didn't want her to know.

Gran, legs elevated in the recliner, tried to fluff herself up at the sight of unexpected company.

"Hello." Junie's hand went out as she sailed toward her next. "You must be Rainey's grandmother. Carrie Melton thinks the world of you. She's Debbie Melton's daughter, who is my best friend, who is seeing some silly little man that roars around town on a motorcycle." She shot Tack a look. "Of course, you wouldn't know about any of the doings around here because I understand you have been confined. But not to worry, I can catch you up on all gossip in Tenikah in nothing flat." Behind her Tack was nodding indulgently.

"I see." Gran smiled graciously. "I love Carrie. And it's very nice to meet you."

Junie addressed her next speech to Seth. "I intended to call ahead while we were on our way to church, and give you plenty of warning," she said, while her husband's smile became fiendish behind her back. "But Tack here let the dang cell phone go dead again. We would have come for a visit a lot sooner, but I have been under the weather. Debbie kept me up to date on that awful tragedy with the Slaughters and all, and of course, it was in the paper. But land's sake. I could not believe it when I heard you got yourself an instant family this way, Seth."

"Let's meet these boys." Tack finally got a word in edgewise.

"They're in the backyard, tossing a football," Rainey said. Aaron, in particular, never tired of catching passes.

Seth went out back and called them in.

When the sweaty trio came ambling in the patio door, Rainey got nervous. The boys had never been subjected to the scrutiny of polite Sunday company before.

The visit was a bit forced, but overall the boys did

just fine. Dillon actually shook Tack's hand. He was imitating everything he saw Seth do these days, with amazing accuracy. Maddy read the faces around him and smiled a lot. Aaron hung back, clutching the football with a solemn expression.

"You boys like football?" Tack indicated the pigskin. It was the perennial question asked by old men of young boys in Tenikah, Oklahoma.

Dillon signed for Maddy. All three nodded.

"I bet Coach would be interested in meeting these boys," Junie chirped.

"Now, Junie, I don't think—" Tack started.

"You know," Seth interrupted, and shot Tack a covert look as he went on. "Maybe he should meet them."

"Maybe he should." Junie smiled. "Especially that one." She looked over her spectacles at the beefy Aaron. "He looks like he could do the Tenikah Pirates proud as a linebacker someday."

CHAPTER EIGHTEEN

THE DOORBELL STARTLED Rainey. The constant feeling that the next shoe might drop left her nervous anytime Seth wasn't around. They had agreed that one or the other of them would remain with the boys at all times now.

They had been home from school only long enough for the boys to grab a snack and plead to go outside and toss the football. On her way out the door, Carrie Melton reported that Gran was exhausted from her therapy and was down for a nap. So in the interest of quiet, Rainey relented on the homework for once.

"Thirty minutes," she told the boys, "then chores and homework." The kids required so much tutoring that she sometimes felt as if she was home-schooling them.

She peeked around the sheers over the side windows by the front door and saw a burgundy Lincoln Continental in Seth's driveway…and caught a glimpse of a large male shoulder in a gray sweatshirt. She opened the inner oak door, but did not unlock the outside glass one.

"Yes?"

"I'm Coach Hollings, Miss Chapman," the man said through the glass. "From over at the school." He was ruggedly handsome, graying. Dressed in coaching clothes—warm-up pants and a hooded sweatshirt with the ubiquitous black pirate stamped on the front. One side of his mouth lifted in an obsequious smile that gave Rainey a chill. "I've come to talk to you about Seth's foster kids."

Rainey's heart started to pound, but she knew what to do. Their emergency plan was in place. She had to act normal. Seth would come.

"I wanted to talk to you, or Seth, about helping the boys get started in the football program."

Rainey thought of Aunt Junie, undoubtedly the innocent conduit.

She wanted to say, *The head coach in this town makes house calls?* But there was no room in this situation for sarcasm. What was he planning to do?

She slid her hand over the object around her neck and pressed the little emergency alarm they'd ostensibly bought for Grace. It was rigged so that Seth got the signal directly.

"May I come in?" the coach asked.

"Of course." With sweaty fingers, Rainey twisted the lock on the outside door and opened it.

He stepped inside and surveyed the room. "You all have a nice place." *You all?* Rainey wondered what the word was in town, about her and Seth. Coach was already looking around for the boys. She had to be calm and stall.

Seth's living room was a long, low-ceilinged space,

with the entrance at one end and a double patio door at the back. Through the open drapes they could plainly see the boys, passing the football. "I hear they're very talented," Coach said as he walked toward the wide expanse of glass, moving slowly around the furniture, as if drawn by gravity.

"Rainey!" Rainey jumped at Gran's reedy voice calling from back in the bedroom.

"That's your grandmother, right?" Coach turned. "The one who hurt her knee when those sorry Slaughter brothers attacked her?"

Rainey swallowed dryly. "Yes."

"I was sorry to hear about that. Those guys always were nothing but trouble. This town is well shed of them."

"Rainey!" Granny called again. "Honey! I need a little help."

"You need to go to her?" Coach looked at Rainey levelly. "Don't let me keep you. I'll enjoy watching the boys while I wait." He stepped to the patio door.

Where was Seth? The coach hadn't done anything overt, probably wouldn't right away, but Rainey wanted Seth. She *needed* him. That was the problem with cops. They were always too busy with somebody else's trouble to be there for their own families.

But surely the cruiser would glide into the driveway any minute now. They'd done dry runs. Three minutes from Broadway to the top of the hill. Two minutes from anywhere in town to Broadway with the light bar flashing.

"Rainey!" Gran called. "I'm stuck in here."

"Excuse me," she said, and dashed down the long hallway to the bedroom at the back of the L.

She was only gone a minute, just long enough to hiss that Coach was there, then lower Gran's bad leg to the floor and shove her walker in front of her. But when she hurried back into the living room, the patio door stood open, with the sheers billowing in the autumn wind. Rainey panicked at the sight and ran out into the back-yard. The expanse of brown grass was ominously aban-doned.

"Dillon!" she cried. "Aaron!"

She ran around the corner of the house, then through the gate, which stood open. She reached the driveway just in time to see the Lincoln swerving into the cul-de-sac. "No!" she screamed. "Come back!"

But the Lincoln's tires squealed as Coach threw it into gear, fishtailing down the hill. Rainey's heart leaped into her throat as she caught a glimpse of Dil-lon's frightened face in the passenger side window.

How had Coach gotten the boys to go with him so quickly?

INSIDE THE LINCOLN, Dillon thrust a defiant face at the coach. "You're not taking us to no practice field to meet the other kids on the team, are you?"

Coach just kept driving, careening down Kanaly Hill like a crazed race car driver.

"You're *him,* aren't you? You're Howard."

"Shut up."

"And you're the one who killed that girl."

"Kid, I told you to shut up." From the console Coach suddenly produced a small gun. Maddy emitted his bizarre cry and Aaron's face went white under his freckles. "Tell your dummy friends that if any one of you makes a move, I'll shoot first and ask questions later."

Dillon signed to the other boys, but not as Coach had instructed. "Get out when I signal," his hands said.

Coach strong-armed the big car through the town and out onto the highway. There he opened up the Lincoln's massive engine to full throttle.

"Where are you taking us?" Dillon demanded.

"The question is, where are you taking *me*?"

Dillon's eyes got big and he swallowed as his cool liar's facade failed him.

"Yeah. To the bones. I know all about it. And don't pretend you don't know where they are. The twins told me everything before they died, except the exact location of that cave."

"There's no bones." Dillon wasn't sure what he was doing, but if he could get this guy alone, he might have a chance to cut him with the knife he had hidden in his sock, maybe even escape. With Maddy and Aaron slowing him down there was less of a chance.

"What are you talking about?" Coach gave him a nasty squint before his eyes flashed back to the winding highway.

"Seth already has them." For once in his life Dillon was using the truth. It felt weird. More powerful than his lies, even.

"But…" Dillon felt sweat trickling down his ribs "…I never told him I had the skull."

Coach's head snapped around. "You *what?*"

"I hid it in one of the caves."

"You're lying."

"I wish I was. If you let them go, I'll take you to it." Dillon twisted in the seat and with his hands made quick signals to the other boys.

"Face the front," Coach snapped. "Why should I let *them* go?"

"They don't know nothin'. Maddy can't hear. Aaron can't never talk. Look at him. He's a freaking zombie."

Coach glanced in the rearview mirror, weighing his options. Whitman would undoubtedly be in pursuit. He had to move faster, and it would be easier with only one boy in tow instead of three. When they turned off onto the narrow road that rose up Purney's Mountain, he braked the Lincoln with a lurch. "Tell 'em to get out."

As SETH TURNED ONTO the one-way road up Kanaly Hill, he called Rainey but got no answer. He figured her cell phone was in her purse again. He punched the speed dial for his home phone.

Precious seconds stretched out before the phone at the house finally rang.

After three rings Grace picked up. "Hello?" The tinny sound told him she was on the ground extension in the bedroom.

"Grace. Get Rainey. She punched the personal alarm."

"Coach is here, Seth," Grace hissed into the receiver. "Hurry."

"Don't hang up!" he yelled into the phone. "Where's Rainey? Where are the boys?"

"Just a minute."

"Wait—" But he heard the receiver clatter onto the nightstand. He gripped the phone, wanting to pound the steering wheel in frustration. Rainey was right. In his blind obsession to uncover the truth, he'd used the boys, thinking he had the power to protect them no matter what. He cursed himself for letting it get this far. More seconds ticked by. Grace moved as slow as an old turtle these days, and now the line was tied up while she tottered around the house, looking for Rainey and the boys.

He pressed harder on the gas. The road up the hill was full of dangerous curves, but it was one-way, so all he really had to worry about were cars backing out from driveways.

CARRIE MELTON FOUND Seth's front door standing wide open. "Rainey?" she called out. "Boys? I've come back for my ankle weights."

Grace emerged from the hallway, pushing her walker like a steamroller. "Carrie!" The old lady looked flushed. "What are you doing here?"

"I forgot my ankle weights. What's going on? The door was wide open."

"Lord." Grace flattened a hand on her chest. "Where's Rainey? And the boys? Oh Lord, oh Lord. Please tell me that man doesn't have them."

"Grace?" Carrie stepped in and took her arm. "What is going on?"

"I don't know. Rainey said Coach was here. And now everybody's gone and Seth is on the phone. He said Rainey set off her emergency device."

"Her emergency device?"

"One of them thingies—" Grace flapped her hands at her neck "—so she could raise Seth in a hurry, in case there was more trouble."

"More trouble? Why would he think that? The Slaughters are dead."

"Because that coach, he was mixed up with those Slaughters somehow, long ago, before Seth's brother died. On account of that missing girl."

"KayAnn Rawls?" Carrie's chest went tight as memories of that time choked upward.

"Yes. Seth's been trying to flush this Coach fella out ever since we came to town."

"Oh God," Carrie breathed. "And he's been here? I've got to talk to Seth." She marched to the kitchen and picked up the extension.

"Seth? It's Carrie. Grace is saying something about Coach, Coach Hollings, being involved with the Slaughters. Is that true?"

Seth only deliberated a second. "I don't have time to explain everything, Carrie, but I think Coach was covering for the Slaughters. I think they were responsible for KayAnn Rawls' disappearance. This is urgent. I have reason to believe Coach may harm the boys because they are witnesses to some…evidence. Let me talk to Rainey. *Now*."

"She's not here. Grace thinks Coach has her, and the boys."

She heard Seth curse, but kept talking. "Listen to me, Seth. It's important. I never told anybody this, but Coach, he…he tried to come on to me back in high school. He…he put his hands—" She choked, then forced herself to tell the next part. "KayAnn Rawls told me he did the same thing to her. He made me feel so dirty, but I never… I should have realized when she ran away…." Carrie couldn't bring herself to finish. Her head was pounding and she could hardly breathe.

That's when Seth spotted the burgundy Lincoln below, turning off the one-way down Kanaly Hill onto the highway. "Carrie, wait there in case Rainey shows up. Tell her I'm tailing Coach. And take care of Grace, okay?"

Seth executed a lurching turnabout on the narrow blacktop, with the light bar blazing and the siren blaring.

If that bastard had his hands on Rainey, if he touched a hair on the head of one of those boys… He pushed the cruiser's eight-cylinder engine to full throttle and hurtled down the hill at top speed.

RAINEY PRAYED. Prayers more fervent than any her gran ever said.

Her little Honda was no match for the powerful Lincoln, but she kept Coach's vehicle in sight long enough to see that he took the highway out of town, in the direction of the Winding Stair. She headed for Purney's Mountain as fast as she dared to drive while she fumbled in her purse for her cell phone. She panicked when she realized she'd left it on the counter, hooked to the charger.

What was she going to do way out here, facing a man like Coach alone?

She didn't know, but she'd die, literally, before she let the man harm the boys. *Please let me get them back,* she prayed. *Let us be like a family again. And please let Seth come. Let him find us.*

At the base of the mountain she saw them. Maddy and Aaron, running down the middle of the road in the waning evening light. When they recognized her car, they started waving their arms frantically.

When she stopped the car and threw open the door the boys fell upon her before she could even get out of the seat. She wrapped an arm around each of them and hung on. Her boys. These were her boys. Nothing, no one, was ever going to separate her from them again.

"Dillon?" she signed. But Maddy was shaking so hard he couldn't sign back.

"Dillon," a voice she'd never heard before croaked. She turned her head to see Aaron's face, streaming with tears, alive with emotion, with urgency. "Dillon t-took th…that Coach up th-there." He spat out the words with extreme difficulty, as if his lips were stiff from long disuse. "To get the sk…skull. I heard him tell that coach about the skull. He…he…"

Rainey clasped the child's shoulders to strengthen him.

"He's the H-Howard guy." Aaron forced out the words.

The lights of Seth's cruiser came into view just as the boys were climbing in the Honda.

Rainey told them to get in, and dashed toward Seth's vehicle before he'd even braked. He leaped out and, with a mutual cry, their bodies crashed together. Seth clasped his arms around her so hard it lifted her off her feet.

For one moment, they were too overcome to do anything but press their faces into each other's shoulders with eyes closed, rocking back and forth. Then Seth kissed her with a fierce possessiveness that was more about joy than passion. "I thought that man had *you*," he breathed.

"I think he's snapped." Rainey swallowed and again buried her face in his neck. "He came to the house and tricked the boys into getting into his car. I got Maddy and Aaron back." She kept her face pressed to Seth's throat as she choked out, "But Aaron told me Coach has Dillon, up on the mountain."

"*Aaron* told you?"

She nodded, choking back her emotion. "He talked, Seth. He finally spoke." Rainey fought for control. There was no time to rejoice. "It's like a miracle. But Dillon's—"

"I'll get him. You just stay strong for the other two, Rainey." They turned their heads and saw the other boys, gawking at them from beside the Honda. "I promise," Seth vowed. "I will bring Dillon back to you."

SETH CAUGHT UP WITH COACH on the ledge. The man had a death grip on Dillon, with a gun pressed under his ribs.

Seth crouched behind a rock and yelled, "Coach! Drop the gun and let the boy go!"

Coach spun Dillon in front of him and pressed the gun harder while he gripped the boy's neck.

"Seth!" Dillon squealed.

"Coach." Seth gave his gun barrel a jerk. "Don't make me shoot you."

Against the glare of the lowering sun, Coach's eyes narrowed to snakelike slits. "You don't have the balls."

"Let him go," Seth repeated calmly.

But Coach only gripped Dillon harder and narrowed his eyes more. His contemptuous expression reminded Seth of the way the man had looked at him under a glaring August sun during two-a-days. He would remove his reflective sunglasses and watch Seth's performance as if he were a piece of meat on the hook.

"What a waste product you have become," Coach spat as he backed Dillon up with him along the ledge. "You had talent, even more than your brother. You could have gone pro. But you never understood teamwork. You should have stayed in the rodeo, boy. That's the place for loners. You'll never be happy in Tenikah.

You'll never fit in. You'll never be anything but a misfit, just like your daddy."

Dillon croaked again as Coach's fingers tightened, dragging him by the neck around a bend.

"Coach, let the boy go." Seth stepped out from his cover. "This is between you and me now."

"How's that?" Coach stopped with his bulk behind a rock and Dillon sticking out in front of it. "She wasn't *your* girlfriend."

It took all of Seth's willpower to keep his finger from pressing the trigger. If he could only get a clear shot, he just might take it.

"You wanted her, though, just like all the other boys," the older man said. "But you stepped aside for your brother, same as you always had."

Seth's eyes flicked to Dillon's. The boy was signaling something. Seth continued to aim the gun while the man he had once looked up to as a mentor spat out a rant that had been waiting ten years to spew forth.

"Well, I didn't step aside. I had her. Your brother just wouldn't let it go. At first I thought he was angry because I favored Lonnie. Had to. The coach is the coach. He's the one who makes the decisions. Lane should have accepted that. But he was so stuck on that silly little girl. She came on to me, you know. You boys didn't get that, either. How the girls are always drawn to an older man with power. How they wiggle their little fannies to get your attention. It's enough to make any man crazy."

Dillon was tilting sideways, ever so slightly. He was

inching his long arm, his long fingers, down to the thick cuff above his hiking boot.

"If your brother only had the sense to let it go. But he had to become a cop, had to keep resurrecting something that should have been buried—"

"Along with her. Is that what you started to say?" Seth stated it flatly, steadily. Dillon needed a distraction. The boy's hand was sliding, sliding down into his sock. An inch at a time.

"You made them bury her out here in these caves, didn't you, Coach?" Seth pressed. "After you raped her? After you killed her?"

Coach just shook his head, then jerked Dillon upright by the neck. The boy yelped, but a flash of something in the fading light told Seth he'd already accomplished his goal.

Seth didn't look at the shiny object that glinted in Dillon's fingers, but he realized it was the razor. The boy had gone back to get it despite Seth's orders. He only hoped Dillon was as good with the weapon as he claimed.

"If this kid means anything to you at all, you'll toss that gun over the side of the cliff, Seth. Right now."

"And if I do, then what?" Seth stalled while Dillon slowly maneuvered his fingers in a good grip around the handle.

"Then we'll take a little trip down to Mexico, down where Lonnie and Nelson have a place that nobody could find in a million years."

"Leave the boy with me."

"Can't do that. He's insurance. I don't want to have to reason with the law at every little crossroad."

"I'll just hunt you down myself."

"I believe you would, you crazy bastard. But you'll have do it alone. You'll have no proof. No way to convince the authorities of anything."

"What about the boy? Kidnapping's a felony. And the bones. Or did you already get what you came for?" Seth knew the answer. He hoped Dillon understood that all of this was merely a stalling tactic, hoped he understood that Seth meant for him to take his time, to make sure of his moves. Once Dillon swung that razor, Seth prayed he'd be able to move fast enough to save the boy. Timing. He felt the seconds ticking away now, as if he were holding tight to the back of a bull. Everything came down to timing.

But timing had always been his strength, on the football field, in the rodeo arena, at a tense crime scene.

Dillon's hand flew up and swiped. Coach screamed and his head flew back. Seth dived forward and tackled.

MAX SAW TO IT that the story was reported factually and fully through Virginia, and the town went into a state of shock. Dillon, of course, told the tale to anybody who would listen. In his version, Seth was always the hero. In Seth's, Dillon was.

But out of the shock and confusion one clear thing emerged. Seth Whitman was the man of the hour. People were saying he was sure to be the next chief of police.

The chief refused to accept his resignation. Flat refused. Seth had to admit he wasn't sorry. Seeing justice served was the most fulfilling thing he had ever experienced, besides the love he had begun to feel for Rainey Chapman. And being a daddy to the boys was a close second.

One Sunday back when he'd let Junie drag him to church, the preacher had talked about how a man could only focus on three or four priorities if he was going to keep his life balanced. Seth wasn't a real churchy guy, but that particular sermon had stuck with him. He liked the sound of a focused life, a life of purpose, with Rainey at the rock solid center.

But part of that center was also about being a cop, he realized now.

He did not look forward to telling Rainey that he had decided to remain on the force, after all.

RAINEY SLOWLY PACKED her few belongings. It was funny how she hadn't needed much when she was with him. Life at Seth's house had been so clean, so simple. But also so tense and so draining.

She closed her eyes, remembering their kisses, and told herself to stop it. Physical attraction wasn't enough. Apparently love wasn't even enough.

"You are going, then." Seth's voice came from behind her at the bedroom door.

Rainey turned to face him. For ten excruciating seconds they studied each other's eyes.

Finally, she nodded stiffly. "I'll take Gran home,

stay with her a few days. Then I'll start getting paid at the school for being Maddy's interpreter. I've found a rental in town I can afford. Thank you for letting the boys stay, for letting me be near them."

"I wouldn't even have the boys in my life if not for you. And this is their home now. I wish..." His voice dropped. "I wish you'd considered it yours."

"I told you. I need security. I can't change that."

"And I can't change who I am, Rainey."

"I am not asking you to." With tears threatening, she turned back to her packing.

CHAPTER NINETEEN

SETH WAITED UNTIL it was almost Thanksgiving to visit Grace. The pain of not seeing Rainey had grown acute at times. She saw the boys at school every day, and often e-mailed them on the laptop he had bought them, but she never had a word for him.

Grace was his only hope of contact. Returning to her place, he found it exactly the same, except these days the smell of wood smoke hung in the crisp mountain air. She now walked with a barely perceptible limp, but otherwise life on Grace's mountain had been restored. Seth followed her to the homey kitchen as memories of Rainey assailed him like physical blows.

"My girl's not happy," Granny said after she set a simple dinner in front of him.

"She'll be okay, eventually," he said glumly. "Rainey's too beautiful to stay alone for long. I imagine plenty of men will beat a path to her door."

"Men? I wouldn't call them that. The last man in her life bugged out on her when she gave up her fancy job at the law firm. Did you ever hear of such a thing? A young man only prizing a woman because of her income? That boy was a wimp by half. Not like some people I know. She's never gonna find another one like you, Seth." Grace's voice dropped to a hush. "Her heart is broken, you know."

He looked up and caught the twinkle of a tear in Grace's eye. The catfish and home fries she'd fixed stuck in his throat.

"All right then," she said when he swallowed tightly. "I'm not aiming to make you uncomfortable. Let it rest at this—my granddaughter thinks she doesn't want anything to do with a cop, on account of her daddy, on account of the way he died. But that's plain nonsense. Rainey's got passion inside of her and she deserves a man who's got the passion inside of him to match it. You and Rainey and those boys are a family if I ever saw one. There. I have spoken."

Seth wiped his mouth on the cloth napkin. "Grace, I appreciate what you're trying to do here. But Rainey's got to make up her own mind about us. There simply is no other way."

Gran's lips pressed together tighter than a French seam. "She's running away from what she really needs. You see that, don't you, Seth?"

"Then I can't stop her." He pushed up from the table.

Grace grabbed his arm. "If you can't, then who can?"

Good question. But Seth could only look sadly at Grace. In his mind, he was the last person who should be trying to tell Rainey what she needed. If she couldn't love him freely, if she couldn't accept him for who he was, he wasn't going to put pressure on her. He wasn't going to go crawling and begging some woman to love him. With him it was all or nothing.

"Thank you for supper." He put his hat on.

"She's making a dern fool mistake. And you're a dern fool if you don't try to stop her." Like Rainey said, Gran always had to have the last word. So Seth allowed the old girl to have it. Quietly, he let himself out the door.

A WEEK LATER Seth stood in the frozen food aisle of the Wal-Mart Super Center, clutching the handle of one of those glass doors that fogged up if you kept the thing open too long.

An older lady who seemed vaguely familiar—didn't the whole town by now?—rolled a shopping cart up alongside his. He touched the brim of his Stetson, a reflex.

She nodded and reached in the case next door, grabbed a couple of boxes and started comparing labels. Seth did likewise. Chicken Bistro Medley, the one in his hand said. Whatever the hell that meant.

He turned the box over and started reading about fat and calories and other stuff he didn't give a hoot about, because he could feel the older woman's curious sidelong glances.

He was wearing a black Stetson, a fitted rodeo shirt, his favorite broke-in black jeans and his old scuffed boots—certainly nothing that resembled the police uniform people had seen in the paper. But still, folks recognized him. There hadn't been anything about the case on the news or in the paper for well over a month now. Coach was in jail, awaiting trial. But even the slightest bit of scrutiny in the Wal-Mart made Seth uncomfortable.

He got so itchy with the lady's peeking, with her acting as if she might actually speak to him, that he almost decided to move on. But something important had been niggling at the back of his brain before she came up, something that had been chewing at him all day, all week, ever since he'd left Grace's that night, and it felt important. He wanted to stand here and snatch it before it flittered away. He didn't care what this nosy matron had on her mind.

He *was* hungry. The boys would be, too, after football practice. Aaron, especially, needed something more than frozen dinners to eat. Seemed like he had grown two inches since he'd started on the team. Maddy and Dillon could pack it away, too.

These days his constant need seemed to be finding something quick and nutritious for their dinner. Something to keep body and soul together, as Granny would say. But he was so very sick of fast food. It was stupid to say he missed Rainey's cooking, or Gran's cooking, or the utter satisfaction of having all of them together. But he did. They had been like a family. A real family.

Junie and Tack had told him to bring the boys out to the ranch to eat dinner with them. Anytime, they said. He knew they could tell that he was still plenty hung up on Rainey. He knew they thought he was a fool for letting her go off that way. He knew they felt sorry for him.

Aunt Junie had even sat him down at the dining room table one recent Sunday afternoon to give him a strange little lecture about "intimacy versus isolation." Some more of that psychobabble she had learned when she had studied to be an LPN at the local vo-tech school, no doubt.

"You see, Seth," Junie said with that pained expression she always got when she was sticking her nose in where it didn't belong, "it's like this. You have a little trouble bonding with people and all, on account of your alcoholic parents. But the boys and Rainey, they got to you. They got to your heart."

Junie cleared her throat and folded her hands before her on her carefully pressed tablecloth, and Seth thought how sweet it was, really, that his aunt had braved telling him all this. Junie was good people, even if she was a terrible busybody.

"But on account of Lane, on account of you being so young when he died—well, you were at a bad age then. Right at an age when people must make up their minds—am I going to love and be loved or am I going to just sit here in my little shell? I imagine your subconscious was puzzling things out like that right about the time Lane died. With him being the only person you ever really bonded with, well…now you're just plain scared. You don't trust your feelings. Can't you see that?"

"For crying out loud, Junetta, leave the boy alone," Tack had hollered from the living room.

"I appreciate what you're doing here." Seth had patted his aunt's hand. "But the fact is, there are two people involved. Rainey's got to make up her own mind."

"Sometimes folks need a little help to do that," Junie had intoned. "Sometimes somebody's got to get the thing off high center."

A youngish woman rolled by with a shopping cart stacked high with boxes of frozen entrées like the ones Seth was pretending to look at. Her hair was cropped, exceedingly blond, meticulously fixed in one of those spiky styles, as if she'd just stuck her finger into a socket.

She smiled. Seth smiled back, but not with his eyes. He touched the brim of his Stetson. Again, just a reflex.

He looked back into freezer, wholly unfascinated with the food, and with her. It wasn't that the blonde wasn't pretty. She was. Sort of. But the first thing he'd noticed about her was that hair, and then her bulging bosom, not her face. And certainly not her eyes. Even as she rolled away, even as she turned to give the back-side of his snug black jeans an obvious glance, he couldn't have told the nosy old lady across the aisle what color her eyes were.

But he could see the exact shade of Rainey's, right now, right here in the frozen-food aisle. Rainey's eyes were the color of the mountains at sunset in the fall just before the leaves started to turn. A rich, lush golden-greenish-brown that drew you into their mysterious depths and wouldn't let you look away.

He rolled his sleeves up a notch.

He was supposed to be buying something for dinner, something to satiate the boys and to keep body and soul together, which of late had seemed sorely divided. Ever since Rainey left he'd felt as if he'd lost his center.

Concentrate, he ordered himself. *Decide what the boys might like to eat. Something filling. Anything. Just get it and go.* But his mind seemed as frozen as the box of food in his hand.

Where was she? Where was Rainey, right now? This very minute? Out on a date? He checked his watch. At seven o'clock on a Friday night that seemed likely. *And why aren't you out on the town, Cowboy? Why are you mooning over the Healthy Choice entrées instead of hooking up with some willing woman?* He thought about the blonde who'd just made it clear she liked the way he filled out his jeans. She was probably over in the next aisle. He could make a move. Rent the kids a video and go out on the town for once.

He could wheel his basket over there, strike up a conversation. All he had to do was give her the polite cowboy routine, then work into the conversation the fact that he was actually a cop. An off-duty cop. A bored, lonely off-duty cop. All he had to do was tell her she was pretty. And it wouldn't be a lie. She was. But pretty as she was, he knew she couldn't satisfy. Not after Rainey.

The women he'd dated before Rainey all seemed kind of like the pretty pictures of food on these boxes he was staring at. They looked good, but the inside never delivered what the picture promised.

Rainey.

He picked up another entrée, cocked a knee, planting one scuffed boot a little closer to the case, as if he was actually shopping. But he just kept thinking of Rainey. *Rainey.*

What could he do to win her over? What could he do to make her see that he'd changed? That he'd changed because of her? What could he do to make her see that he could love a family and still be a good cop?

And then it hit him, like a two-by-four between the eyes. A *real* family. He grinned and slammed the freezer case closed, so hard the nosy old lady next to him gave a startle.

He was practically whistling as he took long strides out to the main aisle, past the produce, past the baked goods, past the checkouts, past the long rows of baskets, through the automatic doors and out into the brightly lit parking lot, where he finally stopped and looked up. He sucked in a massive draft of cold night air while his mind sang out *Hallelujah!* Junie was right, bless her. Sometimes you had to do something to get life off high center. The first wisps of a light snow were circling the parking lot lights with soft coronas of moisture.

Why hadn't he thought of it before? After all, the boys were wards of the state—there would be no parental rights to terminate. And Seth had the squeaky-clean reputation, the stable lifestyle, that DHS required.

How complicated could it be? Max would know what to do. No matter how many papers Seth had to fill out or how many hoops he had to jump through, this was what he wanted. He knew that now. Somehow he'd known from the start. This was what he wanted. The boys. A family. Rainey.

If she said no, then she said no. But he had to try.

The snow started coming down faster and thicker now, as if the sky had burst open, like his mind. As if it was pouring down its abundant whiteness just because he'd made his decision.

Snow. Just in time for Thanksgiving. The boys would love it.

And by Christmastime, one way or another, they'd be a family.

THE PAPERS WERE LONG, legal-size, crisp and smooth, bound at the top with one of those fat black alligator clips found in a law office. Rainey turned the sheaf so she could read it, and recognized the documents immediately. She gave Seth a questioning look and felt the beginnings of tears smarting behind her eyes.

Outside the plain square picture window of her little house, it was snowing. In only a few days, it would be Christmas, and Rainey didn't have a single decoration up. Not even a cluster of red candles on the coffee table. She seemed to be living her life on hold these days.

Seth stood over her, looking enormously pleased with himself. He tapped the pile of papers he'd laid on her small rolltop desk. "It took a month to get this done."

"Only a month?" Rainey said senselessly as she lifted the thick stack of papers. Adoption papers. A set for Dillon. A set for Maddy. A set for Aaron.

For some reason she couldn't talk about what was right before her. About the boys. About the family Seth obviously intended to have. About how she might fit into all of this. The print on the decrees began to blur. Why had he come back?

Seth walked to the window and folded his arms over his chest. His pose was casual, satisfied, as if nothing all that significant was happening in this room. He peered out at the worsening winter storm as he spoke. "I've been looking at a place out in the country, up in the Winding Stair. It's got a barn, even if the thing is leaning to one side. Plenty of flat pasture between two mountains. I might raise breeder bulls out there. Tack said he'd help me. It's a pretty little spot. A creek, an old house—you like old houses, don't you?—and the mountain behind. There's room for a horse or two. Room to run wild and play. Room for a little garden—an acre or so. Everything the boys got used to while they were living at Grace's. Everything we would want."

"We?" The word came out in a croak and Rainey cleared her throat. "Everything…" But the tears were coming through in her voice. "Why are you talking about this farm all of a sudden?"

Seth came and stood over her, his pose bold, his

voice even. "Because, Rainey, it's for us. I've decided
to give up being a cop if that's what I have to do to win
you over." Out of the corner of her eye, through the blur
of tears, Rainey could see his boots, the ones with the
white eagles emblazoned on the vamps, planted wide.
"I want us to be together, Rainey. You, me, the boys,
even Grace if she wants. We always were a family, at
least in my heart. In yours, too, I hope. This—" he bent
and flattened a palm on the papers "—will just make it
official."

"A family?" she echoed. She gazed at his hand while
she fought her tears and tried to make sense of the emotions that were flooding through her. He was buying a
farm? He was giving up his career as a cop? For her?

But was he talking about marriage or about living together, the way they had in his house here in Tenikah?
What had Gran called it? *Playing house.* "What do you
mean...a family?" she asked.

"The only kind there is. A real one. That's why I'm
making the boys legally mine. Man, you should have
seen how those DHS people checked me out. Good
thing I'm nothing but a boring cop. And good thing I'm
in tight with the local judge. Good old Max speeded
things up considerably. I guess that's one more favor I
owe him."

All Rainey could think was, *You, Seth Whitman, are
far from boring.* What kind of man would do this?
Adopt three half-grown boys? Give up everything that
had defined his life?

The kind of man a woman could trust, the kind of

man a woman could love with every fiber of her being. That's what kind of man.

Seth had waited patiently, but finally he urged, "Well, haven't you got anything to say?"

"I'm…I'm speechless."

He dropped to one knee in front of her. "Girl, if I'd known that's all it would take to make you speechless, I would have done this a long time ago."

Through her tears, she gave him a wan smile then picked up papers. The adopter named was Seth Whitman. Her name wasn't anywhere on the documents. "I'm happy for you and the boys. But I can't ask you to give up your profession."

Seth's heart sank for one instant. Was she going to use such a flimsy excuse to reject him? First it was because he was a cop, and now because she couldn't let him give up being a cop? In his heart, he knew they were right for each other, but a man could only take so much.

"You can ask anything of me, Rainey. Don't you see that?"

"And what, exactly, are you asking of me, Seth?"

"I'm asking you to share my life with me, whether I'm a cop or not. Whether we've got three boys or not. This is about you and me now. Oh…" His tone suddenly shifted. "Which reminds me." He straightened his shoulders, dug around in the pocket of his Levi's for something. What came out was the blue velvet cube of a ring box.

At the sight of it, Rainey's heart started to pound.

Seth popped it open to reveal a solitaire diamond ring. Rainey looked at the ring for only a split second, just long enough to make sure she wasn't seeing things, then her eyes went up to Seth's face, the face she loved more than any other.

His gaze traveled slowly from the ring until he was looking directly into hers. "If you marry me…" his voice was soft now, low with import, not light, not teasing "…you'll be the boys' mother. Do you still want that?"

With tears spilling over, Rainey let the papers fall back to the desk. "Oh, Seth. You are the most amazing man."

He swiveled her desk chair to face him and bracketed his hands around her thighs. "Then say yes."

She stared at him, feeling a joy so pure it boggled her mind and struck her mute.

"Say yes. Come on…." He gave her thighs a gentle squeeze.

"Yes!" The word came out in a strangled whisper.

"God, I do love you," Seth whispered as his mouth sought hers.

Rainey's mind raced with a hundred questions, while her heart raced with joy and her husband-to-be kissed her senseless. But the one thing she didn't question, would never question, was Seth Whitman. She knew that no matter what, they would forge a future together…as a family.

In her mind a string of happy years unfolded on a small farm, or in the house on the hill in town—it didn't matter. She could see three sons teasing their parents whenever they caught them kissing this way. She could see the boys grown to young men, winking at each other, signing. And she could see Mr. and Mrs. Seth Whitman, growing old together.

When their hunger was satisfied and they broke off the kiss, she looked into his eyes. "Life really is all about timing, isn't it, Seth?"

Seth thought he detected a twinkle in Rainey's pretty green eyes.

"Yes, sweetheart, it is. It's all about timing."

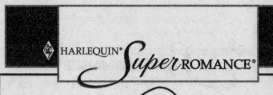

HARLEQUIN *Super*ROMANCE®

On sale May 2005

With Child by Janice Kay Johnson
(SR #1273)

All was right in Mindy Fenton's world when she went to bed one night. But before it was over everything had changed—and not for the better. She was awakened by Brendan Quinn with the news that her husband had been shot and killed. Now Mindy is alone and pregnant…and Quinn is the only one she can turn to.

On sale June 2005

Pregnant Protector by Anne Marie Duquette
(SR #1283)

Lara Nelson is a good cop, which is why she and her partner—a German shepherd named Sadie—are assigned to protect a fellow officer whose life is in danger. But as Lara and Nick Cantello attempt to discover who wants Nick dead, attraction gets the better of judgment, and in nine months there will be someone else to consider.

On sale July 2005

The Pregnancy Test by Susan Gable
(SR #1285)

Sloan Thompson has good reason to worry about his daughter once she enters her "rebellious" phase. And that's before she tells him she's pregnant. Then he discovers his own actions have consequences. This about-to-be grandfather is also going to be a father again.

Available wherever Harlequin books are sold.

www.eHarlequin.com

HSR9ML0405

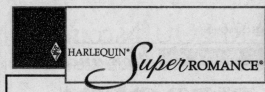

YOU, ME & THE KIDS

On sale May 2005

High Mountain Home
by Sherry Lewis
(SR #1275)

Bad news brings Gabe King home to Libby, Montana, where he meets his brother's wife for the first time. Siddah is doing her best to raise Bobby, but it's clear that his nephew needs some male attention. Can Gabe step into his brother's shoes—without stepping into his brother's life?

On sale June 2005

A Family for Daniel
by Anna DeStefano
(SR #1280)

Josh White is trying to care for his late sister's son, but Daniel's hurting so much nothing seems to reach him. The only person the boy responds to is Amy Loar, Josh's childhood friend. Amy has her own problems, but she does her best to help. Then Daniel's father shows up and threatens to sue for custody, and the two old friends have to figure out how to make a family for Daniel.

Available wherever Harlequin books are sold.

AMERICAN *Romance*®

THE ABBOTTS

A Dynasty in the Making

A series by

Muriel Jensen

The Abbotts of Losthampton, Long Island, first settled in New York back in the days of the *Mayflower*.

Now they're a power family, owning one of the largest business conglomerates in the country.

But…appearances can be deceiving.

HIS FAMILY

May 2005

Campbell Abbott should have been thrilled when his little sister, abducted at the age of fourteen months, returns to the Abbott family home. Instead, he finds her…annoying. After a DNA test proves she isn't his long-lost sister, he suddenly realizes where his prickly attitude toward her comes from—and admits he'll do anything to ensure she stays in his family now.

Read about the Abbotts:

HIS BABY (May 2004)
HIS WIFE (August 2004)
HIS FAMILY (May 2005)
HIS WEDDING (September 2005)

Available wherever Harlequin books are sold.